Bring Me Back

KRISTEN GRANATA

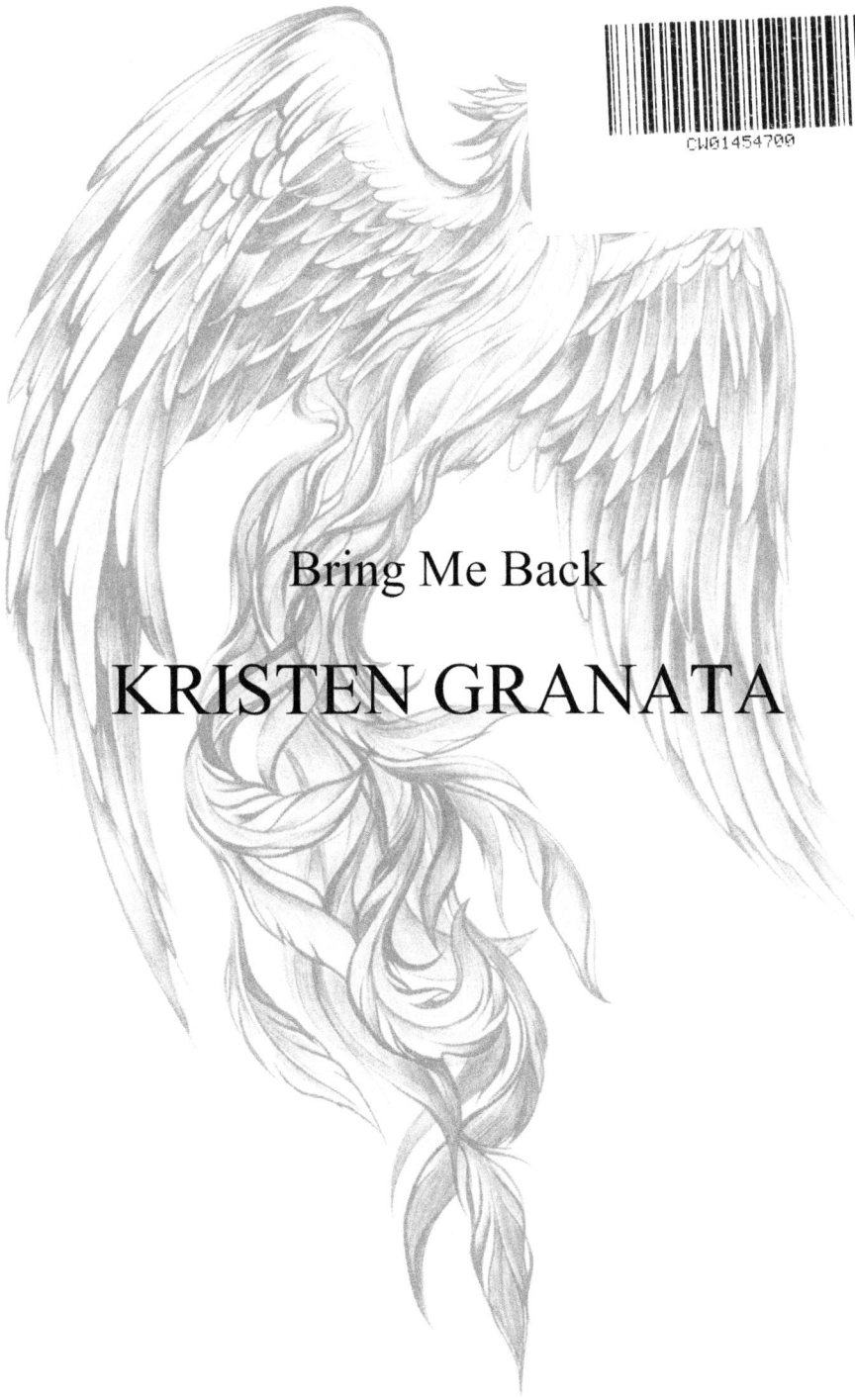

Bring Me Back

Dedication

This story is for me.
I might get knocked down, but I will always get back up.
I will always keep fighting.

Bring Me Back

A Note from the Author

I have suffered from depression and anxiety since I was a child.

I know firsthand what it's like to feel helpless and alone, even with the most amazing support group surrounding you. I know what it's like to feel as if you can't trust your own thoughts. I know what it's like to constantly fight a war inside yourself. I know what it's like to be told you "shouldn't" be depressed. I know what it's like to feel like no one gets you. I know what it's like to feel less than everyone around you.

I almost took my own life when I was a teenager. I've been through some pretty dark times, but through it all, I held on to that faint ember of hope that things might get better one day. I'm lucky to be here to see that they can get better. My mission is to deliver that message to everyone who needs to hear it.

It's okay to not be okay, but it's not okay to not exist anymore.

If you're someone who is triggered by suicide, I encourage you to read this book. It might be a little difficult. It might make you cry. But I think you should push through. It's a beautiful story with an important message of hope, second chances, and learning to embrace who you are—scars and all.

"It's the Joshua tree's struggle that gives it its beauty."
—Jeannette Walls

Bring Me Back

1

Phoenix

Daily Affirmation: "I will stop worrying. I will learn to deal with my worries in a logical way."

I stare up at the beige siding along the front of the house and blow out a heavy sigh.

It's kind of funny, seeking refuge in the one place I've avoided for so long. Life always seems to turn out this way. You waste so much time and energy steering yourself away from a particular path, yet you end up on that path regardless.

A deep-orange rust covers the three metal birds hanging above the garage. Dad loved those birds. I told him they looked tacky, but he insisted they stay. So, my brother Tyler and I named them and it became a running joke.

I tap out a text to Tyler: *Buffy, Willow, and Xander say hi. We wish you were here.*

I kill the engine and let my head fall back against the headrest. I don't know what I'm waiting for. I can't sit in my car all day—I have nowhere else to go, and it's twenty-six degrees outside. Besides, it's not like Dad is going to come out to greet me. His wide smile flashes in my mind, and my cheeks push up the slightest bit. It was impossible not to smile whenever he was around. He illuminated any room he walked into. I swear, the world got a bit darker when he passed.

Cancer can go fuck itself.

I close my eyes, count back from ten, and then swing open the car door. I hoist my bags out of the back seat, lug them up the driveway, and I don't stop moving until I'm twisting the key in the jiggly knob of the front door. Quick, like ripping off a Band-Aid, I step inside.

My eyes bounce around the entryway like a scared animal approaching a watering hole. Maybe if he didn't die here, I'd feel differently. Maybe we all would. My mother hasn't stepped foot in this house since his body was rolled out the front door, and my brother never looked back since he left after he graduated high school. I think that's why Dad left this shore house to me. He knew I'd need it one day. Somehow, he knew this could be my safe haven.

He was the only one who always knew what I needed.

Grief sinks into my stomach like a lead ball, splashing the bile around. For years, Mom hounded me to sell this place. *"You're throwing away your money. It's foolish."* But it wasn't foolish to me, and I'm glad I stuck to my guns on this one because it feels right being here after everything I've gone through. It's the only comforting thing I have left to hold on to.

I do a quick tour of the first floor. Eat-in kitchen where I used to watch Dad cook breakfast; living room with the brick fireplace we never lit because we only lived here during the summer; glass sliders that lead out onto the deck we'd jump off of every Fourth of July. Everything is exactly how I remember it, only now it's cold and empty. The vivid memories with Dad have been drained of their color.

Everything might look the same, but everything is different.

My combat boots echo off the wooden stairs as I head upstairs to my old bedroom, keeping my head down as I walk past my parents' room and focus on the thought of sleeping on a mattress bigger than a twin for the first time in almost two years. I drop my bags in the corner of the room and flop facedown onto the puffy white comforter.

My phone buzzes, and I scramble to get it out of my pocket. My heart sinks when Tyler's name isn't the one flashing across the screen, but only for a second. I clear my throat and try to mimic a cheery tone.

"Hey, Drew."

Drew's assertive voice blares through the speaker. "You're free. Why do you sound so sad?"

I roll over onto my back and stare up at the ceiling. "Being free isn't all it's cracked up to be."

"Sure, it is. Pizza, privacy, and porn, remember?"

"That was *your* list. Mine didn't include porn."

"Well, it should. Maybe that's why you're so damn depressed all the time."

I smirk. "What are you up to?"

"You know damn well what I'm doing: A whole lot of fucking nothing. The question is, what are *you* doing? How does it feel to be out of the looney bin?"

"Don't call it that." My eyes roam around my bare bedroom. "In a way, it feels like I never left. The world is the same, but there's more pressure now. Like I already fucked up once, so I need to do better this time."

"Dude, you're setting yourself up for failure if you think you aren't going to make any mistakes from here on out. You need to be more like me. Lower the bar. Expect to fuck up, and then when you do something right, you'll surprise yourself."

A slight smile curves my lips. "What am I going to do out here without you and your prolific advice?"

"You'll survive until I get out."

Drew has been my friend for the last sixteen months while I was at Clearview. I don't know how I would've survived that place without him. Not that it was so bad there; everyone was nice for the most part. But staying at a residential mental health facility isn't exactly the same as staying at an all-inclusive resort in Cabo.

"What am I going to do out here? What am I going to do with the rest of my life? I don't have a plan." I slide my thumb along the scar on my left forearm. Some people bite their nails when they're anxious. Some tap their feet. I rub the physical reminder of the lowest moment in my life.

"Stop touching your scar. And don't tell me you're not, because I know you are." Drew clicks his tongue. "You're not supposed to focus on the past, remember? Look forward. Never back, always forward."

"Looking forward is what worries me. I have anxiety, remember?"

"You'll figure it out. You need to give yourself some time. You just got out this morning, for Christ's sake. You're not going to have all the answers on day one, so tell your anxiety to fuck right off."

If only it were that simple. I practice my deep breathing for a few seconds and try to slow my racing mind.

Focus on what you can control.

"What's on your to-do list? I know you made one."

I put Drew on speaker, and tap on my notes app. "I need to unpack, obviously, and I should stock up the fridge, so I'll need to go grocery shopping."

"Fuck that boring shit. Order a pizza and worry about substantial food tomorrow. You've been living on this organic free-range kumbaya chicken over here. Let yourself indulge on your first night out. Celebrate."

Celebrate what? The fact that I had to be deemed stable enough to live among normal people again? Or the fact that my mother disowned me because she took my suicide attempt as a personal attack against her? Or how about the fact that my schizophrenic friend who has limited phone privileges managed to check in on me before my own brother did?

Drew's voice cuts through my thoughts. "Hey, stay out of your head. You're going to be okay, Nix. It's just going to take some time to adjust."

"Thanks for calling." A pang of sadness pricks my heart. "I miss you already."

"Good, you better. I used my one call for you, which means I can't call the phone sex hotline later."

"Eww. Please don't tell me you actually do that."

"I wouldn't have to if you were game. Come on, Nix. Talk dirty to me."

I throw my head back and laugh. "Not a chance in hell."

"Prude. I'll call you tomorrow to check in. Have a slice of pizza for me."

As soon as I end the call, I search for a nearby pizzeria and order a large pie.

While I wait, I log onto Facebook. Clearview had a strict policy against social media, so it's been sixteen months since I've connected to the internet world. I used to be into scrolling through my feed. There's something oddly comforting in seeing that everyone else's lives turned out to be just as mediocre and meaningless as mine.

Notifications flood my account, all from people I haven't seen or spoken to since high school nearly ten years ago:

Nicole Paisley: You should've died.
Roger Clementine: There's always next time.
Jessica Armando: Selfish bitch.
Billy Jenkins: Her poor family.
Tarryn Desai: Loser couldn't even kill herself the right way.
Jared Martino: The world would be better off without people like you.

Each comment pierces my heart like a bullet. I know I should stop reading them, but I can't bring myself to look away. These are people I grew up with. People I sat next to in history class. People I worked on science projects with. These aren't sad internet trolls living in dark basements with nothing better to do. They're regular people with jobs and spouses and children.

And *this* is the way regular people view depression and suicide.

I don't know why I'm shocked. I was raised by someone just like this. Humans tend to shun and judge whatever they don't understand. But that doesn't make it hurt any less.

"Insensitive assholes." I deactivate my account and delete the rest of my social media apps. I survived without it at Clearview, and the world really is more peaceful when you don't have instant access to everyone's thoughts and opinions.

Instead, I open the romance novel I'm in the middle of reading and try to convince myself that love isn't one big crock of shit.

Bang!

It's difficult enough falling asleep in a house by yourself when you have anxiety but being woken up by a loud noise only confirms your irrational fear that someone has in fact come to kill you.

I sit up, spine straight, and strain to listen. In Clearview, I learned all of the nighttime sounds, like the clanking of the vents whenever the heat was about to kick on, or the cries of the patients in need of sedatives, and the differing footsteps of the aides making their rounds. But I can't identify where this bang came from, or what caused it.

I have three choices:

I can call the police. But I don't know if I'm in danger yet, and it might be for nothing. I'd hate to wake the neighborhood with sirens and lights over a pan falling in the kitchen cabinet. Not a great way to make a first impression.

Choice Two: I can jump out the window to escape the possible intruder. But if I broke my ankle, I wouldn't be able to run away. Plus, the last thing I need is for someone to think I'm jumping off the roof to try to hurt myself again. I'll be back at Clearview in less than twenty-four hours.

My last choice is my least favorite: I can be a big girl and go downstairs to find out what the bang was.

After weighing my options, I grab Tyler's old baseball bat—the one I found in the closet earlier and propped against my nightstand in case I needed it for a moment like this—and tiptoe out of the bedroom.

It's fine. It's probably nothing.

Or it's an escaped convict here to murder you.

No, that's not helpful. Maybe a bird flew into the window.

Birds don't fly at night, you idiot.

Shit. That's actually true.

I peer over the railing at the top of the staircase, and moonlight spills onto the tile from the open door—the front door that was locked shut before I went up to bed. It's an intruder. It has to be. How else does the front door magically swing open in the middle of the night? My heart races. I need to get back to my bedroom so I can call the police. But before I can move, a dark figure appears at the bottom of the stairs.

"Hey!" His deep voice thunders, shaking me to my core.

My knees lock up, and I stand there frozen.

He bolts up the stairs, taking them two at a time to get to me.

Fuck, fuck, fuck!

I shriek.

I panic.

Then I throw the bat.

I legit throw the only weapon I have at the crazed killer.

Not the smartest move, but it ends up paying off. The bat cracks the man in the head and sends him tumbling back downstairs, buying me time to run and lock myself in my bedroom. I grab my phone off the nightstand and dial 911. The operator promises someone will be here soon, so I hide in the closet and pray the maniac doesn't kick down my door before the cops get here.

I'm not waiting long before I hear muffled voices. I creep across the room and press my ear against the door until a booming voice says, "Ma'am, this is the Beachwood Police. I'm entering your home."

That was quick.

I glance out the window, and my eyebrows press together. No police car with flashing lights. Not even an unmarked vehicle. The cul-de-sac is desolate at this hour.

It's not a cop. It's the murderer trying to trick me!

"Nice try," I yell through the door. "I know you're not the police. But you'd better get the hell out of here, because I called them and they're on their way."

"My name is Officer Russo." His footsteps are slow and heavy on the stairs, and his voice gets louder as he ascends. "I received a call about an intruder. I can show you my badge if you open the door."

"Where's your car?"

The hallway light flicks on, shining through the sliver of space under the door. "I live next door in the gray house to your right. Dispatch sent me to check it out before sending anyone else."

"Did you see the man downstairs who broke into my home? He needs to be arrested."

"Yes, ma'am. I saw him. You gave him a pretty nice bump on his head." His tone hints at amusement. "You said this is your home. Can I please see your ID?"

I snatch my purse off the floor and fish around for my wallet. "I'll slip it under the door."

After a moment of silence, he says, "Miss Bridges, the address listed on it does not match this one. Would you please explain why you think this is your house?"

Shit. "My name is on the mortgage, and the deed. But I just moved in today and haven't had a chance to change my license."

"Why don't you open up so we can talk?" Then he adds, "My badge won't fit under the door."

"Is the intruder in handcuffs?"

"No, Miss Bridges. He—"

"I'm not coming out until he's cuffed."

He chuckles under his breath. "All right."

A deep voice says, "You can't be fucking serious."

"You heard the lady. Place your hands behind your back." Metal clanks together, followed by Officer Russo's voice. "Okay, he's cuffed."

I crack open the door and peer into the hallway. An older man in uniform stands beside the younger intruder.

The man in handcuffs grunts. "This is ridiculous."

And that snaps my last thread of patience. "What's ridiculous is *you* breaking into *my* house and trying to attack me."

"I didn't attack you." He glares down at me. "You're the one who assaulted *me*."

"No, I defended myself after you started chasing after me." I gesture at the egg-sized mound on his forehead. "You got what you deserved."

The police officer frowns, and his forehead creases. "This place has been vacant since we moved next door. Figured it belonged to the bank."

The man in cuffs lowers his voice as if I'm not standing right in front of him. "How do we know the house is hers? Maybe she's lying."

I cross my arms over my chest. "I am not lying. I have the paperwork to prove it. And whether the house is mine or not doesn't justify the fact that you broke in, so you don't have a leg to stand on."

Officer Russo claps him on the shoulder. "She's got a point, kid. Care to explain what *you* were doing here?"

His jaw clenches. "Not now, Dad."

My head jerks back as my eyes bounce between them. "Dad?"

"I'm Jim Russo." He gestures to himself, and then to the asshole beside him. "And this is my son, James Russo."

I almost laugh. The cop's son is a criminal? "You're kidding."

"I'm sorry about my son's behavior. If you can believe it, he had good intentions when he came into your house tonight."

Good intentions for breaking into my house, and scaring the life out of me? I arch an eyebrow as my gaze roams over the cop's son.

He towers over me. With a square jaw and dark features, he bears a strong resemblance to his father—except for his thick brown hair, which is unfortunate for him because he won't be keeping much of it judging by his father's bare scalp. He's dressed in a white T-shirt with gray sweatpants—every woman's dream, if they're not also worn with the pair of handcuffs he's sporting—and he's as broad as his muscles are thick.

James Russo is one exceptionally good-looking criminal.

Figures.

"I think you owe her an explanation, James." Officer Russo's eyes soften with his voice as he addresses his son.

James drops his gaze to the floor and shifts his weight from one foot to the other in silence. "I was looking for my brother, and when I saw the light you left on in your kitchen, I thought…" He swallows before he pushes out the rest of the words. "I didn't expect you to be here."

"And there's supposed to be an apology in there somewhere," his father whispers loud enough for me to hear.

James's jaw tics before he sets his eyes on me. "I'm sorry for scaring you."

Damn. This guy barrels into someone's house in the middle of the night in search of his brother, and mine can't even shoot me a simple text to wish me luck on my first day out of a mental facility.

Curiosity urges my next question. "Why did you think your brother would be in *my* house?"

His father answers for him. "We haven't seen him in a while. Sometimes he squats here instead of coming home. He—"

"Can you uncuff me now?" James cuts in.

Officer Russo gives me an apologetic smile as he unlocks the handcuffs. Without another glance in my direction, James turns around and heads down the stairs.

Officer Russo pinches the bridge of his nose. "He gets upset when his brother disappears like this."

"He does this often?"

He shrugs like he doesn't know what else to say. "My boy will turn up when he wants to be found. Always does."

What does that mean? But it's not my business to keep prying into his family drama. "If there's anything I can do to help you find your son, please let me know. I watch a lot of *Cold Case Files*."

Officer Russo chuckles. "That won't be necessary." He turns toward the staircase and pauses. "We're a sorry attempt at a welcoming committee, but welcome to the neighborhood, Miss Bridges. If you ever need anything, feel free to come by. Call me old-fashioned, but I don't like the idea of a young woman living here all by herself."

Warmth pools in my chest. "You don't have to worry about me, sir."

No one else does.

After he leaves, I close the door behind him and wedge a chair under the damaged knob in an attempt to secure the house.

That fucker broke my lock.

2

Phoenix

Daily Affirmation: "I am on the right path in life, and I am going in the right direction."

I wake up to the sound of banging.

Again.

I shield my eyes from the sun streaking through the blinds and sit up with a groan. This is a different type of noise than the one that jolted me out of bed last night. It's a steady hammering, followed by a high-pitched drilling sound.

Throwing on my oversized sweatshirt, I pad down the hall, but my feet falter at the top of the stairs. I squint to make sure I'm seeing this correctly.

The front door is wide open, the chair I had propped against it now lying on its side in the entryway. James kneels in the doorway as he drills a screw into my doorknob—a shiny *new* doorknob.

What the…?

I trot downstairs, studying him as I approach. In the daylight, I have a much better view than I did in my dim hallway last night. His expression is a perma-scowl—dark brows pushed together, eyes narrowed and focused while he works. *Is there a term for resting bitch face for men?* Because he'd be the poster boy for it. Harsh, intense lines make up his profile, as if each detail was hand carved out of stone by an angry artist. Smooth, olive skin surrounds his dark features. He's intimidating and beautiful at the same time.

My baseball bat left a nice purple knot on his forehead, and I almost feel bad about it. Almost, but the man continues working as if he doesn't see me standing in front of him, and that irritates me.

I clear my throat. "Isn't there a law about making noise before a certain time in the morning?"

He glances at the watch on his wrist. "It's noon."

"Yeah, well, some asshole broke into my house last night so I didn't get much sleep."

He presses the trigger on the drill, and the noise makes my shoulders jump.

Jerk.

After the noise stops, he reaches down for another screw.

I cross my arms over my chest. "I could've done this myself."

"That's a funny way of saying thank you."

My eyebrows shoot up. Is he shitting me? "Oh, yes. Thank you for replacing the doorknob *you* broke when you illegally let yourself into my home last night."

"You needed a better one anyway."

"Why do you care?"

"It's not safe without a lock on your door."

"That's not what I asked."

He lets out a long exhale, and the muscles in his jaw work under his skin as he stares down at the screw between his fingers. "I feel bad about scaring you last night. Figured I should replace the lock so you can feel more secure here."

I pause. A criminal wouldn't care about how I felt. Neither would an asshole. And when was the last time someone cared enough to make sure I felt safe?

I swallow the retort climbing up my throat and glance at my new doorknob. "Well, how much do I owe you for this?"

He shakes his head as he pushes off his knees to stand.

"No, no. This one's much fancier than the one that was on there before. Tell me how much it was."

He collects the garbage and places the key on the railing before turning to make his way down the stairs.

I throw up my hands. "I know you hear me."

He glances over his shoulder, and his eyes finally meet mine. His irises are a light-yellowish-brown color, like honey reflecting in the morning sunlight. They're beautiful and warm, despite the way his skin tightens around them to scowl at me.

"Just let me do this, okay?" He asks the question with a desperate edge to his voice, like it'll pain him if he doesn't do it, and I'm only making it worse by trying to get him to take it back.

"Sure." I avert my gaze to the doorknob again and chew on my bottom lip. It looks so much nicer than the rest of the house. "This place really went to shit. My father would hate to see it like this." Sadness seeps into my bloodstream, coursing through me like a slow and subtle poison.

James gives the house a quick appraisal—the overgrown, weed-filled landscaping, the rusted railing, the dilapidated garage door, and the rotting shutters. He hesitates a moment, and I wait for him to say something. But James just turns around and walks back to his house.

Good talk.

Returning my attention to my house, I start making a mental checklist of all the things I can see that need fixing. I head inside to write them down and sort them into tasks I can do on my own, versus jobs I need to hire people for. I'm not too handy, but I'm not incapable either. I'll fix whatever I can from YouTube and pay for a professional to fix whatever I can't.

Keeping busy is important when you have depression. When your mind is occupied, you don't have time to think or wallow in despair. People with a purpose are less likely to kill themselves, which is good news for me because I can't leave anything unfinished. Not books or shows or projects. I have to see it through to the end. I figure if I start a project in the house, it'll lead to another, and another. At the very least, it'll get me through the upcoming dark winter months.

I stan the House of Stark, after all, and *winter is coming.*

I've been spackling all day, going from room to room like a tornado.

The walls will look nice with a fresh coat of paint after I'm finished filling holes and fixing nail pops. It would've made Dad happy to see.

Not sure how much the noise carries outside, but even though it's after nine o'clock at night, I raise the volume on my Bluetooth speaker. It's "Bodies" by Drowning Pool, and you can't not rock out to this. Hopefully the neighbors will understand.

Music has a way of making me feel as if I'm not alone in my pain because there's someone out there who feels as much as I do. The lyrics articulate the things I can't bring myself to admit to anyone, sometimes not even myself, and for those few minutes, it heals my broken soul.

Draining the last of my water, I make my way into the kitchen for another bottle. I close my eyes as I belt the chorus down the hallway. But when I open my eyes, a bloodcurdling scream tears from my throat. A man in a black baseball cap is halfway through the window above the sink. Glass shards are scattered across the counter and on the floor. And I'm frozen where I stand as an intruder breaks into my home.

Again?!

His dark eyes meet mine as he hoists himself into my kitchen and plants his feet on the tile. He raises a tattooed index finger to his lips. "Shh. You're going to wake the neighbors."

The neighbors. My neighbor is a cop. Go!

I spin around and bolt down the hallway. Skidding to a stop in front of the door, I flick the lock, swing it open, and run face-first into a brick wall on my porch.

James grips my shoulders to steady me. "What's wrong?"

I point toward the kitchen. "There's s-someone… in my house."

He pushes me behind him as he stalks down the hall.

I pull out my phone and stop the blaring music. "Is your dad home? Should I call the cops?"

"I *am* the cops."

My head jerks back. *What?* But before I can ask what the hell that means, James spots the man in my kitchen and his hands ball into fists.

"Hey, big brother," the stranger says, as if it's the most normal thing in the world to smash in a window and climb into someone else's kitchen.

Wait, brother?

James lunges at him, but the man darts away and runs straight for me. I don't have to do much to stop him though. He slips on the tarp I have laid out on the floor in the entryway where I've been spackling, and his legs go up while the rest of him slams down onto the tile. His hat flies off, and then James is on him. He bends down to grip his hoodie and drags him toward the door like he weighs all but two pounds.

I step aside to let him pass and follow him out onto the porch. "Did he just say he's your brother?"

James ignores me as he slides the guy's body down the stairs like a sack of potatoes.

"Ow! Jesus, fuck. Watch my spine, dude."

James lets out a sardonic laugh. "Oh, I'm just warming you up for what's coming."

"Hold on a second." I run down the stairs behind them. "Is this the brother that's been missing?"

His brother answers while he's being dragged across my lawn. "I just took a little vacation."

That strikes James's last nerve. He lets his brother fall onto his back as he mounts him and slams his fist into his face. "You selfish piece of shit!"

His brother chuckles, revealing a bloody mouth. "And where does being selfless get you, James? Tell me, how's that Captain America bullshit working out for you?"

James lands another punch. He hammers him again, and again before he pushes off the ground to stand, and swings his foot, the toe of his boot connecting with his brother's ribs.

The quiet, composed man installing my lock this morning has been replaced by an explosive angry one. He's kicking the shit out of him, and I can't say I blame him. If my brother went missing and acted as nonchalant about it as this guy, I'd be pissed too. But if I've learned anything about family over the years, it's that you can't make them be who you want them to be no matter how hard you try. Beating his brother's ass won't make a difference.

James winds back for another punch, but I catch his elbow. "Enough! You're hurting him."

He freezes, and his brother rolls over onto his side, coughing and clutching his midsection.

"Breathe." I slide my palm over James's shoulder in slow circles, hoping to soothe his rage.

He blinks as if he's clearing his vision, and the warmth returns to his wild eyes. He stares down at his brother and uncurls his fists. "Dad will be home soon."

His eyes flick to mine, and in that instant, I know how he feels. You don't fight for the shit you couldn't care less about. You only fight for the people you love, and the things that matter. James loves his brother very much.

And that resonates with me.

I bend down and hold out my hand to the bleeding stranger. "Come on. I've got a first aid kit in my house." I toss one of his arms over my shoulder, and James takes the other. We hoist him up and walk him back inside.

He groans as we prop him up on my toilet seat. "I think you broke my ribs, bro."

James doesn't say a word. *At least I'm not the only one he ignores.*

His brother, however, has no problem continuing to fill the silence. "So, who are you?"

I lean forward and dab his lip with a cotton ball. "I'm your new neighbor. This is my house."

His eyes flick to the open buttons on my Henley. "Sweet. I've always wanted a hot neighbor."

I grip his jaw hard. "Eyes up here, buddy. There's nothing in there for you."

He chuckles, until I put peroxide on his cut, and then I'm the one wearing a smirk as he hisses.

"I'm Leo. Where are you from?"

I toss the bloody cotton ball into the trash and pick up another. "New York. This was my family's shore house."

"Was?"

I steal a glance at James who's staring down at the box of Band-Aids before I focus back on Leo. "Why didn't you tell your brother where you were? He's been looking for you."

Leo's Adam's apple bobs. "I don't need to answer to him. I'm a grown-ass adult. He needs to worry about his own life and stop worrying so much about what I choose to do with mine." I press more peroxide into the gash on his lip, and he jerks his head back. "Take it easy. That shit burns."

James finally pipes up. "Dad was worried."

Leo's jaw clenches. "Everyone needs to stop worrying so much. I can take care of myself."

"Is that why you broke into my house tonight? Is this you taking care of yourself?" I shake my head. I should mind my business, but he came into *my* house, so in a way, he made this my business—and I can't help the words from tumbling out. "You know, you're lucky to have a family who worries about you, and actually fucking cares about your well-being."

Both of their heads snap to me.

I snatch the box of Band-Aids out of James's hands and pull one out. Without meeting either of their curious gazes, I peel off the backing and smooth it over Leo's eyebrow. "You owe me a window."

I leave them in the bathroom and make a beeline into the kitchen, picking up Leo's baseball cap along the way. Footsteps sound in the hall a moment later, and then the front door opens and closes. I breathe out a sigh of relief, and slump against the counter, rubbing my forehead in small circles.

Despite the fact that my neighbors seem pretty dysfunctional, I can't help but feel jealous. I've been here for two days, and my brother has yet to call or text. I shouldn't be surprised—he barely called to check in on me while I was in Clearview—but that doesn't mean it hurts any less. My own mother disowned me when I was at my lowest. I truly have no one who cares about me, other than Drew, who's only my friend because we were stuck in a mental facility together.

How did I get here?

Hot tears sting my eyes, but I blink them away, not wanting to give in to feeling upset about people who clearly don't feel upset about me. Or miss me. Or think about me.

It's easier to be angry than it is to feel this disappointed.

Fuck them.

I toss the larger glass shards into the recycling bin and sweep the smaller pieces into a dustpan. Just then, the front door opens and closes again, followed by the sound of heavy boots clomping down the hall. James appears in the kitchen holding a piece of cardboard and a roll of duct tape.

I lift an eyebrow. "You going to tie me up and finish what you started last night?"

He shakes his head as he walks over to the sink. "This will do until I can get you a new glass pane tomorrow."

"Why isn't your brother here fixing it?"

"You don't want my brother fixing anything, trust me."

I dump the contents of the dustpan into the garbage and watch James while he works. He presses the cardboard to the window and secures it with tape around the edges. That's when I notice the skin on his knuckles, red and swollen from pummeling his brother's face.

I snatch the dish towel hanging from the handle on the stove and dig into the ice bucket in the freezer. "Give me your hand."

He hesitates, so I step closer and take his right hand.

He jerks it back, but I grab it again and press the ice against the top of it. "Hold still. Don't be a baby."

"You've helped enough." His eyes meet mine for all of two seconds before dropping to the towel. "Thank you, by the way. For dealing with my brother."

"Your dad seems nice. I didn't want him to see the two of you fighting like that." I pause before asking, "Where's your mom?"

"She passed."

I drop the conversation because I know all too well what that's like. No wonder he's fighting so hard to keep his family together. These Russo men are all each other has.

I shrug and try to lighten the situation. "Just figured I'd ask in case there are any other Russo members I should expect to come crawling through my window. What is it with your family and breaking into people's houses?"

The corner of his mouth twitches.

"I mean, I should just make each of you a spare key. That way, you don't have to keep breaking my shit."

His warm honey eyes meet mine. "I promise it won't happen again, Phoenix."

My body stills at the sound of my full name. His father must've told him after he saw it on my license last night. "No one calls me that. It's just Nix."

He cocks his head to the side, watching me for a moment. "You don't like Phoenix?"

"I don't." I take the ice and dump it back into my freezer, needing to turn around so he stops looking at me like a science experiment. "Thanks for boarding up the window. I'll see you tomorrow."

He takes the hint, and I wait until I hear the front door click shut behind him.

Only later as I lie in bed does it dawn on me that I have no idea why he was standing on my porch tonight in the first place. I'm grateful he was there to handle his brother when he came through my kitchen window, but...

What was James doing here?

3

Phoenix

Daily Affirmation: "I let go of thinking about the past and the future and trust my inner wisdom to guide me in the present moment."

"Are they hot?"

I roll my eyes. "Does it matter?"

Drew clicks his tongue. "Of course it matters. Looks always matter."

"And why is that?"

"Think about it. If an unattractive Shrek-like woman breaks into my house, I'm calling the cops. But if she's good-looking—let's say a smoking brunette with big boobs—then I'll be more apt to play break-and-enter before I enter her."

A loud laugh rips out of me. "Oh my god. You're sick. Are they even doing anything for you in that place?"

He chortles. "You know I'm right. That's why you're laughing."

I can't argue the fact that the Russo brothers are attractive—in very different ways. Leo's tattoos definitely draw the eye. He's the leaner, scrappier of the two. The fallen angel. The bad boy. Lots of women like that type, the kind they think needs saving. James is the larger, clean-cut version of his younger brother. His muscles are thicker, and his eyes are captivating. Plus, he's got the whole quiet and brooding thing working for him.

Apparently, it's working for me too.

I let out a frustrated sigh, but I can't deny it. "Fine. James is good-looking. But that's it. He's just… nice to look at."

"Well, don't go and get a boyfriend before I even get out of here. We need to enjoy some single nights out first."

"I'm not getting a boyfriend. Don't worry."

The doorbell rings, saving me from enduring the rest of this conversation. "He's here, let me go." I end the call and scurry toward the door.

It's been well over two years since I've so much as kissed another man. Depression, my father's death, my suicide attempt, and spending the last year and a half in a mental institution haven't exactly been great for my love life. So it's no surprise the sight of my attractive neighbor has me fanning myself. He's hot. No big deal.

Until I swing open the door and see James standing on my porch, and all of the air leaves my lungs. He towers over me in a short-sleeve navy-blue button-up tucked into matching pants. The uniform conforms to his muscular arms and legs, hugging his trim waistline, and putting his strong forearms on display. His hair is neatly styled, shiny from the product he used to slick it into place, and dark aviators conceal his eyes.

But despite the eye candy standing before me, it's the holstered gun hanging from his hip that has my jaw hanging wide open.

James Russo is a police officer.

I bite the inside of my cheek to keep the laughter from bubbling out. "You're shitting me." A giggle escapes me, and I clamp my hand over my mouth. "You're a cop? The man who broke into my house is an enforcer of the law?" More laughter spills out of me until I can't control it.

James shifts from one foot to the other, clenching his jaw. "It's not that funny."

I hunch over and brace my palms on my knees for support. I wheeze, each word barely coming out. "You were in handcuffs the other night." A tear forms in the corner of my eye, and I swat at it as I try to catch my breath.

James pushes past me, clearly out of patience, and he lumbers into the hallway with his measuring tape. "I need the dimensions of your window. I'll be back with the glass tonight after my shift."

I sniffle as the laughter subsides and follow him to the kitchen. "I can do that myself if you have to get to work. Then I can have the glass waiting here for you when you have time to install it."

He stretches over the counter, measuring the window as if I didn't just speak.

I cross my arms over my chest. "What, do you think I'm not capable of taking accurate measurements or something?"

"That's not what I said."

"I'm capable, you know."

"I don't doubt it."

But then it dawns on me. This is what he's used to doing. Leo fucks shit up, and James swoops in to make it all better. He's the fixer.

How much of his life has been spent trying to clean up his brother's messes?

"What were you even doing here last night?" I lean against my counter. "You were already standing on my porch when I opened the door."

"I was coming to tell you to turn down your music."

I snort. *Of course he was.* "You don't bat an eye when you break into someone's home, but loud music is where you draw the line?"

He retracts the measuring tape with a snap and spins around to face me. "Are you going to keep throwing that back in my face? I said I was sorry, and I fixed the lock on your door. What more do you want?"

"Easy, officer. I was just kidding. I'll keep the noise down. Jeez, someone's grumpy in the morning."

"I'm not grumpy. I'm just..." He pulls off his sunglasses and blows out a long stream of air through his lips. "I'm stressed, and I shouldn't be taking it out on you. I'm sorry."

"It's fine. I get it."

"Do you?"

More than you know, buddy.

"Why don't we start over?" I stick out my hand between us. "Hi, I'm Nix. I just moved in."

Amusement flashes in his eyes. "It's nice to meet you. I'm James."

His hand engulfs mine in a firm shake, and warmth spreads up my arm. I try to think of something witty to say, but with those beautiful eyes of his on me, my brain turns to mush. He needs to put those sunglasses back on.

Still holding my hand, he says, "Well, have a nice day, Phoenix."

I yank my hand away. "I told you not to call me that."

"What's wrong with your name?"

"I just don't like it, okay?" I give his chest a light shove. "Now, go. I have a lot of shit to do today."

My pace slows as I round the corner of my cul-de-sac on the way back from my evening run.

I smell a skunk.

Some of the houses on the block are owned by retired locals who live here all year round. Any one of them can be the cause of this scent. Baby Boomers love their marijuana. But a cloud of smoke rises from the alley between the Russo's house and mine, and I have a sneaking suspicion I know who it's coming from.

Leo smiles wide as I enter the alley. "Hey, neighbor."

I arch a brow. "I knew I smelled trouble."

He looks happy as a clam despite the scabs and bruises on his face. "What you're smelling is *fun*. The scent often gets confused with trouble when uptight pricks get a whiff of it."

I chuckle and lean against my house facing him. "Fun wouldn't be hiding out here in the alley if it weren't causing trouble."

"Touché, neighbor girl. So, does that mean you came out here looking for some trouble?" He holds out his joint and wiggles his eyebrows.

"Trouble's not my thing."

"Ah. That's too bad." His eyes trail down the length of my body, lingering on my spandex-clad thighs. "We could've gotten into some together."

"Look at me like that again, and I'll make the beating your brother gave you last night feel like a tickle fight."

He throws his head back as he laughs, and then winces, clutching his ribs. "Okay, okay. No need to get all Black Widow on me. I can take a hint."

"Something tells me you need more than a hint. Maybe a giant flashing neon sign."

"Nice hat, by the way."

I tap the brim of Leo's black hat I decided to wear today. "Call it my consolation prize."

He spreads his arms out wide. "I'll be your consolation prize, baby."

I roll my eyes so hard it hurts. "I'd rather an apology instead."

"I'm sorry. Your house has been empty for years. I wasn't expecting anyone to be living in it." Leo jerks his chin toward my house. "I envy you, with that house all to yourself."

"Is that why you came through my window last night? You wanted to be alone?"

"To be fair, I tried the front door but it was locked."

I laugh. "What's wrong with your house?"

"It's too suffocating in there."

"Well, I envy *you* with a houseful of people who care about you."

"Maybe we can do some *Freaky Friday* shit, and switch bodies."

I snort. "All you'd do is play with your tits and get yourself off."

"You're not wrong." He winks. "So, what's your name?"

"Nix."

"Like Stevie?"

"No, and don't ask me to sing." I stuff my hands into the pockets of my bubble vest. "Why is it so suffocating in your house?"

He digs the heel of his hand into his eye. "They want me to be someone I'm not. They expect me to be like them."

"And you're not?"

"There are two types of people in this world, Nixie: The do-gooders, and the fuckups. I'm the latter, and they can't handle that."

I hum. "That puts me in the same category as you then."

His dark irises meet mine. "Is that why you're here alone? You're the fuckup of your family too?"

"Yup. But I don't think your theory is correct. Life isn't so black and white. I think we're all a little fucked up, and it doesn't mean we're bad people. You can't lump us into the same category as the Ted Bundy's of the world."

"I did break into your house."

"You just said you thought it was empty. You weren't trying to hurt me. You don't go around kicking dogs, do you?"

He shakes his head. "People don't see it that way though. Everyone looks at me like I'm a piece of shit. I'm just the loser junkie."

"People resort to drugs because they're in pain."

Leo watches me through narrowed eyes. "It never goes away though. When the high wears off, the pain is still there."

The pain is always there.

"We all carry around the weight of our traumas and try to survive. We do what we have to in order to cope." I glance up at the night sky. "It's not us who's fucked up. *Life* is fucked up."

He takes a long pull and holds his breath before blowing out the smoke. "How do *you* cope with your trauma?"

Not very well. I swallow, rubbing my scar. But I don't have time to answer because footsteps crunch on the concrete path followed by his brother's deep voice. "Goddamnit, Leo. I can smell you from here."

I snatch the blunt from Leo's fingers just as James comes into view at the end of the alley.

His eyes bounce between me and his brother before dropping to my hand. His lips press into a firm line, nostrils flaring. "Give me that."

I hand over the contraband, feeling like I'm back in high school even though I'm a twenty-eight-year-old woman.

James doesn't take his eyes off me when he speaks. "Leo, get inside."

"Maybe you should take a hit of that, big brother. You need to loosen up." Leo pats his shoulder as he slips past him. He walks backward and mouths "thank you" before he disappears.

I squirm under James's hard glare. "It's just weed, James."

"He doesn't need to be around it. He needs to get clean."

"Weed isn't like other drugs. Some people need it to calm down. It helps them."

"I don't give a shit."

His clipped tone makes my shoulders jump. "Well, you should. There are more important things in life than right and wrong. You should try being his brother, and not his parole officer."

"You've got a lot to say for someone who doesn't know us at all."

"You've inserted yourselves into my life, so it feels like I have a right to offer some friendly advice. In fact, here's another: He's not your responsibility."

"Says the one who took the blame for him." He holds up the joint he confiscated. "I know this isn't yours."

I plant my hands on my hips. "You should cut him some slack."

He towers over me as he steps into my space. "Who are you to tell me what I should do with my family?"

"Blood isn't everything. He needs a friend."

"How would you know what he needs?"

"Because I know what it feels like to have no one."

James's eyes bounce between mine as my words hang between us. I wish I wouldn't have blurted them out, but it's too late now. So, I pluck the joint from his fingers, take a puff, and then blow the smoke in his face just to be a brat.

His head rears back, and he lowers his gaze to my outfit. "Running and smoking pot don't exactly mix."

"Sure they do. They both help with anxiety."

His eyebrow arches. "You have anxiety?"

I don't normally go around telling strangers I have a mental disorder, but it's easier to say that I have anxiety than it is depression.

"Yep. I've had it my whole life." My eyes narrow. "And if you tell me to *just relax*, I'm going to kick you in your balls."

He grunts. "People tell you that often?"

"It's as if we didn't already think of relaxing. Like yes, Martha, thank you for that very helpful advice. The next time immense, uncontrollable fear seizes my body, my lungs constrict, and I stop inhaling oxygen, I'll be sure to remind myself to fucking relax. What a revelation."

The corner of his mouth twitches. "Still, marijuana is illegal."

"Barely. And it's your fault anyway. Two break-ins in the last forty-eight hours aren't exactly great for my nerves."

His shoulders droop as if I stuck a pin in his bravado. "So much for starting over, huh?"

I lift my hand and let it fall. "Look, I don't want to fight. He's your brother, and I'll mind my business." I move around his large frame, but he surprises me by reaching for my hand.

"I can come by and fix your window. Is now a good time?"

"Sure."

James walks me to my front porch, where a pane of glass is propped against the first step. "I was going to throw some frozen pizza in the oven. You want a slice?"

"You're going to eat pizza after a run?"

"Okay, Judgy Judgerton. You telling me I can't afford to have some pizza?"

"No. That's not what I meant at all. Your body is... you're..."

My feet slow on the porch, and I turn around to meet his worried gaze.

He scratches the back of his neck as his eyes trail down my body. "I mean, you're perfect."

Perfect? I laugh it off. "Hardly. But I can't cook, and frozen pizza is all I've got right now."

He's quiet as he follows me inside, and I go about making my dinner of champions while he works on installing the new glass.

I may or may not glance at his round, muscular ass several times as he stretches over the sink. I've never been particularly drawn to a man's rear end before. But every now and then, one demands you take notice. And I'm definitely taking notice.

If he can look, then so can I, right?

4

James

"Wait, she made Dad *handcuff* you?"

I glare at Leo as he doubles over with laughter, clutching his stomach.

Dad's belly shakes as he laughs, and even though I'm furious with my brother, I can't help the relief seeping into my stomach. Seeing Dad happy makes the anger subside.

"God, I would've loved to see that." Leo stuffs a piece of bread into his mouth. "The almighty James Russo with his hands behind his back."

"I did what I had to do. Poor thing was scared shitless." Dad glances at me over the rim of his glass. "She looks to be around your age."

Leo shoves another piece of bread into his mouth. "She's hot."

I shoot my brother another look.

"What? She is. Don't act like you didn't notice her in those spandex pants tonight." He wiggles his eyebrows. "Girl's got curves in all the right places."

Oh, I noticed.

Long brown hair, plump lips, and those big doe eyes. And yes, she has a fit little body. She's gorgeous. But my new neighbor also has a snarky remark for everything, telling me what to do with my own brother as if she knows better.

Hell, maybe she does.

I shouldn't have snapped at her tonight. Maybe that's the reason why I made her a container of food and left it on her porch. Blame it on the guilt, instead of the fact that I wanted to provide her with a decent meal that hadn't come out of a freezer.

"Leave the girl alone, Leo." Dad sets down his glass. "Why don't you tell me about what happened to your face?"

Leo chokes on his bread and slaps his chest as he coughs.

I shake my head. *Idiot.*

"This bread is dry as fuck." He chugs his water. "Tell the chef he needs to do better."

I kick his shin under the table. "You're lucky the chef is letting you eat any of his food at all."

"Dinner tastes great, as always." Dad nudges my arm. "Don't listen to him."

Leo smirks. "Does your ass ever get sore from Dad's head being up there?"

I squeeze the steak knife in my right hand. "I can ram this knife up your ass and show you what it feels like if you're jealous."

"Enough." Dad's voice makes us both jump. "It's the first time we're sitting down together in a long while. Can't we get through one meal without arguing?"

Leo and I exchange glances.

Dad sighs and glances at Leo. "You're fighting again, aren't you?"

Leo nods, and it's not so much of a lie as it is a stretch of the truth. He'd fight whether it was with me or someone else. "I like fighting. I'm good at it."

"Doesn't mean you should do it. Those underground rings aren't safe."

"I'll be safe."

"It's not you I'm talking about." Dad balls his napkin in his fist. "People fight dirty. I've gotten calls about those fights down at the station. It's only a matter of time before someone dies."

"I need to fight, okay? Just let me have this."

"Why?"

31

Bring Me Back

"I'm clean."

My fork drops onto my plate, and Dad stops chewing.

"Have been for over a month now." Leo rubs the back of his neck, looking between the both of us. "I know you think I won't be able to stay clean, but I can. I want to."

Dad watches him as if he doesn't believe him. "That's why you disappeared?"

He nods. "I didn't want you to see me detoxing. It was… ugly."

"Why?" I can't help the disbelief in my tone. "Why now?"

Leo stares down at his plate, the muscles in his jaw clenching and releasing. "My friend overdosed. The one I've been staying with. I found him in his basement."

I shake my head. "So, you came back home because you couldn't stay at your friend's house for free and get high anymore."

"No, that's not it." He lifts a shoulder and lets it fall. "I don't want that to be me. I don't want one of you to find me like that, cold, in a pile of vomit."

"That's good to hear, Leo. Because I don't want to find you like that either." Dad swipes a tear with the back of his hand. "I'm sorry about your friend. But sometimes it takes a loss like that to kick you in the ass and send you in the right direction."

"What does you getting clean have to do with underground fighting?" I'm not trying to be a dick, but I need to understand.

Leo wipes his palms on his jeans, something he's done since he was a kid whenever he's nervous. "Some people drink when they want to numb their pain." His eyes flick to Dad before dropping back down to his lap. "If I'm not getting high anymore, then I need to replace that feeling. I need to feel… something."

"And getting punched in the face does it for you?"

"It's the rush of adrenaline when I'm in the fight."

I blink at him. "Shit, I can kick your ass every night if you want me to. Why didn't you say something sooner?"

Leo flips me off, but he's smiling. Dad laughs too, and that's all I need to see.

"I just want my boys happy and healthy." Dad reaches across the table and covers Leo's hand with his. "I'm glad you came home, son. And I'm proud of you for wanting to get clean."

Dad and his hopeful heart. We both know Leo declaring he *wants* to stay clean is much different than Leo actually staying clean. But I don't have the nerve to say it. Dad needs something good to hold on to right now. It feels like the three of us have been drifting through the underworld for years. Lost souls, barely alive. Or maybe Mom took them with her when she left us.

Maybe this is all our lives are meant to be without her.

Nighttime is the worst.

After dinner, I cleared off the table, washed the dishes, packed Dad's lunch for tomorrow, watched a movie, and folded my laundry. Now I don't know what to do with myself.

I roll onto my back and stare into the darkness of my room. Sleep never comes easy. Not since Mom died. It's the reason I take as many night shifts as I can. I try to recall the happy memories—her bright smile, her warm hugs, the sound of her voice. Until the last vision I have of her flashes through my mind and destroys everything that came before it.

A soft light streaks through my window, drawing my attention. I sit up and lean over to see where it's coming from. My room is on the side of the house, overlooking the alley I caught Leo smoking pot in earlier. But as I stare out my window, I realize Phoenix's bedroom is on the side of her house as well.

Directly across from mine.

My eyes dart away on instinct, but curiosity gets the better of me and my gaze wanders back. Her long dark hair is wet, and she's wearing a white robe as she lowers herself onto her bed. I should look away. I'm invading her privacy. But I can't bring myself to turn my head. Something about the way she sits there staring down at her hands in her lap calls to me.

Something's wrong.

I squint, moving closer to the window until it fogs up from my breath. She lifts her hand and swats at her cheek. Once, twice. She blows out a stream of air through her lips and looks up at her ceiling, as if she's sending up a silent prayer. Then she covers her face with both of her hands, and her shoulders shake as she bends forward.

My gut twists. Why is she crying? What happened? My first instinct is to go over there and find out, but how would I explain myself? *Hi, Phoenix. I saw you crying while I was watching you through the window like a Peeping Tom.*

I shake my head. I don't know anything about this girl. She's crying—so what? We've all cried. We're all going through shit. Why should I care? For all I know, she's upset over something ridiculous, or insignificant.

But her voice floats through my head like a sad song.

I know what it feels like to have no one.

You're lucky to have a family who worries about you.

She's alone. So, I watch her until she lies down and cries herself to sleep. I'm with her in this moment, even if she doesn't know it.

Since sleep isn't happening anytime soon for me, I trot downstairs for a late-night snack.

Dad and Leo are already sitting at the table.

"We're a sorry bunch." Dad chuckles as he pulls out the chair beside him. "Can't sleep?"

I shake my head and dump the box of Lucky Charms into a bowl. "Not tired."

Leo smirks. "Just go next door and bang the pretty neighbor. We both know that's what's keeping you up."

Dad smacks Leo in the back of his head before I can get to him. "What's wrong with you? Who taught you to talk about women like that? You're twenty-three years old. You should know better."

I lower myself onto the chair. "What do we know about her? Did you run the background search?"

"So you *are* thinking about her." Leo pumps his fist into the air. "Fuckin' knew it. I swear, I just know shit."

Dad shakes his head and talks around the spoonful of cereal. "I didn't think we needed to. She's not causing trouble, and it's an invasion of her privacy if we poke around like that without a cause."

Not half as bad as watching her through her bedroom window. I rub my temples in small circles. "You're right."

"I think she's been through some shit." Leo stares down at his bowl. "And she doesn't have anyone to turn to."

I lean my elbows onto the table. "And how do you know that?"

"We were talking earlier."

Dad nods like he agrees. "There's a reason she's living in her family's shore house without her family."

Leo wipes his mouth with the back of his hand. "I'm going to look out for her."

I cross my arms over my chest, irritation spiking in my veins. "You need to look out for yourself."

"I have you for that, don't I?"

"Boys," Dad warns. "I don't have the energy for your shit right now. It's after one in the morning."

Leo holds up his hands on either side of his head.

"The last thing we need is you two fighting over a pretty girl."

"No one's fighting over a girl." Leo smirks. "Besides, she shot me down."

An odd sense of relief blankets me. "You already made a pass at her? You've known her for five minutes."

"Like I said, she's hot." He shrugs. "And she gets me."

"Shit." Dad laughs. "Then we better get her a Nobel Peace Prize for figuring you out."

Leo balls up his napkin and tosses it at Dad. "You guys understand me too. You just don't want to admit it, because then that means you could end up like me."

Dad and I fall silent. He's right. I don't blame Leo for turning to drugs. I'd love to escape reality every once in a while. But I don't have the luxury of forgetting all my problems. I'm the one who has to hold everything together. I'm the one who has to keep Dad going. Which is why I can't let myself believe Leo will stay clean, because if he lets me down again, I don't know if I'll be able to take it.

Sometimes, it feels like one more heartbreak will ruin me for good.

5

Phoenix

Daily Affirmation: "I am open to receiving new changes, new lessons, and new adventures."

"Well, look who it is."

I wrap my arms around Drew's shoulders. "Surprise."

"I thought they were fucking with me when they said I had a visitor." He pulls back and eases himself into the chair across from me. "What are you doing here?"

"I have therapy today, so I came a bit earlier to see you." I glance at the reddish-purple marks around his wrists. "You okay?"

He shrugs. "Had a rough night."

A rough night in a place like Clearview means more than the usual *I couldn't sleep*. "What happened?"

"Trish was annoying me. You know how she always tries to get on my nerves to set me off."

I frown. "How long did they restrain you for?"

"I don't know." He chuckles. "I punched Billy in the face though. Got him good."

"Poor Billy. He's always getting beat up."

"The man needs a raise putting up with me, that's for sure." He pulls his knees up to his chest. "So, how's the renovation going?"

"Good. It's keeping me busy."

"I can't wait to see the place when I get out of here."

"June tenth. Only a few more months."

"Just in time for summer." His green eyes widen. "Let's throw a Fourth of July party!"

"And who are we inviting to this party? We're the only friends we have."

"You'll make friends for the both of us."

I laugh and shake my head. "We'll talk about it when the time comes."

"Fine." His expression changes, and he rubs his wrists. "Thanks for coming to visit me, Nix. Seriously. It means a lot to me that you're still keeping in touch."

I reach across the table and squeeze his shoulder. "I told you I wasn't going to forget about you once I left."

Dr. Erica waltzes into the room and smiles. "Phoenix, it's so good to see you."

"It's nice to be back. Sounds weird, but I miss this place."

"It's not weird at all. It's common for patients to miss the safety and security of a place like this."

Drew holds up his marked wrists. "Can't imagine I'll miss this."

Dr. Erica frowns. "I'm sorry that happened to you, but you know the protocol. If you're a danger to yourself or others—"

"I have to be restrained and sedated." Drew rolls his eyes. "I know, I know."

Dr. Erica turns to me. "Are you ready?"

I nod and hug Drew. "Try to keep your cool, okay? Whenever you get mad, just think about our Fourth of July party."

He ushers me toward the door. "Don't worry about me, Nix. I'll be fine."

I follow Dr. Erica down the hallway and into her office.

"It's strange being back here when I'm not a patient."

She smiles. "You've come a long way."

I sit in the familiar yellow chair and smooth my hands over the armrests. "Sometimes it feels like I'm in a different place than I was, and other times I feel like I'm right back where I started when I came here."

"That's because you're still the same person, with the same core beliefs and values. As you experience life, you learn and you grow, and you become different versions of yourself, but you're still the same person essentially."

Wish I could change into a different person altogether.

"Tell me, how has your first week been?"

I let out a soft laugh, gazing out the window behind my therapist's chair. "Eventful."

Her eyebrows lift. "How so?"

"I've been keeping busy with renovating the house."

"That's good." She scribbles something on her notepad.

"I've been running every day."

"Excellent. That's important."

"And I met my new neighbors."

"Oh?"

"The father is a police officer, and so is his oldest son, James. I'd say he's around my age, late twenties. His brother Leo is a few years younger."

Erica glances at me over the rim of her glasses. "Making friends is a great way to become part of the community. I know you were nervous about living on your own before you left here. How have you been feeling?"

"I get nervous at night, but it helps knowing there's a family of cops next door."

Even if they're the ones scaring me in the middle of the night.

"And you've been taking your medication?"

I nod. "I wish the antidepressant didn't dehydrate me. I'm drinking so much water, half my day is spent running to the bathroom to pee."

She chuckles. "That's an irritating side effect."

"But hey, I guess it's better to feel thirsty all the time than to feel like I want to die, right?"

She writes something on her pad again. "Yes, that's the point of your medication. Have you had any suicidal thoughts since you've been out?"

"No." I glance down at my wrist. "It's strange. I don't feel like I want to die, but I also don't feel excited about living."

Erica sets down her pen and slides off her glasses. "So then it bears asking: What do you think would make you feel excited about living?"

"I don't know."

"Think about it. What makes you happy?"

I heave a sigh and focus on the clouds drifting past the window. "I enjoy running and reading. I like going out to eat and trying different foods. But I don't have anyone to go with."

"You'll make friends in time, but you don't need anyone to go to a restaurant with. You can sit by yourself and enjoy your own company." She lifts a finger. "Or you can take a cooking class. You'd probably make some friends there too."

A cooking class would be interesting. I could learn how to cook something other than frozen pizza.

"You know, Nix. Your father left you a lot of money. He'd want you to spend it on the things that make you happy."

Other than buying things to maintain the house, I haven't spent any of it for myself. "I don't want to spend it. I don't want anything. I just want my dad back."

The money doesn't mean anything without him.

"Not spending it won't bring him back."

I drop my chin. "I know."

"Have you been writing in your journal?"

I chew my bottom lip. "No. But I've been reading the affirmations."

"What's stopping you from writing?"

"I don't know. I guess I'm just not sure what I should be writing."

"There are no rules, Nix. You can write whatever you want, whatever comes out in that moment. You can write what you're feeling, what's weighing on your mind. Many people find it helpful to write down a few things they're grateful for, and some positive affirmations of their own."

I snort. "I can't write affirmations."

"Why not?"

"I don't know. They're so… cheesy. What would I even say?"

"An affirmation is a way to praise yourself. Think of the things you appreciate about yourself. The things you're proud of."

My thumb rubs idle circles around my scar while I think. "I haven't done anything to be proud of."

"According to who?"

I shrug.

"You're living every day with depression. You overcame a suicide attempt, and you're working on building a new life in the wake of that. I'd say you have a lot to be proud of. Your strength. Your courage. Just because you don't see it doesn't mean it's not there." She points to her chest. "Go to the core of who you are as a person. The things you value. The things you consider to make yourself a good friend, or family member. And it doesn't have to be cheesy. It doesn't even have to be something you believe."

My eyebrows press together. "Why would I praise myself for something I don't believe to be true?"

"Because everyone has to start somewhere. You've been working on self-love, and self-worth, so you're not going to have a list of things you love about yourself right off the bat. But the idea is to practice saying it until it becomes the truth. Force a new pathway of thought patterns. Take control of what you think by feeding your mind positive thoughts." She shrugs. "Eventually, you'll start to believe it."

I laugh. "You're telling me to fake it until I make it?"

"Exactly."

"That I can do."

After spackling for the rest of the day, I clean up and head outside with a bag of scraps to toss into the trash.

But when I get to the side of my house, my garbage pail is missing.

"I rolled out the garbage for you, Miss Bridges. Pickup is tomorrow."

My head snaps up toward Jim Russo's voice. He's standing on his porch in his uniform.

"Thank you, sir. You didn't have to do that."

"It's not a problem at all." His gaze flicks down to my stained clothes. "How's it going in there? My boys mentioned you're doing some renovating."

"I'm just doing minor things for now. I'll have to hire someone to take care of the roof, and the deck out back." I give him a sheepish smile. "It's overwhelming when I think about it all at once, so I'm starting slow."

"I have a guy who can take a look at your bulkhead. I have a roof guy too." He chuckles. "I know a lot of guys. I'll get you their business cards."

"That'd be great. Thank you so much."

I turn to walk down the driveway, but he calls out to me again. "Miss Bridges, do you have dinner plans?"

"No, sir."

"Why don't you join us tonight?"

I shake my head. "I wouldn't want to impose. Thank you for the offer though."

He waves a dismissive hand. "Nonsense. It's not an imposition. We'd love to have you."

I stare into his kind eyes. *Won't it be awkward to have dinner with people I hardly know?*

His round cheeks push up as he smiles. "All my sons do is argue at the table. Put me out of my misery so I have someone to talk to."

I bite back a smile. "They do argue a lot, huh?"

He scrubs a hand over his jaw. "Miss Bridges, you have no idea."

I take a deep breath. "Let me get cleaned up, and I'll be there."

"Fantastic. I'll see you soon."

I change into a pair of jeans and pull on a black long-sleeve top. I rake a brush through my long strands and staring at my plain reflection in the mirror, I figure a little mascara won't hurt either. I know I'm not as put-together on the inside as I look on the outside right now, but Dr. Erica told me to fake it until I make it. It's the first time I've put effort into my appearance, and it feels kind of good.

After I grab a box of cookies from the mini-mart down the road, I head over to the Russo's. My father taught me to never show up anywhere empty-handed, and I smile down at the box in my hands.

Miss you, Dad.

The door swings open, and Leo's wide grin greets me. "Hey, neighbor."

I sweep my hand in front of my body. "See this? This is how to enter a neighbor's home. One person rings the bell, and the other person lets them in."

"Very civilized. I prefer climbing in through the window." He smirks as he grips my forearm and yanks me into the house. "Come on. We can watch my brother have a meltdown in the kitchen."

"Why is he having a meltdown?" My eyes bounce around as I'm dragged through the hallway. Their house is the exact model as mine, except theirs looks more like a home. Lived in. Pictures hang from the walls, and shoes are scattered around the entryway.

"Because he takes his cooking very seriously, and you're the first guest we've had in forever." He eyes my chest. "Well, the first female guest."

I swat his arm. "Don't look at my boobs unless you want to eat your dinner through a straw tonight."

Leo throws his head back and laughs. "God, I'm glad you're here, Nixie."

Affection warms my chest. He's so open with his emotions. His laugh is loud, his smile is huge, and he isn't afraid to say whatever's on his mind. He's a breath of fresh air, and I hope his family appreciates that. I know I do, and he deserves to hear it.

"I'm glad you're here too, Leo."

His steps falter as he looks down at me. "You sound like you mean that."

"Wouldn't have said it if I didn't mean it." I shove the box of cookies at his chest. "Here, take these."

When we reach the dining room, Leo tosses the cookies onto the table, and breaks open the seal. "Chocolate chip is my favorite."

Jim stands from his seat at the head of the table and smacks his hand. "Don't eat them now. You'll ruin your appetite." He shakes his head as he leans in to hug me. "I swear, it's like these boys haven't aged a day since they were five."

I chuckle. "I can believe it."

"James is in the kitchen." He points toward the doorway. "Leo, show her around and get her something to drink."

Leo salutes him and takes my elbow. "I hope you're not looking for alcohol because this is a dry house."

"Water is fine with me. I don't drink."

"Why not?"

I shrug. "Never liked it."

It's an easier answer than the truth: Alcohol is a downer, and it fucks with my meds.

Leo enters the kitchen and whispers, even though he's being loud enough for the whole house to hear him. "Here we see the chef in his natural habitat. We cannot disturb the artist while he's in the middle of creating his masterpiece."

James sighs. "Do you ever shut the fuck up?"

I roll my lips together so I don't start laughing. "Also, that might be the worst Australian accent I've ever heard."

"I'm working on it." Leo slaps James on the back and massages his shoulders. "When's dinner? Our guest has arrived, and I'm starving."

James doesn't turn away from the stove as he speaks. "Considering I didn't know we were having a guest up until ten minutes ago, you're going to have to wait."

My stomach sinks. "I'm sorry. I told your father I didn't want to be an imposition, but he insisted."

James turns around to look at me with regret etched on his face. "That came out wrong. I don't mind that you're here. I just want to make sure I have enough for everyone."

I step forward to stand beside him at the stove. "Anything I can do to help?"

He shakes his head. "Guests don't help."

"I'm your neighbor, not Queen Elizabeth."

"Is there a difference? A guest is a guest."

"I told you, Nixie. He takes his work very seriously." Leo taps the doorframe before he heads back to the dining room.

My eyes bounce around the room, trying to settle on anything other than the way James's arms look in his fitted black T-shirt. "Well, can I set the table at least?"

"You want to help? Tell me how this tastes." James lifts the spoon from a large pot filled with creamy red sauce and brings it to his lips to blow on it first. Something about that thoughtful gesture has my heart rate kicking up a notch.

His warm honey eyes watch me with rapt attention as I lean forward to sip from the spoon. It's sweet with a zing of spices. "Wow. This is delicious, James. You made this from scratch?"

He nods and then swipes the excess sauce from the corner of my mouth with his thumb. Instead of wiping it on a napkin, he licks it off his finger. And I feel that one gentle lick all the way between my legs.

This shouldn't be the single most erotic moment in my life, yet here I am, panting like a dog in heat.

I clear my throat and take a step back. "That reminds me, thank you for leaving that container of food on my porch last night."

He shrugs like it's no big deal. "You should eat protein after a run."

"Pfft. A pizza hits three of the major food groups."

He shakes his head, but the hint of a dimple sinks into his cheek.

"It was really good. I wish I could cook like you. I've actually been thinking of enrolling in a cooking class. Do you know of any in the area?"

"I learned to cook from my mother." He twists the knob and shuts the burner. "I didn't take any classes."

"I guess I can Google it. There has to be something."

"I can teach you."

My eyebrows jump. "You'd do that?"

"It'd save you the money."

"I can pay you for your time."

He shakes his head. "I won't take your money."

"Well, if you're sure you don't mind, then I'll take you up on that offer. Just a few simple dishes, nothing fancy."

He nods. "Sure."

"I'm going to drop dead from hunger in here," Leo yells. "And Dad's looking a little pale. I think he has low blood sugar."

James pinches the bridge of his nose. "Why don't you set the table if you're so hungry?"

"I'm too weak to move."

I stifle a laugh. "Just think, last week you were looking for him to come home."

"It was a lot quieter here without him."

I pat him on the shoulder and snatch the bread basket off the counter. "You know you wouldn't trade it for the world."

James carries in a bowl for each of us, and then we're shoveling forkfuls of pasta into our faces.

"This tastes just like your mother made it." Jim dabs his mouth with a napkin. "You've outdone yourself, James."

"Was she a chef?" I look around the table, posing the question to anyone who wants to answer.

Jim shakes his head. "She just loved feeding her family. I never saw her as joyful as she was when she was in the kitchen. It came naturally to her." The boys remain quiet, staring down at their bowls as their father continues.

"Leo never had the patience for it, but James was like his mother's shadow. They were really close."

Leo glances up at me. "Dad and I would tinker with our toys in the garage until we'd smell dinner."

I smile. "That's how I was with my dad. I wanted to learn whatever he was doing. Whether he was under the hood of his car, or mowing the lawn, I was right out there with him asking him a million questions."

Jim laughs. "And I bet he answered every one of them."

"He did."

Leo takes a gulp of his iced tea. "What about your mom? Were you close with her too?"

I almost laugh at the notion. "No. We couldn't be more different. My brother learned how to navigate her personality, but I never did."

"Is he the older sibling?"

I nod. "By a few years."

"Ah, that explains it," Jim says. "The older one usually gets more patience."

"And the younger one?"

"The younger one gives his patience to everyone else because they're the ones who need it by the time he arrives."

Leo shoots me a wink across the table. "Younger siblings gotta stick together, Nixie."

"Where's your brother now?" James asks.

"He's down in Tennessee. He recently had a baby, so he's busy. We don't talk much."

"And your mom?"

"She's still in New York. She'll never leave, and I don't know if it's because she actually loves New York, or if she just hates change that much." I stab a few pieces of macaroni with my fork. "Our relationship pretty much went out the window after I lost my dad."

"When was that?" Leo asks.

"When I was fourteen. Cancer."

"I was sixteen when Mom died," Leo says. "Dead parents make high school fun, don't they?"

I let out a humorless laugh. "You're not kidding."

Silence blankets the table like it usually does after someone drops the dead parent card.

"That's why I'm fixing up the place." I gesture with my fork in the direction of my house. "He left it to me, and I couldn't bear to sell it."

I can hardly bear to live *in* it without him, but it's the easier option of the two.

Jim covers my hand with his. "I'm so sorry you lost him. I'll get you those business cards I was telling you about, and they'll give you a good deal. They'll help you with whatever you need."

"I appreciate that, sir."

"Call me Jim, will ya?"

I nod, and he squeezes my hand before he lets it go and turns his attention to James. "How did it go with all those dogs the other night?"

James shakes his head. "We got them to the shelter, but I don't know what's going to happen to them."

Leo's eyebrows pinch together. "What dogs?"

"We got an anonymous call from someone about a puppy mill down on Bay Street. The assholes were gone by the time we got there, but they left all the dogs behind." James shakes his head. "They were filthy."

I set down my fork. "Poor things. How many were there?"

"We counted twenty-six. A couple of them were, uh…" He scratches the back of his neck. "Already gone when we arrived."

I gasp and clamp my hand over my mouth.

Jim frowns. "No telling how long they'll make it at the shelter."

My head whips to the right. "What do you mean?"

"There's no room at these shelters."

I dip my chin. "So, you're saying…"

"They'll put them down," Leo finishes.

"Kill them?" My eyes bounce between James, his brother, and his father. "Why would they do that?"

"If nobody adopts them, they don't have the room to house all these animals." James looks down at his plate as if he can't bear to look at me when he says, "So, they euthanize them."

I balk. "That's horrible. There has to be something we can do."

Jim's eyebrows lift. "We?"

"Put flyers around town, spread the word somehow." I shrug. "Something other than just sit here and let innocent puppies get killed."

Leo chuckles. "You're passionate, Nixie. I'm in. Let's save the puppies."

My eyes widen. "Really? You'll help?"

"We'll all help you." He pats James's shoulder. "Isn't that right, big brother?"

James's eyes meet mine, and he holds my gaze for longer than he has since we met. "Sure."

I squeal. "We can set up an adoption event and invite everyone in town. Once they see how adorable the dogs are, they won't be able to leave without taking one home. We can get local businesses to contribute, and we'll promote them there. We'll need a dog grooming service to clean them up. Oh, and maybe we can get the local high school kids to volunteer to save money."

By the time I finish rattling off ideas, the men are all staring at me. I avert my gaze and take a bite of bread. "Okay, someone say something. Is that a dumb idea?"

"Not at all." Jim gives me a reassuring smile. "It's a great idea, actually. Getting the community involved will raise awareness."

Everyone returns to eating, but James's eyes linger on me. He's not checking me out the way his brother does, and his usual glare isn't in place. It's less like he's staring *at* me, and more like he's *watching* me—a strange new animal he's trying to study and figure out.

It's unsettling.

After dessert, I slip on my jacket and thank the Russos for having me.

Leo walks me to the door. "Well, we're both younger siblings, and we're bonded by our commonality of our dead parents. I guess that makes us best friends."

I chuckle. "As morbid as that is, I could use a best friend."

"And if you want a brother instead, I'll be your brother." He pops a shoulder as if it's the most nonchalant thing. "Either way, I got your back, Nixie."

Emotion lodges in my throat as reality sinks in. If I didn't go through the worst moment in my life, I wouldn't be where I am today. I wouldn't have met the Russos. They've shown me more help and kindness in the last week I've known them than my mother has shown me my whole life.

"Okay, but if you're going to be my brother, then you have to stop making comments about how hot I am. Brothers don't comment on their sister's tits. It's weird."

Leo grins as he wraps his arm around my shoulders. "You got it, sis."

"And I'm here for you too, you know." I side-eye him. "If you ever feel like disappearing again, you call me first."

His smile fades, and he nods. "I can do that."

James takes tentative steps into the entryway, his eyes bouncing between the two of us.

Leo gives me a nod. "Night, Nix."

James waits for his brother to get to the top of the stairs before he turns to me. "Be careful with him."

I give him a dubious look. "We're just friends. I'm not going to hurt him."

"I'm talking about you. He'll let you down."

"Well, I'll give him that chance."

He nods like he figured as much. "If you're free tomorrow night, I can come by with a few ingredients and we can cook something."

"Sure. Whatever works for you and your schedule."

He lifts a white shopping bag and holds it out to me.

I take it from him and peer inside. "What's all this?"

"I picked up a few things at Lowe's today to help you with your sanding. I noticed the tools you have aren't the right ones. If the sandpaper is too coarse, you'll sand right through the spackle and you'll have to start over again."

I blink down at the contents in the bag. "Thanks. That's very… nice of you."

"You say it like you're surprised."

I *am* surprised. Surprised at the act of kindness. Surprised that he cares. Surprised that he thought of me at all.

I hike a shoulder. "You are a cop, after all."

"I can be nice." He smirks. "When I want to be."

Now ask me why that sends a shiver down my spine.

6

Phoenix

Daily Affirmation: "I am attracting a new person into my life, and I won't let myself question this person's intentions."

"How are you with loud noises?"

"Fine, I guess." I scrunch my nose. "Why?"

The owner of the animal shelter, Sadie, grimaces. "When I open the next door, all the dogs start barking. It can be really overwhelming." She leads me down a short hallway. "The dogs either get excited or agitated when they see someone. Some can be really aggressive. Poor things have been through so much."

I frown. "I hate that a place like this even has to exist."

"Better than living on the streets."

"True." *Until they get put down.*

Sadie swings open the door, and my shoulders jump up to my ears. She wasn't kidding about the noise. The barking ranges from high pitch yapping to larger dogs with deep bass, mixed with sad howls. Floor-to-ceiling chain-link gates line the room. Some dogs look like they haven't had a meal in months, while others are missing patches of hair.

"I wish I could take them all home."

Sadie heaves a sigh. "I think about it every night when I clock out of here." She points to the far end of the room. "That's where your crew is. I kept each litter in the same cage because they're so young. A litter needs to keep each other company."

When we stop, I crouch down, linking my fingers through the first gate. "Oh my god. They're adorable."

Playful puppies tumble over each other, wrestling and nibbling on whatever they can get their little teeth on.

"These are Labs. There are Malteses and Yorkies over there." I follow her finger as she rattles off the different breeds. "Beagles, Dachshunds, and over in the last stall are the Pits. Those will likely be the first to go."

To go? My eyes widen as I push to stand. "What? Why?"

"Everyone wants the small, cute dogs. Pit bulls are commonly used for fighting, and they have a stigma surrounding them. The dangerous ones get euthanized immediately."

I head to the pit bull cage, and my heart thunders in my chest. "How can these guys be dangerous? They're so cute."

"They get big, and they're strong. They get a bad rap."

"Look at that one." I point to the puppy curled up in the corner. He has a black body with a white face. "His nose is in the perfect shape of a heart."

Sadie laughs. "You're right."

"Why isn't he playing with his brothers and sisters?"

"He's a lot smaller than them. He looks like the runt of the litter."

The corners of my mouth turn down. "So, they won't play with him because he's smaller?"

"Unfortunately, that's the animal kingdom's way of weeding out the weak ones."

My lips part in surprise. "Can I… am I allowed to hold him?"

"I can let you in for a bit. But I don't recommend getting too attached. It only makes it that much harder."

A lump rises in my throat when I step inside the concrete space. The puppies swarm me as soon as Sadie closes the gate behind me, and I laugh as I bend down to pet them. "Easy, easy. You're trampling each other."

I approach the tiny dog trembling in the corner, and his black eyes are locked on me. I press my back against the wall and slide down beside him. The tip of his tail looks like it was dipped in white paint, but it's matted and missing hair in places. It wiggles furiously as I reach over to pet him.

"I see that tail wagging. Come here." I scoop him up in my hands, and his tongue sneaks out to lick my nose. "You're a little lover boy, aren't you?" I snuggle his small body into the crook of my neck. He lets out a big sigh and nuzzles his nose against my skin.

"You're lonely, huh?" I stroke his matted fur and close my eyes. "I'm kind of a runt like you in a lot of ways. Sometimes I think we're not made for a world like this."

His brothers and sisters climb all over me, trying to get into my lap. But I give them a gentle nudge and push them on their way. This runt needs some extra attention.

Sadie laughs when she comes back to check on me after a while. "Looks like you made a friend."

"How could anyone harm these babies? They're so innocent and helpless."

"We try our best to find them good homes, but there's just not enough out there."

I rest my cheek against the puppy's body, squeezing my eyes shut.

I'll do everything in my power to make sure every single one of these dogs finds a good home.

The doorbell rings, and I wipe my palms on my pants before opening the door.

Out of all the encounters I've had with James, this one is different. It's planned, and I don't know what to expect. I've seen the authoritative asshole side of him, the worried brother, and the quiet, brooding side.

Which James will I be getting tonight?

I swing open the door. "Right on time."

"I live next door. It'd be pretty pathetic if I was late, don't you think?"

Snarky James, it is.

The ends of his hair look slightly damp, like he took a shower before he came, and his fresh scent surrounds me as he steps inside the house.

His eyes scan the walls. "You did good with the spackling."

I give him a triumphant smile. "I found a good YouTube video. It was pretty easy."

"Why not hire someone to do the renovations?"

"I like doing it myself. It keeps me busy." I take the two shopping bags from his hands. "So, what are we cooking tonight?"

"Shrimp and rice. It'll be quick for you to throw together on your own."

"Quick is good." I side-eye him as I set down the bags on the countertop in the kitchen. "Thank you for taking the time to teach me."

"It's no big deal."

"Well, it is to me. I appreciate it."

He moves around my kitchen with confidence and ease. He doesn't ask where anything is; he just rummages and takes what he needs. I stand back and watch, thoroughly enjoying my view for the night. He pushes up the sleeves of his black thermal, putting his strong forearms on display, and he's wearing those damn gray sweatpants again.

He sets a pan on the burner. "So, how bad would you say you are in the kitchen?"

"On a scale from one to grease fire, I'd say I'm a solid four. I'm not going to burn the house down or anything, and I know the basics." I shrug. "But I also haven't enjoyed anything I've made in the past. It never tasted good."

"Well, this recipe is pretty basic. The worst thing you can do is overcook the shrimp, but that won't be a problem for you if you follow my directions." He jerks his chin. "Come stand here."

I inch closer, but it's apparently not where he wants me because he grips my hips and moves me until I'm standing in front of him, sandwiched between the stove and his body.

The rumble of his voice in my ear sends goose bumps rolling over my skin. "Pour the oil onto the pan, and I'll tell you when to stop."

I tip the bottle of olive oil over the pan and wait for his signal. "Shouldn't I measure it so I know how much to use?"

"No." He takes the bottle from my hand and sets it on the counter. "You just need enough to coat the pan. Now turn on the burner and set the flame to medium."

I glance over my shoulder at him. "You're bossy."

"I prefer *assertive*."

I snort. "Of course you do."

James coaches me through the next steps and I try to focus on what he's saying, but he's surrounding me and guiding my hands, making it hard to think straight. I can't promise I'm going to remember any of these directions.

Once the shrimp is in the pan, I step to the side and busy myself with the bag of frozen rice. "I went to the animal shelter today."

His eyebrows lift. "Really?"

"I wanted to see the dogs you rescued. They were so cute." My lips tug downward. "It was sad seeing them in there."

He nods and turns his attention to the shrimp. "We're looking for the scumbags who were breeding them."

"I hope you catch them, and the judge throws the book at them." I splay my palm on my chest. "There was this adorable black-and-white pit bull with a tiny heart-shaped nose, and he really wasn't bonding with his brothers and sisters. He was just cowering in the corner. Sadie called him the runt of the litter. He was such a little lovebug. I could've held him forever."

"You held him?"

"I couldn't not hold him. He's so tiny and sweet, and he just needs love. He doesn't deserve to be in there, getting ignored by his family members."

"Shrimp only need a couple of minutes on each side, so you'll flip them in another minute." He hands me a fork. "Are you really going to plan an adoption event?"

"Sadie gave me the phone number of this agency that finds foster homes for the dogs until they get adopted. I have a meeting with them tomorrow."

"Will you adopt one?"

I shake my head, staring down into the pan. "I need to focus on myself right now. Get back on my feet. Plus, I have my hands full with the renovations here."

"Get back on your feet after what?"

Regret spikes through my veins. "Uh, you know, my family and I had a falling-out so it's been tough coming back from that."

That wasn't a total *stretch of the truth.*

He's quiet as he watches me flip the shrimp, as if those honey-colored eyes can see right through my lies.

I keep the conversation going so he doesn't have time to question me. "Have you ever owned a dog?"

He nods. "She died a week after my mom. She was old, but she wasn't sick or anything. I think she missed my mom too much."

Without thinking, I reach out and clasp his hand. "I'm so sorry you lost your mom. It really sucks."

He blinks down at our contact, and his jaw flexes. "After she died, Leo went off the deep end. He'd always been reckless, but his drug use became less recreational, and more of a necessity. I left my apartment and moved back home to be with my dad. He was in pretty bad shape. I tried to get a handle on my brother, but…" He shrugs. "I'm still afraid we'll lose him, and my father won't be able to take it."

"Addiction is a tricky thing. You can only do so much."

His eyes flick to mine. "Leo said he feels like you get him."

A smile tugs at the corner of my lips. "I think I do."

"Why is that?"

"When you have darkness inside you, it helps you recognize darkness in others."

His thumb strokes my hand, an idle motion I'm not sure he realizes he's doing. "Why do you have darkness in you?"

"I think we're all born with it. It's like the alcoholic gene that only comes out if you're in the right kind of environment."

His eyebrows press together. "What kind of environment were you in?"

I'm saying too much… or he has too many questions. Either way, I need to steer him away from this conversation.

I pull back my hand and let out a nervous laugh. "Okay, officer. That's enough interrogation for one night. I think the shrimp are done."

"I don't mean to pry. I'm just… trying to get to know you."

"Why?" The question comes out before I have time to stop it.

Why? Why are you here? Why are you wasting your time helping me?

His eyes bounce between mine like he's searching for the answer, and the truth smacks me in the face. He doesn't really *want* to get to know me. He just feels bad for me. That's what this is. Pity. He's a helper, and he wants to help anyone who seems like they need it. And I guess I look pathetic enough to need it.

I swallow down my embarrassment. "Look, I appreciate your help with the meal. You can go now."

His head jerks back. "You want me to leave?"

"I'm just saying, you wanted to help and now you're done. You don't have to stay. I'm good."

He shuts the burner and turns to face me. "What just happened? We were talking, and now you're telling me to get out. Did I say something to offend you?"

I press my thumb against the scar on my wrist and dig my nail into the raised skin. "I shouldn't have bothered you with this. I can just Google a recipe when I'm hungry."

He shakes his head and grabs the pan handle. He scoops the shrimp out of the pan and pours them over the rice. He sets the pan back down on the stove, and I wait for him to leave, to make his way into the hallway and go back to his house. But he opens each cabinet door until he finds the plates and pulls out two. He brushes past me and sets them on the table. Then he carries the bowl of shrimp and rice to the table and sets it down between the two plates.

"Come on." He pulls out a chair. "Let's eat."

"You don't have to—"

"Stop telling me what I don't have to do," he cuts me off. "I don't do anything I don't want to do. Now sit."

Warmth pools in the pit of my stomach and spreads out into the rest of my body. "Okay, Mr. Bossy Pants."

"*Sir* sounds better, but we'll work on that."

I bite back a smile as I take a seat at the table and start eating.

"This is so good, James." I shove another forkful into my mouth. "Like, ridiculously good."

"Now you can make it any time."

"I don't think it'll come out like this."

He tilts his head. "You don't believe in yourself much, do you?"

I shrug and swallow. "I do when I'm good at something."

"You can be good at anything if you believe in yourself."

I chuckle. "You sound like my therapist."

His fork stops moving. "You see a therapist?"

My stomach clenches, but I refuse to be embarrassed about it. "Yeah. It helps. I think everyone should see one at some point in their lives."

He nods, gazing down at his plate.

"You've got darkness inside you too, you know. I saw it the night you kicked Leo's ass on my front lawn."

"I'm fine."

"You don't have to pretend like you are. Not with me at least. I know how heavy it gets carrying around that weight all the time."

"I can handle it."

"You shouldn't have to. Not alone."

"I'm used to being alone."

My heart breaks at those words, because I know how lonely life can be when you're destined to be alone. "Just because you're used to it doesn't mean that's the way it should be."

He pins me with his hard stare. I can feel the emotion radiating off him, the things he's keeping inside and too ashamed to share. I can see it all burning behind his eyes.

Then he asks, "Why did you have a falling-out with your family?"

I inhale, long and slow, thinking of how to navigate this question. "I don't think my mom wanted to have me so soon after my brother, and I think I ruined her plans. That's the way she's always treated me. Like I was a nuisance."

"And your brother? How did she treat him?"

"They tried for my brother, so she always wanted him. He's the golden child." A sad smile touches my lips. "I always looked up to him. He knew what he wanted; he knew who he was."

James takes a sip of water and sets down his cup. "You don't feel like you know who you are?"

I shrug, pushing the shrimp around my plate with my fork. "My mother wishes I were someone else."

"That's not what I asked."

I pause. "I know who I am. I'm just not anything special. Not like my brother."

His grip on the glass tightens, and his eyes narrow. "You don't have to be like your brother to be special. Everyone's different."

"Tell that to my mother."

"Screw what she thinks."

I laugh. "Yeah, screw her."

"I bet your dad thought you were something special."

I lift my eyes to meet his. "He was the best person I've ever known."

James is quiet for a moment. "I think my brother was my mom's favorite."

"How so?"

"He was funny. He got all the attention." He swipes at the condensation on his glass. "I was shy and responsible, and I followed the rules. He was more... outgoing."

"Like you said, you're both different. Nothing wrong with that."

He nods. "She would always tell me that I needed to look out for him. Protect him. The only thing he needs protecting from is his own damn self."

"I can see that."

"So, what happened between you and your mom?"

A stabbing pain pierces my heart as the memory replays in my mind. "Shit was building between us since my dad passed, and we fought a lot." I swallow hard. "The last time I saw her, she said I was dead to her."

James frowns. "I'm sorry."

"It's okay."

"No, it's not."

I look down at my lap. "No, it's not."

"Sounds like you're better off here."

"It has definitely been interesting with your family around."

He chuckles. "You're welcome."

I lift my glass between us. "Here's to fucked-up families."

He clinks his glass against mine. "And to new neighbors."

"New neighbors who can cook."

It's quiet while we finish eating, each of us off in our own heads. James stays to help clean up even though I told him not to. He washes while I dry, and we remain in comfortable silence. My nerves have dissipated since our talk over dinner, and I'm enjoying his company more than I expected to. When he makes his way to the front door to leave, I almost ask him to stay and hang out some more. But I lose my nerve.

He pulls out his phone from his pocket. "Let's exchange numbers, and I'll let you know the next time I'm free to come by for another lesson."

I type out my number and hand back his phone, and he does the same with mine. "Thanks again for tonight. I'm sure you have better things to do with your time than to teach me how to cook."

"Don't say that." He steps out onto the porch and turns to face me. "Being with you is time well spent."

Butterfly wings flap against my rib cage, and I open my mouth to speak but no sound comes out.

The corner of his mouth twitches before he trots down the stairs. "Good night, Phoenix."

I shoot him a text:

Me: It's Nix. Not Phoenix. Get it right.

I swear I see him crack a smile when he reads it before he goes inside his house.

7

James

"Officer Russo. What a pleasant surprise."

It's a surprise to me too. "Hi, Sadie. Just came by to drop these off."

Her eyes widen when she spots the two officers behind me, each holding two boxes as large as the ones I'm carrying. "What is all this?"

"Supplies." I step into the shelter and lower the boxes onto the floor. "You said you were low on some things, so I wanted—*we* wanted to make sure you had everything you needed for the puppies we unloaded on you."

She touches her fingertips to her lips. "Oh, my goodness. Thank you so much. This is too generous."

I'm as much of an animal lover as the next person, but something made me want to go out of my way to make sure Sadie was able to care for the dogs. Or maybe it was some*one.*

My head has been all sorts of fucked up since Phoenix moved in next door. I find myself thinking about her at random times throughout my day. What she's doing, if she needs help renovating, if she's hungry. I tell myself not to get distracted by her, that I need to focus on Leo right now.

Yet I can't get her off my mind.

So here I am, bringing supplies to the shelter, knowing it'll make Phoenix happy.

"Your girlfriend was here earlier," Sadie says. "She's been stopping by to spend time with the puppies, and she's been such a huge help."

My partner, Phil, slaps me on the back. "You got a girlfriend, Russo? You've been holding out on me. I knew something was up with you lately."

My head jerks back. "What do you mean, something's up with me?"

"You've been acting strange. Stranger than usual. Mumbling to yourself and shit. Barely listening to anything I've been saying." He shakes his head. "I should've known it had something to do with a female."

Sadie waggles her eyebrows at him. "She's very pretty."

"Oh, I don't doubt it. My man right here can pull just about any lady he wants." Phil sucks his teeth. "It's a damn shame he doesn't take advantage of his powers."

I roll my eyes. "You're an idiot."

"It's true, and you know it." He drapes his arm around Sadie's shoulders. "Tell me more about this pretty girlfriend of his."

She beams up at him, and I shake my head. Phil has enough charisma to choke a horse, and he can manipulate any conversation with a flash of his smile.

"She's got long brown hair and pretty dark eyes. She looks a little sad until she smiles and her entire face lights up." Sadie nudges me with her elbow. "That runt pup makes her smile. You want to be boyfriend of the year? Get her that puppy."

I'd be lying if I said the thought hadn't already crossed my mind.

"Yes." Phil points his index finger at me. "I second that. Chicks love puppies. That'll get you major pussy points."

I cringe. "I'm so sorry about my partner, Sadie. Would you mind taking us back to see the dogs? Then we'll be out of your hair."

"Of course." She waves a hand, and we follow.

Phil leans in. "Seriously, bro. Why didn't you tell me you're seeing someone?"

"Because I'm not. She's just my neighbor."

"The one that moved into the vacant house next door?"

I nod.

"So why does your pal Sadie here think she's your girlfriend?"

"I don't know." *Because I didn't correct her.*

He arches a brow. "But you're into her though."

"Didn't say that."

"Didn't have to."

I shoot him a look, and he grins.

Sadie pushes open the back door, and dozens of dogs jump at their gates, barking and wagging their tails as we pass by.

Phil winces. "Shit, it's loud back here."

Sadie nods and gestures to the last pen. "They're in the back there."

My eyes scan the litters of puppies until I spot the tiny black-and-white one with a heart-shaped nose. He's trying to get to the water bowl, but his brothers and sisters crowd around it.

Sadie points to him. "That's your little guy." She swings open the gate and ushers me inside. "Take all the time you want."

I crouch down and scoot the puppies aside to make space for the runt to drink. I stroke his back while he laps the water, feeling each bone in his tiny body. These dogs were so scared when we found them in the abandoned house. It breaks my heart knowing they were ripped away from their mother, unable to form that important bond with her before some piece of shit did God knows what with her.

Once again, I arrived too late.

"These guys are going to be monsters," Phil says. "Look at the size of their paws."

I scoop the runt into my arms, and he nuzzles into the crook of my neck. "Pit bulls get such a bad rap. They're all innocent, gentle animals until someone gets his hands on them."

"How's the adoption event coming along?"

"Phoenix is handling it." Her wide eyes flash through my mind. "She's really excited about it. I hope the dogs get adopted, otherwise she's going to be heartbroken."

Phil sits down, and several of the puppies crawl onto his legs. "So, tell me about her. What's going on?"

I shrug. "I don't really know her."

"But you're trying to?"

I let out a sigh, and the puppy licks my cheek. "My gut tells me there's something wrong with her."

Phil's eyebrows shoot up.

I shake my head. "Maybe *wrong* isn't the right word. I don't know. Something's off. Something happened to her. Something she's going through. I can't put my finger on it, and it frustrates me."

He chuckles. "You can always read people. You're telling me you can't read this chick?"

I don't tell him how she cries every night before bed. I don't tell him how she barely smiles, and that when she does, she looks so incredibly sad when it fades. I don't tell him about the subtle comments she's made in passing, about not having a family, about being alone, about having darkness inside her. I don't tell him how she doesn't think she's worth someone's time, how she views herself as a burden for needing the tiniest bit of help. And I definitely don't tell him how I can feel her from all the way inside her house, like she's calling out to me, drawing me in.

I don't tell him any of these things because then it'd sound like I know her better than I said I did, and I can't explain how because we've only just met, yet there's something so familiar about her that it feels as if I can see into her soul.

My gut twisted when Phoenix looked up at me last week, expecting me to leave her to eat by herself. It twisted even more when I watched her cry herself to sleep later on through her bedroom window.

I shake my head at my own stupidity. *As if hanging out with me would be enough to take away her sadness for a night.*

"Leo likes her."

Phil cocks his head. "Yeah? How's he been since he came home?"

"I think he's going to get clean. It feels different this time."

"I hope so, for you and your father's sake. I'd hate to see you get let down after everything you've been through."

My walkie crackles on my shoulder, and Phil groans after the dispatcher finishes talking. "Really? Those punk kids at the skate park again?"

I give the puppy one last kiss on his head before setting him down with his siblings. "Let's go scare them straight."

When we arrive at the scene, the group of teenagers spray-painting the side of the skate ramp scatter in different directions.

"Fuck, I hate running." Phil bolts out of the car and pounds the pavement after them.

We've received multiple calls about these kids for the past couple of weeks. They're vandalizing the new skate park and terrorizing the younger kids who want to skate. They're bored sixteen-year-olds who haven't had proper parental supervision or discipline.

The fuckers are fast, but not fast enough to outrun me and my partner. We each grab a kid by the collar of his shirt, while the rest get away.

"Get off me." The boy tries to squirm out of my grip but fails. "You can't manhandle me like this. I'm a minor."

"I'm holding your shirt, not manhandling you. And you shouldn't have been spraying graffiti everywhere if you didn't want to be manhandled by the police."

He grunts. "There's nothing wrong with art."

"There is when it's on public property."

"What about the children you've been fucking with all month?" Phil tugs his offender's elbow. "That part of your art too?"

He grits his teeth and says nothing.

"Oh, you the strong and silent type?" Phil snorts. "You'll do well in jail."

He scoffs. "Jail? I'm only sixteen. I can't go to jail."

"There are kids younger than you sitting in the juvenile detention center because of the dumb choices they've made."

I look down at the boy in front of me. "You want to do art? Go to school. Take a class. Set up a studio in your garage."

He rolls his eyes. "Yeah, like my parents would let me do that."

"Have you asked?"

He looks down at his shoes and shakes his head.

"Another dumb move, assuming instead of asking. What's your name?"

"Cory."

"You have any plans on going to college, Cory?"

He shrugs like he hasn't thought about it.

"There are plenty of art schools you can get into. You can start building your portfolio now and do some volunteer work to look good on your college applications. Start thinking long term about your art, and you could make this a future for yourself."

He kicks a rock with his shoe. "I'm not that good. I just spray paint to mess around."

I gesture to his mural on the side of the half-pipe. "That's good. You should believe in yourself and your abilities."

His friend pipes up. "If you're not going to arrest us, then you have to let us go. We don't need a lecture from you, Grandpa."

Phil's eyebrows shoot up. "Grandpa? Boy, I'll run circles around your ass. Watch your mouth when you're talking to authority and show some respect."

I keep my focus on Cory. "You become the company you keep. You should surround yourself with people who are going places. People who will lift you up. Not the kind of people who drag you down with them."

"Yes, sir." He lifts his eyes to mine, and something familiar tugs at my heart. There's an innocence in his eyes, something I once saw when I looked at Leo.

I release his wrists and cross my arms over my chest. "I'm letting you go with a warning."

Phil's mouth drops open. "Another warning? Come on, man. These punks will just do the same thing again tomorrow."

"Then we'll bring 'em in." I shrug and glance between the boys. "This is your last chance. Don't fuck it up."

They take off running in the direction their friends ran before.

"You're too nice for your own good." Phil blows a low whistle and shakes his head. "You know you're gonna regret this decision, right?"

"Probably."

I pull off my shirt and toss it into the hamper before collapsing on the bed.

I slip my legs under the covers, telling myself I won't look into Phoenix's window even though I know I will. I can't seem to help myself when it comes to her.

What would she think of me if she knew I spied on her every night before bed? Would she be creeped out? Angry? Would she stop speaking to me?

I crack open the book on my nightstand and settle against my headboard to read. But I keep reading the same sentence over and over again, until I toss the book onto my comforter, and lift my eyes to the window.

She's sitting up in bed with her elbows resting on her knees. She's staring at her phone, the glow from her screen illuminating her face in the darkness. Then she wipes her eye with the back of her hand and hangs her head between her knees.

What is she looking at that's making her so sad?

She didn't tell me the whole truth about what happened between her and her mother. I didn't want to pry, but I could tell there's more to the story than what she told me.

My heart thumps a quick rhythm as I watch her body shake with her sobs. I can't go over there. It's late, and I can't let her know I was watching her. Yet it pains me to see her upset and not be able to do anything about it.

I snatch my phone off the charger, and type out a text:

Me: You up?

I watch as her head pops up to look at her phone. Her lips curve up, and my chest squeezes at the mere sight of her almost smile. I hold my breath in anticipation until my phone vibrates in my hand.

Phoenix: Yup. What are you doing up?
Me: Just got home from my shift.
Phoenix: Catch any bad guys?
Me: Not tonight. Just some punk teenagers.
Phoenix: Ever shoot somebody?
Phoenix: Wait, is that too personal?
Me: Yes, and no.
Phoenix: You killed someone?!
Me: I said I shot someone, not killed.
Phoenix: *phew* Breaking and entering is where I draw the line.
Me: Gotta have standards.
Phoenix: I bet the guy deserved it. Where did you shoot him?
Me: In the leg. He robbed the Wawa down the road.
Me: He fired first.
Phoenix: Wow. I could never be a cop. I don't think I could shoot someone if I had to.
Me: You would if your life was on the line.
Phoenix: I don't like that you have to put your life on the line.

Warmth spreads in my chest. My eyes flick to her window. She's lying down now, with her phone resting on her chest as she waits for my response.

Me: Why not? I'm protecting people.
Phoenix: But who's protecting you?
Me: I protect myself. Plus, my partner has my six.
Phoenix: Your six? Is that cop code?
Me: It means he has my back.

Phoenix: Then I have your six too.

Emotion constricts my throat. Phil has my back because it's his duty. When was the last time someone had my back because they wanted to? I stare at the blinking cursor on the screen, unsure of what to say, until another text pops up.

Phoenix: Goodnight.
Me: Night, Phoenix
Phoenix: It's Nix
Phoenix: N - I - X
Phoenix: Three letters. One syllable. It's not that hard.

I chuckle as she rolls her eyes before she plugs the charger into her phone and sets it down on the nightstand. At least she's not crying anymore. I wait until she's asleep and then I type out one more text:

Me: I've got your six now too.

8

Phoenix

Daily Affirmation: "Today will be a great day. I look forward to what's ahead of me."

This stupid smile hasn't left my face all day.

It's ridiculous.

It's pathetic.

Nobody should feel like this just because a man texted her.

But he did, and I do.

Butterflies flap away in my stomach whenever I reread our texts from last night—which I've done three times.

It's not like James said anything spectacular. I've been trying to rationalize the reasons why he texted me in the first place, but I keep ending up at the same conclusion: He was thinking about me. Why else would he have asked if I was up in the middle of the night?

There goes the stupid smile again.

I put down the paint roller and take a break for lunch. On my way into the kitchen, I check my phone and spot a missed call from Drew. We've been playing phone tag for the past week. I click on his name and sandwich the phone between my shoulder and my ear while I stick leftovers in the microwave.

Drew's snippy tone chirps through my ear. "Well, look who it is. Miss Busy Bee."

"Hey, I'm so glad I was able to catch you. How are you?"

"Oh, just living the dream. How are you?"

"I'm good. Been busy with the renovations on top of planning the adoption event."

"How does the house look? You haven't sent me any pictures."

"I will when I finish painting. I picked out some soft grays and light blues. It's very calming."

"I'm gonna start calling you Joanna Gaines from now on."

I chuckle. "Hardly."

"You're really into this dog event, huh?"

"I feel excited about something for the first time in a long time. I just hope all the puppies go to good homes."

"You should adopt one."

I frown. "I can barely take care of myself right now."

"Not true. You're doing good out on your own. Besides, nobody can be depressed with a puppy."

I laugh. "Maybe."

"What's new with your hot neighbors? Tell me some juicy stories before I have to get off the phone. Give me something here. I'm bored out of my mind."

I bite my bottom lip to stop the goofy smile from making yet another appearance. "Well, James came over last week to teach me how to cook."

"Oh, that's sexy. I love when someone can feed you."

I take my bowl out of the microwave and carry it to the table. "It certainly was sexy watching him cook."

"Has he made a move yet?"

"Oh, no. I think he just likes to help. It's in his nature."

"Men aren't that helpful unless they want something from you."

I'm quiet for a moment. "He texted me late last night after his shift. It didn't seem like he wanted anything from me. It was almost like… like he needed someone to talk to."

"It was late?"

"Yeah. After two."

"Dude, that's a booty call."

I shake my head. "He didn't ask to come over, or to see me. We were just talking."

"Nix, this isn't one of your romance stories. When a guy texts you that late, he's only got one thing on his mind. Trust me."

My stomach sinks. "I don't know."

"I'm just saying, don't be too naive. I'm looking out for you."

We chat for a few minutes longer, and then I tell him I have to go even though I don't.

Maybe Drew's right. James didn't text me during the day. Why was I on his mind so late at night? What did he really want? Questions swarm my mind, and I go down the rabbit hole of *whys* and *what-ifs*.

Why would he be interested in me?

What do I have to offer him, or anyone for that matter?

My own family can't even stand to be around me. Why would James be any different?

Several minutes later, my heart is racing and my palms are sweaty. Then I remember something my therapist once told me: I need to stop overanalyzing everything. It doesn't serve me to sit here and waste time wondering why someone did something. It doesn't matter why James texted me last night—what matters is that he did. For whatever reason, I was on his mind, and he reached out. The conversation was harmless, regardless of what his intentions might have been, and I enjoyed it. End of story. I finish my lunch so I can get back to painting and leave the worrisome thoughts behind.

Or at least I try to. Drew's voice echoes in my head for the remainder of the day, and I end up rage painting half of the bedrooms upstairs.

I'm in bed reading around nine o'clock when the doorbell jolts me out of my thoughts. I trot downstairs and swing open the door.

I gasp when I see Leo's face. "Oh my god. What happened to you?"

He shrugs. "Got into a fight."

"Clearly." I tip his chin. Purple splotches cover his jaw and cheekbone. A scab runs down the middle of his bottom lip where it was split open, and one of his eyes is still swollen shut. I haven't seen him in a few days, but the wounds are still pretty fresh. "Is the other guy even alive?"

"Barely."

I usher him inside and then freeze. "Please tell me your brother didn't do this to you."

He laughs. "Nah. Some random guy."

"What was the fight over?"

He pulls a wad of cash from his pocket. "About five hundred dollars. It's an underground fighting ring. No rules. Last one standing wins."

I roll my eyes. "You're in *Fight Club*? Seriously?"

"Don't knock it till you try it, Nix."

I stare at the money as he tucks it back into his pocket. "Why fight for money? Why not just get a job?"

"I don't do it for the money."

"Then why? You like getting your ass beat that much?"

He lifts an eyebrow. "Something like that."

My stomach flutters. He *does* like getting his ass beat. It's the pain. The need to feel something physical to dull the ache of the mental anguish.

He glances down at my arm. "I know why you're always rubbing that wrist, Nix. I know you like the pain too."

I swallow, embarrassment coloring my cheeks. "It's not like that."

He drops his chin and looks straight into my eyes. "You can't lie to me, Nixie."

I pull my sleeves down and grip them in my palms. "I don't *like* the pain. I want to escape it."

He takes my hand and lifts it between us. "Will you show me?"

I shake my head and pull back my arm.

He lifts his palms on either side of his head. "Okay. You don't have to tell me."

"Why are you here? You need me to patch you up again?"

"Nah. I'm bored. Wanted to see if you wanted to hang out with your little bro."

I chew my bottom lip. "Maybe you can take me the next time you go. That is, if you're allowed to bring a guest to *Fight Club*."

A wide grin spreads across his face. "How about tonight?"

Nerves trickle through my veins. I could stay in my comfort zone with my nose in a book, reading about other people's adventures, or I could go out and try something new.

"I'm in."

I've officially lost my mind.

I'm standing in a dimly lit auto body garage. People push against me from all sides, waving fists of money and placing their bets. Their shouting echoes off the walls.

It's the last place I'd ever choose to be. Confined, crowded, and unpredictable. Yet here I stand, holding on to Leo's hand like a lifeline.

"Back again?" Someone claps Leo on the back as he pushes past us.

"Just spectating."

"That's too bad. You put on a good show the other night, man."

Leo grins, beaming with pride.

It makes me wonder what else he's good at, and if anyone ever praised him for it.

"Bring me the next time you fight," I shout into his ear. "I want to watch you."

He shakes his head. "If I'm fighting, I can't keep an eye on you."

"I can keep an eye on myself."

He arches a brow. "Pretty sure my brother would actually kill me if anything happened to you on my watch."

"You let me deal with your brother. He's all bark and no bite."

"Only when it comes to you, Nixie."

My chest tightens, and I want to ask why that is, but this isn't the best place for a heart-to-heart about his brother.

We watch the first fight, and I'm equal parts enamored and disgusted. I've watched UFC matches on TV, but this is different. It's raw and dangerous. These people aren't fighters in the literal sense of the word. They're regular, everyday people—the cashier at ShopRite; the gas station attendant; the bank teller at Chase. We all recognize each other from the area. But we don't say hello. We don't acknowledge that we know each other, because down here we're someone else. And isn't that all anybody wants? To step into someone else's shoes for a little while? To forget who we are, and let it all go?

The fight ends when one guy clips the other on his chin, and it's lights out for him. While we're waiting for the next fight to start, the crowd grows restless, amped up from the first. Leo's grip on my hand tightens as we're jostled around. Someone knocks into me from behind, and I fall against the person in front of me.

"Sorry about that." I steady myself, and glance at the person I was pushed into.

The woman spins around and places both palms on my shoulders before shoving me backward. "Watch where you're going, bitch."

I stumble. "It was an accident, I'm sorry."

Leo pulls me to his side. "Come on, let's head over there for a better view."

"You want a good view?" The woman grins and swings her arm wide, gesturing to the makeshift ring. "How about a front-row seat, Bambi?"

My eyebrows push together. "Oh, no. I'm not fighting."

She sucks her teeth, and steps so close to me I can smell the sour scent of beer on her breath. "What's the matter? You scared?"

I shake my head, squeezing Leo's arm. "I came here to watch."

"That was before you crossed my path." She yanks my elbow. "Now you can watch as I kick your ass."

Fear courses through my veins, adrenaline kicking my heart into overdrive. "N-no. I'm not fighting."

"Leave her alone. She said she was sorry." Leo's fingers tighten around my wrist. "Go fight someone your own size."

The crazy woman laughs. "Don't worry, pretty boy. When I'm done with your girl, I'll make sure you get a taste too."

Before I can blink, she charges me, digging her shoulder into my midsection and knocking me back onto my ass. The crowd roars as she mounts me and begins throwing punches at my face.

Leo attempts to rip her off me, but a few men grab him so he can't intervene.

It's just me and this psychopath.

A warm stream trickles into my eyes, making it hard to see. Pain splits into my face from the force of her fists as she lands each punch. It's fight or flight, and with her on top of me, I'm not going anywhere.

"Put your arms up! Block her!" Leo's voice rises above the screams from the crowd.

"What's the matter, Bambi? You're too scared to hit back? Don't want to chip a nail?"

All of a sudden, my mother's face flashes in my mind. She's looking down her nose at me, top lip curled in disgust, and speaking to me with that condescending tone in her voice. *You've got to toughen up. You can't crumble at every inconvenience. People in the world have it so much worse than you. Don't be so weak.*

I gnash my teeth, and buck my hips as hard as I can, throwing her off-kilter. I slip out from under her and scramble to my feet, backing away and putting up my fists to block my face. I bounce around her as she pushes to her feet.

She grins. "You should've stayed down, bitch."

She throws another punch, but I duck out of the way. I step to the side and land a right hook on her cheekbone, but she barely notices it.

The fight continues like this for what feels like an eternity, with me attempting to land a punch here and there in between blocking my face from her heavy fists.

But I'm not a fighter.

I'm not tough.

I can't do this.

I can't beat her.

She rushes me again and slams me down onto my back. All the air is knocked out of my lungs, and a splitting pain shoots through my side. My arms are tired, and I don't have any fight left in me. I just want this to be over. I let her hit me until someone jumps in and calls the match.

Leo dives down beside me and scoops me into his arms.

And that's when everything goes black.

9

James

My phone buzzes on my nightstand, and I roll over to see my brother's name on the screen.

This can't be good. It's after midnight, and Leo only calls me when he's in trouble. I swipe my thumb across the screen. "What did you do now?"

"James, you need to come next door."

The alarm in his voice and his use of my name has me shooting up out of bed. "What's wrong?"

I glance at Phoenix's bedroom window, but it's dark.

"She's hurt."

I bolt into the hallway. "Did you call an ambulance?"

"No. She doesn't want me to."

"How bad is it?"

"Just get here."

I'm already out the door and sprinting across the lawn. When I get to her porch, I burst through Phoenix's front door. "Where are you?"

"Up here," Leo's voice calls, as light spills into the hallway from the bathroom.

I take the stairs by twos and hear Phoenix's feeble voice say, "Why did you call him?"

I don't know what I expected to see when I got into the bathroom, but the sight of her lying in Leo's arms on the tile, covered in blood and bruises wasn't it.

A strangled groan slips out of my throat, and my stomach lurches. I drop to my knees beside my brother. "Who did this to her?"

Leo swallows. "It's my fault. I took her to the fight—"

"You *what*?"

"She wanted to go. We were only supposed to watch."

"I'm okay," she croaks out. "Just have a headache."

My eyes roam over her injuries. Most of the blood is coming from a cut above her eyebrow, but she's hugging her midsection, curled in a ball. She might have a broken rib, or internal bleeding.

I could kill my brother for taking her to a place so dangerous. But now's not the time to lay into Leo about the dangers of underground fighting. I need to focus on helping Phoenix.

I cut a glare at my brother. "Go home."

His eyes widen. "What? No. I can help."

"You've done enough. She wouldn't be in this situation if it weren't for you."

He drops his chin, but Phoenix slips her hand inside mine. "Let him help, James. Please."

I stare down at her small swollen hand in mine, and it's in this moment I realize I'll do anything she asks me to.

"Fine." I heave a sigh and jerk my chin at my brother. "Get ice and wrap it in a dish towel. Then find something for the pain."

Leo jumps up and dashes into the hall.

"He needs to do this." Phoenix's eyelids droop closed, her split lips barely moving when she speaks. "Don't push him away."

I brush her hair away from her face. "I'm gonna need you to stay awake, babe."

She blinks a few times, and then her eyes trail down my chest. "Where's your shirt?"

I glance down at my gray sweatpants. "I came as fast as I could. I didn't think about clothes or shoes."

She shakes her head. "I told him not to bother you."

Acid fills my stomach. *Bother me?*

I cradle her face between my palms, careful to be as gentle as I can. "Why do you keep thinking you're bothering me, huh? Who told you that you're a bother?"

Her eyes bounce between mine and her voice lowers to a whisper. "Everything hurts, James."

The vulnerability in her voice cracks open my heart. She's being strong for Leo, but with me, she's letting her guard down.

"I'm going to take care of you, Phoenix."

She groans. "Stop calling me that."

My lips twitch. *Got her ass beat, yet she's still as stubborn as an ox.*

Leo bursts into the room with the supplies. He presses the ice on her eye, and she hisses.

"We need to get this swelling down." I look up at Leo. "I still think she should go to the hospital."

"No!" Phoenix recoils, clutching her ribs. "Ow. Please, no hospital."

Leo lifts a shoulder. "We can easily carry her to the car."

Phoenix pushes off the floor and tries to get up, the ice scattering onto the tile around her. "I won't go. You can't make me." She winces and holds her head as she sways. "Please. I can't go."

"Okay, okay." I hold her steady.

Leo slips the Tylenol into her mouth and tilts her head back as she washes them down with water. He collects the ice cubes and wraps the towel around them again. "Keep this on, Nixie."

Within minutes, the towel is soaked with blood.

"You guys can go now. I'll be fine. I just need to sleep it off."

My grip on her tightens. "You can't sleep yet. Not like this. I need to get you cleaned up so I can see what's going on under all that blood."

Leo and I wrap each of her arms around our shoulders as we stand. Phoenix grits her teeth, breathing hard through her nostrils. She has a bruised rib, at the very least.

"A hot bath will be good for your muscles." I reach down and twist the lever on the faucet in the tub. "Leo, I'm going to take it from here."

He looks from the tub to Phoenix.

She rests her head on his shoulder. "As much as you want to see my tits, I can't allow it."

He cracks a sad smile. "You'll call me if you need me though, right?"

"I always need you, little bro."

Something settles in his worried eyes. It amazes me how she knows exactly what he needs to hear when she's only known him for a short while.

"She's gonna be okay." I offer Leo a tight nod. "You did good calling me."

He ducks out of the bathroom and closes the door quietly behind him.

Phoenix props herself against the sink and starts to unbutton her jeans. I turn away to give her privacy and dip my hand into the water to feel the temperature before putting the plug into place. But her grunts as she struggles pull my attention back to her.

I tip her chin and look into her deep-brown eyes. "I'm going to help you. If you feel uncomfortable at any point, you tell me to stop. Okay?"

She nods.

I kneel in front of her and drag her jeans down over her ass and hips, going as slow and as careful as I can. I cup her calf and lift her leg, pulling it out of the pant leg before switching to the other.

I avert my eyes from her black lace thong and try to think of anything but the fact that I'm on my knees in front of her beautiful body, stripping off her clothes.

I return to standing and suck in a deep breath. "This next part is going to hurt. I'm gonna need you to lift your arms so I can get you out of this shirt."

She picks up her arms, and her whimpers of pain are like knife pricks to my heart. I pull off the shirt and tank top underneath in one swift movement so I don't have to do it twice, leaving her in a black sports bra.

I suppress a frustrated growl when I spot the reddish-purple splotch along her ribs. "I'm going to yell at you properly when you're feeling better."

A smirk twists her lips. "Too bad you don't scare me."

"Apparently nothing scares you, because you got the shit kicked out of you and you're over here cracking jokes."

I wrap my arm around her waist and guide her over to the tub. She holds on to me while she lifts each leg and steps into the water, and I take all her weight as she lowers herself down.

"Ow, fuck. I don't think I can lean back." A tear escapes and rolls down her cheek, and she covers her face with her hands. "I'm so stupid. Why did I get myself into this mess?"

Fuck no. I tear off my sweatpants, toss them to the floor, and step into the tub. I lower myself behind Phoenix, my legs on either side of her, and settle her back against my chest as I wrap her in my arms.

"You're not stupid."

She sniffles. "I haven't looked in the mirror. Is it bad?"

"I've seen worse. Did you at least get any hits in?"

"A few."

"Good." I reach for the washcloth and lather it with the soap that's sitting on the ledge against the wall. Then I tip her head back, resting it on my shoulder, and begin washing the blood off her face. I drag it over her cheek, pressing as light as I can.

She's quiet as I continue to scrub her skin clean. "Stay awake, Phoenix. You can't go to sleep yet."

She stifles a yawn. "I'm just so sleepy."

"Yeah, that's part of a concussion. Which is why I wanted to take you to the hospital."

"I don't like hospitals."

"No one does."

"This is different."

I dip the washcloth under the water and wring it out before smoothing it over her other cheek. "Bad memories?"

She nods.

"Will you tell me about it?"

"Maybe one day."

It's better than a no, so I take it. She doesn't owe me anything.

We all have secrets.

"Lucky for you, the cut over your eyebrow doesn't look like it needs stitches. But you'll have a decent scar there for sure."

"Add it to the collection," she murmurs.

My eyes flick to the thin line of raised skin along the inside of her forearm. It boils my blood to think about someone hurting her.

Her eyes droop closed again, so I think of something to keep her awake. "How's the adoption event coming along?"

"I booked the venue. It'll be the week before Christmas."

"That's good. Lots of people will be looking to surprise their loved ones with a new puppy for the holidays."

"That's what I'm hoping for." She pauses for a moment, her eyes searching the ceiling. "Do you think they'll all get adopted?"

"I don't know. But we'll make sure everyone knows about the event."

"We?" Her eyes flick to mine.

"Yeah. The guys at the station and I can leave flyers around the neighborhood. That should help spread the word."

The corners of her lips turn downward.

"What's wrong?"

She sighs. "I just… I can't figure you out."

"What do you mean?"

"You keep helping me, and I don't know why."

"Is it so strange for someone to want to help a person who needs it?"

"It is for me."

My stomach sours at the thought of Phoenix being all alone at a time when she needed someone the most and having no one. "Remember what I said last night? I've got your six now. And so does Leo—even if I'm going to have to rip him a new asshole for taking you to the fight."

She chuckles and then coughs, gripping her ribs.

85

I scrub the bloodstains from her face and run the cloth over her neck and chest.

Her voice echoes off the tile. "Can I ask you something?"

"Shoot."

"Why did you text me last night?"

My hand freezes with the washcloth on her shoulder. "Uh, I couldn't sleep."

She hums. "It was pretty late. My friend thinks you were looking for a booty call."

My chin jerks back. "What?"

"Don't look so disgusted. I told him you're not into me like that."

"I'm not disgusted. I…" Surprise wraps itself around my throat. "I don't do booty calls. Did I say something to make you think that's what I was insinuating?"

"No."

"I know it was late." I try to think of a plausible reason to give her, but her friend is right. It *was* late. And I can't lie to her. I pinch the bridge of my nose, and blurt out, "I saw you crying through your window, and I wanted to make sure you were okay."

Her eyebrows knit together. "You were looking through my window?"

I let out a frustrated sigh. "Our bedrooms face each other. I was about to go to sleep, and I glanced up and saw you. You looked upset."

Her eyes narrow. "What else have you seen through my window?"

"Nothing." I squeeze her hand under the water. "I promise, I'm not some Peeping Tom. If I saw you were getting undressed, I'd have looked away."

She lifts an eyebrow as if she doesn't believe me.

Fuck. How am I going to explain this? What am I *supposed* to say? Because I can't go with the truth, since the truth is me telling her, *Phoenix, I swear I'm not looking through your window because I'm some kind of voyeuristic pervert. It's because I can't not look at you. I can't stop myself from checking in on you and making sure you're okay. There's something about you that draws me in and makes me want to protect you, the same way you want to protect those puppies from life in the shelter, because you're too good and too innocent to deserve a life like this, and something tells me you haven't been protected by anyone your whole life. I couldn't save my mom, and I can't stop my brother from hurting himself, and for once I just want to be enough to make somebody feel like everything's going to be okay because I'm here.*

No, I can't say that.

"I'm sorry, Phoenix. I—"

She squeezes her eyes shut and reaches up to press her palm to her forehead. "It's throbbing so bad."

"Come on, let's get you dried off. I want to keep icing your head to keep the swelling down." I help her stand and wrap a towel around her, easing her legs over the edge of the tub.

She blinks up at me while I squeeze the water out of the ends of her hair. "You're a caretaker."

"I am."

"That's a learned behavior, you know."

I roll my lips together and work the towel down her arms. "What does that mean?"

"It means you grew up thinking you had to take care of your family, instead of them taking care of you."

I drop my arms and let the towel hang at my side. Memories of my mother flash through my mind.

Phoenix lifts her hand to my face, grazing her fingertips against my jaw. "You save everyone, but who saves you?"

I swallow around the ball of emotion in my throat. "Maybe I don't need saving."

"We all need saving every once in a while."

Her big brown eyes stare into mine with such sincerity, I lose all sense for a moment. My fingers move of their own volition, trailing along the hollow of her neck and tracing the curve of her bare shoulder. She sways closer, her lips parting and drawing every ounce of my attention.

But she's taken more than a few hits to the head, and the last thing I want is her to make a decision like this when she's not in the right frame of mind.

87

So I bend down and lift her, cradling her bruised body in my arms. "Right now, it's you who needs saving."

She directs me to her bedroom, and I help her into her pajamas. Then I make her another ice pack for her head.

When she's settled in bed, she presses the ice against her eye. "How much longer until I can fall asleep?"

"Give me another thirty minutes, and I think you should be okay. You haven't thrown up, and your pupils don't look dilated."

"Yes, Dr. Russo." She smiles, but it fades just as fast. "You don't have to stay. I promise I'll follow your orders and stay up for another half hour."

I climb onto the mattress beside her, propping myself against the headboard, and fold my hands over my stomach.

"James."

"Phoenix."

An irritated sound leaves her throat. "Why won't you stop calling me that?"

"Why won't you tell me the reason you don't like it when I call you that?"

"Will you stop if I tell you?"

I shrug. "Maybe."

She lets out a bitter laugh. "That's what I thought."

"You can tell me, you know. You can talk to me."

It's quiet for a few minutes, and just when I think she's falling asleep again, her voice fills the quiet room. "A phoenix rises from the ashes. It's a symbol of strength."

"So, what's wrong with that?"

"I'm not strong."

Ah, there's the truth. "Most strong people don't actually feel like they're strong. Doesn't make it any less true."

"Trust me, I'm not. I don't know what my father was thinking when he picked this name. It's just a constant reminder of how un-phoenixlike I am."

I roll onto my side to face her. "That's not what I see."

She peeks at me from under the ice pack. "And what do you see?"

"I see someone who's still here. Someone who makes the choice to wake up and live every single morning. You're working on the house to make it better. You run to keep yourself healthy. You want to learn new things, like how to cook. You help people, and you help animals. Regardless of what you've been through, you're still standing. That seems pretty damn strong to me."

Her eyes glisten as she blinks up at the ceiling, her chest heaving with shallow breaths.

Is this what she thinks about when she's alone in her room?

I lower my voice to a whisper. "Why do you cry every night?"

She turns her head and sets her questioning gaze on me.

"What's making you so sad, Phoenix?"

Her bottom lip trembles. "Do you ever wish you were someone else? Like not anybody specific, but that you could be… different. A better version of yourself."

My chest aches. "I've felt like that before."

"When?"

"When my mom died."

Phoenix sets down the ice pack and winces as she shifts onto her side to face me.

We're so close, I can feel her warm breath against my lips when she says, "I wouldn't want you to be anyone else."

Heat crawls over my skin, a mixture of calm and comfort, seeping into my pores and settling deep into my bones. "You want to know what I think? I think you call yourself Nix because you don't accept the power in your name. You don't think you deserve it. And I can't for the life of me figure out why." I press my index finger into her chest. "You don't recognize the strength you possess. But I see it. It's who you are. Your soul is a phoenix, whether you believe it or not. And one day, you're going to burn your demons to the ground and rise above it all." Tears stream down her cheeks, and I thumb them away as they fall. "If you want to be a better version of yourself, then be it. Nothing wrong with that. But maybe you already are the best version of yourself, and you just don't see it yet."

A quiet sob racks her body, and we lie like this in silence until her lids close. I let her drift off to sleep, but right before she's out cold, she whispers one more thing into the darkness.

"I'm glad you broke into my house that night, James."

I smile and press my lips to her forehead.

So am I.

10

Phoenix

Daily Affirmation: I am continuously working on myself and my inner peace.

An axe splitting through my skull wakes me out of a dead sleep.

I groan, clutching my forehead as I push to sit up.

"Easy, tiger." James's low voice startles me. "You can't move so quickly."

I crack one eye open. "Why do I smell bacon?"

"Is that a cop joke, or do you actually smell bacon?"

"As much as I'd love to take credit for a joke like that, I'm not that quick first thing in the morning."

He chuckles, and it's raspy with the sound of the morning still wrapped around his voice. "I've got your bacon right here. Just take it easy."

I blink, looking around the room to clear my vision. My eyes fall on James's smooth broad shoulders and sculpted arms. "You still don't have a shirt on."

He shrugs and sets a plate on my lap.

Realization sets in. "Did you not go home?"

He holds out two pills in his palm. "Once you eat, you can take these for the pain."

"You didn't have to stay all night."

His bloodshot eyes flick up to mine, dark-purple crescents staining his under-eye skin. "Google said to watch for signs of a seizure in your sleep."

My heart skips a beat. *He was worried about me.* "I'm fine. Go home and get some rest."

He digs the heels of his hands into his eyes. "I actually have to go get ready for work."

I balk. "But you were up all night."

He waves me off and rises from the bed. "Leo will be over to check on you when he wakes up. Make sure you take those pills."

"Wait." I grab his hand as he turns to leave. "James."

He stops and looks down at me.

"Thank you. That was scary last night, and I'm glad you were here with me."

The corners of his lips turn up, and I make a mental note to figure out how to make him smile more.

He leans down and presses his soft lips against my cheek. "I'll be back to check on you later."

Butterflies go wild in my stomach. I watch him leave my bedroom, the low-slung sweatpants that mold perfectly to his muscular ass, accentuated by the wide span of his smooth, bare back.

But more than his physical appeal is the fact that he cared for me last night. He handled me *with care*, as if I'm this valuable thing. The way he made me feel in the bathtub wrapped in his arms as he washed my wounds, and again in the safety of his embrace in the bed after—I've never felt that secure, that important, that… good. I've never been able to give my pain to someone else and let him help me through it.

And it makes me want to be that for *him*, when *he* needs it. Because we all need it. We all need someone we can let our guards down with.

Maybe James and I can be that for each other.

The doubtful voice in my head whispers, *He would've done it for anybody. He was just being nice.* But my stupid, hopeful heart doesn't want to believe a single word.

I stab the omelet with my fork and shove a huge bite into my mouth. My hand shoots up to my jaw as an aching pain slices through my face as I try to chew. What the hell do I even look like? I slide the plate off my lap and scoot in slow movements to the corner of the mattress. I grit my teeth and breathe through the pain in my ribs until I'm standing, and hobble over to the mirror above my dresser.

Jesus. Puffy purple skin surrounds one eye, and a bandage covers what must be a gash above my eyebrow. There's a decent cut in my bottom lip too, and some bruising along my jawline. I guess it could be worse.

Out of the corner of my eye, I see James walk into his bedroom. I avert my gaze from the window on instinct, but then it slowly travels back as curiosity takes over.

If he can look, then so can I, right?

He slips on the shirt to his uniform, his large fingers working the buttons one by one. He shucks his sweatpants, and I'm reminded of how good he looked in his boxer briefs last night. Strong, thick thighs, big calves, large feet. Everything about him is large. A massive fortress of a man. He combs through his hair, styling it just so, and he even takes his time tying his shoelaces in perfect, even bows. He's so careful and cautious in *everything* he does, but the memory of him losing control when he beat up his brother flashes through my mind. James holds it all together until it explodes, and I wonder just how much he's suppressing under the surface.

Just before he leaves his room, he stops by the tall chest of drawers by his door. I lean closer and watch as he picks up a small square picture frame and stares at it.

My phone rings and my shoulders jump as I cry out and clutch my ribs. Serves me right for spying on my neighbor. "Ow, hello?"

"Ow?" Alarm fills Drew's voice. "What's wrong?"

I breathe and wait for the throbbing to pass. "I'm fine."

"Clearly. What happened to you?"

"Would you believe me if I told you I went to an underground fight club and got my ass kicked by the female version of Thor?"

"I… I don't even know where to start."

I chuckle. "Well, it's true. She beat me pretty good."

"Of course she did. You don't have any fighting skills."

"I think I held my own in there considering who I was up against. I got in a few punches too."

"What the hell were you doing at an underground fighting club?"

I chomp on a burned piece of bacon. "Leo took me. I thought it would be exciting to get out of the house and watch a fight. I didn't think I'd be the main event."

He sighs. "You're having entirely too much fun without me. This is unacceptable."

I grimace. "Yeah, because having my face pummeled is loads of fun."

"So, Leo took you home and patched you up?"

"Until James got here."

"You called James?"

"No, Leo did. He was trying to convince me to go to the hospital, but I didn't want to. I think he thought if his brother was there, he'd get me to change my mind."

"You know, you're going to have to get over this fear of hospitals one day. You might really need to go, and you won't have a choice."

"I know, I know. I'm just not ready to be back there yet." I push away the memory and change the subject. "How are you doing?"

"Ah, I'm good. I have my ups and downs. You know how it is."

I nod. "I'll be there this week for therapy. Want me to bring you anything?"

"A shovel, so I can dig myself out of here *Shawshank* style?"

I snort. "Something less conspicuous."

"Fine. I also accept baked goods."

"That I can do."

I toss my phone onto the comforter and glance at the window one last time.

James really does have an all-access pass to my private space. I'll have to remember to close the blinds from now on.

It's noon when Leo shows up.

His face falls when he walks into my bedroom and sees the aftermath of my face. "Shit, Nix. I'm so sorry about last night."

"You have nothing to be sorry for."

He gestures to my face. "Look at you."

"You don't look so hot yourself."

He scoffs. "I always look hot."

I smile and shake my head. "One day someone's going to knock that ego right out of you."

"Unlikely." He glances down at his phone as it dings in his hand. "God, my brother is relentless. He has texted me every twenty minutes to remind me to check on you and tell you to take your pills."

"Tell him I took them, and to stop worrying."

He heaves a sigh and tosses his phone onto the bed. "Impossible. The man worries constantly. I told him he's going to take years off his life if he keeps worrying so much."

"I don't think he can help it."

He shakes his head. "It's been bad since Mom died. It's like he thinks he can single-handedly stop anything bad from happening to me or Dad."

"It's an awful way to live." I pat the space next to me. "How old were you when your mom died?"

He lowers himself onto the bed. "Eleven. None of us expected it. It really fucked with us. My dad started drinking."

My eyebrows shoot up. "Really?"

He nods. "He almost lost his job. They put him on leave so he could go to rehab and get his shit together."

"I can't picture him like that. It must've been so hard for him to lose her."

"Every night, I wish it was me who died and not her."

My heart breaks thinking about Leo not here, in this moment, on this earth. I clasp his hand and squeeze it as hard as I can. "I used to wish the same thing about my dad. I would've switched places with him. But we can't. We just have to learn how to survive without them."

I'm about to ask how she died when my phone buzzes in my lap. I show Leo the name flashing across the screen, and he snatches my phone out of my hand to answer it. "She took the damn pills, James. I'm not a complete fuckup."

James's impatient voice blares through the phone. "Put her on."

But Leo hangs up on him.

I gasp. "Leo, he's going to kill you. Stop torturing him."

"He's gonna call back. Watch."

Sure enough, my phone vibrates. "Hi, James. I'm fine."

He grunts. "Why does he have to be such a pain in the ass?"

"He's *your* pain in the ass. Just remember that."

He mutters something under his breath. "How do you feel?"

"Just sore."

"I'm going to stop by the store to get a few ingredients before I head home later tonight. I'm making you chicken soup for dinner."

Leo grins and shakes his head.

"You don't have to do that, James. You've done plenty."

"I know I don't have to. Is there anything else I can get you while I'm out?"

I nudge Leo's shoulder and whisper, "Watch this." I clear my throat. "Actually, would you mind stopping at Barnes and Noble?"

"I can do that. What book do you want?"

"I don't know. I read romance novels, so just pick out a variety."

Leo clamps his hand over his mouth as his shoulders shake.

It's quiet on the line. "James?"

"I'm here. Do you mean, like, the books with Fabio on the cover?"

I bite the inside of my cheek to keep from laughing. "No, but that's the section you need to go to. I'll let you pick them out for me. Read the blurbs on the back and pick whatever sounds good to you."

"I don't know if I'm the right person for this."

Leo leans over. "I can make a run if you don't think you can do it, brother."

"No, no. It's fine. I'll go."

We say goodbye, and as soon as I end the call, I double over with laughter. "Oh my god. I can't believe he's going to do it."

"Damn, Nixie. I had no idea you were into spicy porn books." Leo rubs his hands together. "This is going to be fun."

"They're not porn books. They just have…"

"Porn *in* them."

I shove his shoulder. "Shut up and go make me a sandwich. I'm getting hungry."

"Yes, ma'am." Leo salutes me, and then he's bounding into the hall and down the stairs like a kid.

Maybe he still is a kid. Maybe he's stuck in the last stages of his life when his mom was still alive. Maybe that's why we have such a hard time moving on from trauma, because we're still the same person we were before it happened, only everything around us has changed. Life goes on, but we're stuck in purgatory, replaying old memories of the good times.

The rest of the afternoon goes by as Leo and I watch old movies in bed. Neither one of us has anywhere to be, and even if he did, I don't think he'd admit it.

"You know, you're more like your brother than you think. Have you ever thought about becoming a police officer?"

Leo snorts. "The law isn't my thing."

"What about a firefighter? Or an EMT? I can see you helping people."

"I never really thought about it." He stares up at the ceiling. "Never saw much of a future for myself."

A familiar feeling settles into my bones, and I drag my nail over the raised skin on my wrist. "Me either."

"You're young. You can still figure it out." He shrugs. "I guess we both can."

"Want to hear a secret that I've never told anyone before?"

He sits up, eyes wide. "Yes."

"I think I want to write a book."

"Like one of your porn books?"

I laugh. "A romance, yes. But a realistic one. Where there's drama, and heartache, and real-life situations."

"So do it. Start writing."

"Yeah, I guess the only way to know if I can write a book is to just try." A surge of excitement shoots through me. "Let's make a pact: I'll work on a book, and you figure out something you want to do. And we both have to have it completed by the summer."

He arches an eyebrow. "Seriously?"

"It'll be good to motivate each other, and it'll give us a goal to keep us on track." I shake his shoulders. "Come on, let's do it."

"Do what?" James walks into the room, and I suck in a breath.

I don't think I'll ever get used to seeing him in his uniform.

"I'm trying to encourage your brother to do something with his life."

James's dark eyebrows jump. "Like what?"

Leo pops a nonchalant shoulder. "Maybe an EMT. Ride around and help people. I could be good at it."

James's eyes bounce between the two of us. "I think that's a great idea."

Leo makes an attempt to snatch the bag of books from James, but he pulls back before he can get to it.

I shake my head and smile. "I can't imagine what you two were like growing up."

"Exactly like this." James gives Leo a playful shove. "Get out of here. Go tell Dad you're becoming an EMT. It'll make his day."

Leo shoots me a wink. "See you later, Nixie. Have fun writing."

James lowers himself onto the edge of the bed and turns his attention to me once Leo leaves. "Writing?"

My cheeks burn. "I told him I was thinking about writing a book. Maybe. I don't know."

He empties the contents of the bag onto the comforter. "The romance section was very… interesting."

I sift through the books. "It looks like you knew what you were doing. Colleen Hoover is the best."

He rubs the back of his neck. "A worker helped me. She said everyone loves Colleen Hoover, and then I threw in a couple of rom-coms because those other books sound sad."

I imagine this big man in his police uniform picking out romance books, and I can't help the smile that spreads across my face. "You're really sweet, James."

His eyes drop to his lap. "You really like these love stories?"

"I do. It's an escape from reality, even if there isn't a love out there like that for me."

"Who says there isn't?"

"I don't know. I never thought I'd find someone who could love me like that." I pause. "Have you ever been in love?"

His eyebrows pinch together, and the corners of his mouth pull down. "I've dated, and I thought I was in love once or twice. But looking back, I don't think that's what love is." He glances around my room like he's trying to find the answer somewhere. "I watched my father love my mother with every ounce of his soul, and when he lost her, it broke him. I look in his eyes now, and he's not the same man. That terrifies me."

"Love can be scary, but I think it's always worth it in the end, regardless of how it turns out. It's better to be full of love than full of… nothing."

"Even if you end up with nothing in the end?"

I nod. "Even if you end up with nothing. At least you had something. I wouldn't take back the years I had with my father. I'd rather the memories than to never have known him at all."

He picks up one of the paperbacks and turns it over in his hands. "There were a lot of shirtless dudes on the covers of these books. What's that about?"

I bark out a laugh. "Sex sells, didn't you know that?"

"I guess it does."

"Trust me. If your abs were on the cover of a book, it'd sell millions of copies." My eyes widen. "Maybe you can be on the cover of my book when I'm done writing it."

A tint of pink crawls up into his cheeks as he rises from the bed. "All right. I'm going to make you dinner."

"Did you blush? The big bad cop just blushed?"

He walks toward the door. "Enjoy your books."

11

Phoenix

Daily Affirmation: "I am doing my best."

With the adoption event only a couple of weeks away, I have to finalize all the little details.

"How many tables do you think we'll need?" I tap on my notepad. "I found a couple in my garage, and James said he has two."

Sadie waves a hand. "That should be plenty."

"Okay, and you're handling the pet supplies. Do you need extra?"

"Oh, no. Your boyfriend really hooked us up the last time he came by."

My pen freezes on the paper. "My boyfriend?"

"He didn't tell you?" She gestures to the pile of boxes stacked behind her desk. "He and his cop friends donated all of this. He's such a sweetheart. You really lucked out with that one."

My lips part in surprise. "Wait, I'm sorry. He told you he was my boyfriend?"

Her eyes widen. "Oh, well, no. I just assumed. Are you two not dating?"

"No. He lives next door to me. We're friends."

She presses her hand against her cheek. "Oh, I feel so foolish."

"It's no big deal. It was an honest mistake."

She leans in and lowers her voice, even though no one else is around. "Although I must tell you, he didn't correct me when I called you *his* girlfriend."

Heat creeps into my cheeks. "Really?"

She gives me an emphatic nod. "Really. And he spends time with that runt pup you love so much."

"He goes in the back with the dogs?"

She nods again.

I'm about to press her for more information about what James said, but my phone dances across the countertop and the name on the screen stops me dead in my tracks.

"Excuse me, Sadie. I have to take this."

I swipe my thumb across the screen and scurry outside into the parking lot. "Tyler, hi."

My brother's voice warms my heart. "Hey, Nix. How's it going?"

I let out a long breath. "It's going well. How are you?"

"Ah, you know how it is with a baby and all. Have you seen the pictures on Facebook? Jenna's getting so big already. It's crazy how fast they grow."

"No, I actually deleted my social media accounts. But I'd love it if you'd send me some photos of her."

"Absolutely."

I roll a rock under my sneaker. "It's good to hear your voice."

"Yeah, same. I would've called you sooner, but it's been crazy here." He laughs. "Jenna does this new thing where she kicks her feet when she's hungry. It looks like she's auditioning for *Riverdance*."

I smile. "I can't wait to see her. When are you thinking you'll have her baptism?"

There's a pause of silence. "Uh, we're going to have the baptism down here. It's just easier than traveling with a baby."

"Oh, of course. Well, just let me know when it is so I can put it in my calendar."

"Uh, well… about that." He clears his throat. "Gabby and I were talking, and we don't want any drama at the baptism. We're going to fly Mom out, and we feel like it'd be best if you didn't come."

My throat swells, and my heart wrenches. "You know I wouldn't cause any drama. I… I just want to celebrate Jenna and see you."

"Look, you know how Mom is. She's incapable of being the bigger person, and Gabby and I just don't need that kind of stress on Jenna's big day."

I blink back tears. "So, does that mean I'm not going to be Jenna's godmother?"

Tyler lowers his voice. "I'm sorry, Nix. I wish things could be different. But I'm so happy to hear you're doing well right now."

I choke back a sob. "I'm sorry to cut this short, but I have to go. Thanks for calling."

I end the call before Tyler can say anything else, and head back inside the shelter.

"Everything okay?" Sadie asks, eyeing me from over the top of her glasses.

"Yeah. Do you mind if I go back to see the puppies?"

"Of course not, but are you all right?"

I nod, the tears about to brim over. "Everything's great."

She gives me a dubious look and gestures to the door. "You know where they are."

I fling open the door and make my way to the back of the room until I get to the tiny puppy with the heart-shaped nose.

"Hey, bud." The tip of his tiny white tail wags furiously as I step into his cage and scoop him up. "How are you doing today? Are your brothers and sisters treating you well?"

I lower myself into the corner of the small space, and he snuggles against my chest. I close my eyes and count my breaths as I will myself to calm down.

He licks a tear as it rolls down my cheek.

"Yeah, siblings are overrated."

"Come on, you piece of shit."

I grunt, struggling to get my new toilet over the pipe sticking out of the floor. Now I know why the guy who delivered it looked at me funny when I said I didn't need help installing it.

The doorbell rings, and I call out to James. "Come in."

His boots clunk along the floor in the hall until he stops in the doorway. "What are you doing?"

I blow a strand of hair out of my face. "I'm trying to get this toilet on but it doesn't want to go, and it's heavy."

"Let me do it. Your ribs are still healing." He kneels down and nudges me out of the way. "Why didn't you tell me you needed help?"

I stand up and brush off my palms on my thighs. "I didn't know I needed help until I needed it."

"If you don't do this right, it can cause a leak." James bends over, and all my attention is drawn to his plump, round ass. He's wearing sweatpants again—tight gray joggers this time—and I can't convince myself to look away.

I slip my phone out of my pocket and snap a quick picture. Then I send it to Drew.

Me: He's quite handy.

It's not my proudest moment, but I'm not above shameless ogling. I've had a tough day, and if this man's rear end makes it better, then so be it.

James sets the toilet into place and finishes the rest of the job, flushing several times until he's satisfied.

"I'm going to let you start billing me for all of your services." I lead him into the kitchen after he washes his hands. "Is there anything you can't do?"

He chuckles. "Golf. Never been good at it."

"Eh, that's a boring sport anyway." I rub my palms together. "Okay, what are we cooking tonight?"

"Chicken teriyaki with vegetables and rice noodles." He hoists a large bag onto the counter. "And then we're making dessert."

I peer into the bag. "Please tell me it's something made of chocolate."

"It is."

"Chocolate makes everything better."

He side-eyes me as he lines up the ingredients on the counter. "Bad day?"

I wave him off. "No, I was just saying that I love chocolate."

"What did you do today?"

I push away the reminder of the conversation I had with Tyler. "I went to visit the dogs, and I picked up a few things for the adoption event."

"I've been passing out flyers on my shift. There should be a decent amount of people at the event."

"That's great. Thank you."

He hands me a green pepper. "Start chopping."

"You got it, Mr. Bossy Pants."

He removes the chicken from the package and starts snipping away at the fatty parts. "While we're on the subject of the shelter, Sadie mentioned to me that you were upset today."

My knife slices into the pepper and smacks the cutting board with a little too much force. "That Sadie likes to talk, huh?"

"Who's Tyler?"

Smack. "My brother."

"And your brother made you cry?"

Smack. "I wasn't crying."

"That's not what Sadie said."

Smack, smack. "Well, Sadie is mistaken. I had something in my eye."

"So, you had a nice chat with your brother?"

Smack, smack, smack. "As a matter of fact, I did."

"Then why are you murdering that pepper right now?"

Smack. Smack. Smack. Smack.

"Hey." James steps behind me and covers my hands with his. "Stop."

Anger and sadness bubble beneath the surface of my skin, coursing through me like hot poison, and my lips tremble as I try to get out the words.

"He said I'm not invited to the baby's baptism."

"Your brother's baby?"

I nod. "He said he doesn't want my mother to make a scene if I'm there, so he's choosing to invite her over me. And I won't be the godmother either. I won't be anything. The baby won't even know me. I'm his only sister, and he doesn't even care that I'm not in his life. It took him weeks to call me since… since I moved out here. It's like I don't matter to him, and I don't know why." I drop my chin to my chest. "I guess this is what I deserve." Punishment for trying to take my own life. Tyler doesn't want his unstable sister around the baby.

James blows out a stream of air through his nostrils and spins me around to face him. "Come here." He pulls me against his chest and wraps his arms around me. His palm presses against the back of my head, cradling me there. His deep voice is at the cusp of my ear. "You *don't* deserve this. This isn't about you. This is about him, and your mother, and *their* issues. You didn't make him treat you this way." I grip onto him as I listen to his soothing voice. "You don't deserve to hurt or cry. You deserve to smile, laugh, and be loved. You have a big heart, and you're a good person, Phoenix."

I release everything I've been holding in all day, the building resentment toward my brother, and the irreversible hurt my mother has caused me. I let go of it all, because I don't have any strength left to hold on to it anymore.

And James takes it.

He lets me unload it, and he bears the weight.

I cry, and he holds me until I finish.

I step back and wipe my nose with the sleeve of my shirt. "I'm sorry about that. I don't know where that came from."

James grips my shoulders so I can't get too far away. "You don't have to apologize. You needed to let it out."

I shake my head and glance up at the ceiling. "I know I shouldn't care so much about someone who doesn't care about me, but I can't help it."

"He's your brother. Of course you care." James lifts his hands to my face and swipes away the tears. "And it doesn't mean that he doesn't care about you. Most people don't mean to hurt us when they do."

My voice lowers to a whisper. "Sometimes it feels like all they do is hurt us. Everyone. Everything always hurts."

His gentle touch lingers on my skin, trailing along my cheek, and down to my jawline. "Not everyone."

I gaze up at him, this beautiful man staring back at me with warm intensity, and my heart flutters. "Sadie said you donated a bunch of supplies to the shelter."

His thumb sweeps over my bottom lip. "That Sadie *does* like to talk."

My heart rate speeds up as he traces my mouth. "She also mentioned you've been stopping by to see the puppies."

"I wanted to check on them."

"Why?"

His Adam's apple bobs in his throat as he tucks a strand of hair behind my ear. "Because they matter to you."

My eyes bounce between his, searching for the truth. "Why do you care what matters to me?"

His hand slips into my hair and settles at the base of my head, drawing me closer to him. "Because *you* matter to *me*."

I slide my hands up his strong arms, over his wide shoulders, and press my palms against his chest. His heart beats a furious rhythm, matching my own. Underneath the hard, muscular exterior is a gentle, compassionate man. One who fights for the people he loves. One who stands by the people he cares about.

Me.

I'm someone he cares about.

I just can't figure out why.

But maybe I don't have to. Maybe right now, I can just enjoy it.

God, do I want to enjoy it.

A loud ring pierces the air, and we both jump.

"Sorry." James clenches his jaw as he slips his phone out of his pocket and holds it up to his ear. "Yeah?"

I turn around to give him privacy, and finish chopping the pepper I half killed before. The person on the other end of the phone is muffled, but I can make out a man's voice.

"Sure, no problem. See you then. Bye." James sighs and sets his phone down on the counter. "I have to cover a shift tonight. One of the guys called out sick. We have time for dinner, but I can't do dessert."

I mask my disappointment. "That's okay. We can save it for another night."

The corners of his mouth pull downward, and I nudge him with my shoulder. "Finish up with that chicken, will you? I'm starving."

James arches a brow. "Now look who's being bossy."

I grin. "Don't get between me and my food."

We cut up the chicken and the rest of the vegetables, and then he shows me how to sauté them in the pan. We work side by side, our arms brushing on occasion. I steal a peek at him any chance I get, loving the way he pulls his bottom lip between his teeth when he's concentrating, the pinch between his dark brows, and how he devotes all of his attention to each little detail, as if it's the most important thing on earth.

"So, have you been enjoying the books I got you last week?" James pulls out a chair for me at the table.

"Already been through two of them."

His eyebrows jump as he takes the seat across from me. "Are they any good?"

"So good. I loved them both." I fill his glass with water. "Do you read?"

"I do when I have the time. Usually at night when I can't sleep."

"What do you like to read?"

"Mystery and suspense. John Grisham's my favorite author."

"Never heard of him." I close my eyes as I chew my first bite of chicken and noodles. "Oh my god. This is delicious."

He offers me a satisfied smile. "Maybe next time we can do Italian. I'm trying to give you a variety of meals to make so you don't get bored eating the same thing."

"I will eat whatever you make. You're the master chef." I dab my mouth with my napkin. "Why is John Grisham your favorite author?"

He shrugs. "I just find his writing interesting."

I set down my fork and square my shoulders. "I have an idea."

He leans his elbows on the table and folds his hands. "I'm listening."

"Why don't you give me your favorite John Grisham book to read, and I'll give you my favorite romance book. Then when we finish, we can discuss them. Kind of like a book club for two."

"You want me to read a romance novel?"

"Are you secure in your manhood?"

He barks out a laugh. "Yes, I'd like to think I am."

"Then it's settled."

"Deal." He holds out his hand, and we shake on it.

After dinner, I try to shoo James out of the kitchen and tell him to go relax before he has to head out to work. Of course, he refuses.

"I don't need you to help me with the dishes. I have this nifty new invention called a dishwasher. Watch this." I wave a dramatic arm and place two dishes on the rack. "All I have to do is press a button, and then *voilà*! It cleans them for me."

He rolls his eyes. "Smart-ass."

I bend over to place the pan in next, and when I turn back around, James's eyes are zeroed in on my ass.

I plant my hand on my hip. "Can I help you, sir?"

He hikes a nonchalant shoulder. "Figured it's only fair since you have a picture of *my* ass in your phone."

My throat goes dry, and all the bravado I just had left my body. "W-what?"

"I'm a cop. I see everything."

Busted.

My cheeks burn, and I try to come up with any plausible excuse but my mouth just flaps open and closed.

He steps closer to me. "Tell me, Phoenix, who did you send that picture to? Or is it for your own personal use?"

I scoff. "Wouldn't you like to know."

He lowers his voice and dips his head as he whispers in my ear. "Only if it's the latter."

My eyes widen, and goose bumps fly across my skin.

A smirk twists his luscious lips before James walks out and leaves me dumbfounded in the kitchen.

12

James

"So, you're cooking for her and repairing her house, but you're not getting laid?"

I shoot Phil a look from the driver's seat. "It's not like that."

"Then what is it like? Come on, man. Tell me." He crumbles his sandwich wrapper and tosses it onto the floor of the car. "Because I can't figure out why you're doing all this shit for her, and she's not giving you anything in return."

"First of all, you don't do things for people just to get something in return. Second, she's helping with Leo. He's been clean for a couple of weeks now, and I think she's part of that reason."

"You sure she's not into him?"

I shake my head. "She's not."

"Are you sure she's into *you*?"

"I don't know."

"Dude, you know when a girl is into you. It's not that hard to read the signs."

"I caught her checking out my ass the other day. Does that count?"

Phil laughs. "Can't say I blame the girl. Your ass is top notch."

"Fuck off." I shove his shoulder, but I'm laughing with him.

"Look at you, Russo. I've known you for a long time. You haven't smiled this much in all the years we've been riding together. You like her. She makes you happy. Why not tell her?"

I let my head fall back against the headrest. *Why not?*

A call comes in on the radio: Kids at the skate park.

"Goddamnit." I hit the steering wheel before radioing back to dispatch that we're on the way.

Phil shakes his head. "I told you they'd be back."

"Maybe it's not them."

"Yeah, sure. You keep telling yourself that."

We pull up to the skate park without our lights on and spy the usual group of boys.

Cory is there.

"That your little buddy, Cory?" Phil asks, gesturing to the blond-haired boy snorting a line off the picnic table.

I heave a long sigh. "Yup. That's him."

"Can we bring them in now?"

"Yes, we can bring them in."

"Do you want to tell me I'm right before we go, or wait until after?"

"You're right. I'm wrong. You feel better now, or do you need me to stroke your dick too?"

Phil throws his head back and laughs. "I always knew you wanted my dick."

"Shut the fuck up, and let's go."

We walk up on them from the other side of the skate ramp. Phil goes one way, and I go the other, giving them nowhere to run. We won't be able to catch them all, but two out of five is all we need.

Phil strides over to the table as he rubs his palms together. "What are we doing, boys?"

All five of them jump up, stuffing whatever they can into their pockets as if we haven't already seen what they're doing.

I shake my head as I enter the area from the opposite side. "Cory, I gotta say, I'm disappointed in you. I thought we had a good chat last time we met."

One of the boys spits on the ground between us. "Fuck you, pig."

Phil unclips his cuffs. "Oh, I'm not the one who's fucked."

Three of the boys take off running, but Phil and I remain with the other two who are too close to run.

"Such a shame." I shake my head at Cory. "I thought you were better than this. I gave you a second chance, but you blew it."

The spitter edges closer to Cory, and his eyes bounce between us as if he's giving his friend a silent message.

Adrenaline spikes in my gut.

Something's wrong.

"James," Phil warns.

I hold up my palm, my signal that I need more time. "Empty your pockets. Let's see what we're dealing with here."

Cory pulls out a bag of weed and a small packet filled with white powder.

Phil leans in. "A gram and an eighth. Who's your dealer?"

Cory looks to his friend, who shakes his head.

"Ah, come on. This will go a lot easier if you just tell us who you're getting this shit from." Phil crosses his arms over his chest. "You help us, we'll help you."

Cory's eyebrows shoot up. "You'll let us go if we tell you who—"

"No way, man. He's lying. They'll take us in regardless." Cory's friend curls his top lip. "We won't snitch, so you can forget it."

"You think your dealer would take the fall for you? Think about this," I say. "This is your life. Your future."

"You don't know shit about my future."

"Maybe not, but I know Cory could have a successful one if he stops hanging around people like you."

Cory shifts his weight from one leg to the other. "Maybe we should listen to him, Damon."

"Fuck that, Cory. You know what happens to snitches, don't you?"

"No one has to know who gave up your dealer," Phil says. "It'll be an anonymous tip."

"I'll do it," Cory says. "Let Damon go, and I'll tell you whatever you want to know."

Damon sucks his teeth. "You know what? I'll handle this." He reaches behind his back and pulls out a small black pistol.

Fuck.

Phil and I aim our guns, fingers poised on the triggers.

"Put down the gun!" Phil yells.

Damon shakes his head. "Let us leave, and we can all walk away from this."

"Slide the gun over to me, and we will let you guys go." I try to keep my voice low and calm. Yelling at him will only heighten the situation. Once we have the gun, we can get him safely into custody.

"Put the gun down, Damon," Cory whispers.

"No. It's a trick. Now let us walk, or I'm going to shoot."

Phil clenches his jaw. "We don't take orders from a punk-ass kid."

"Damon, don't do this," I say. "Give us your gun, and no one gets hurt."

Cory's eyes are wide as they bounce between me and his friend.

Damon points his gun at me and glances at Phil. His hands shake as he sways. God only knows what combination of drugs are coursing through his veins, making him unsteady and unpredictable.

"Come on, Damon. It doesn't have to be like this."

Without warning, Cory rushes Damon, and they both fall to the ground. Damon's gun fires and the bullet ricochets off the nearby picnic table.

I aim for Damon, but just before I shoot, another gunshot goes off. Searing pain shoots through my right hip, causing me to miss my mark. Damon's gun clatters beside him, and Phil hurries to grab it.

Damon stays on his back, blinking up at the night sky.

"He's hurt." Cory spears me with his crystal-blue eyes. "You shot him."

I glance down at the blood pouring from my abdomen.

And then everything goes dark.

A soft, fluttery sound has my eyes blinking open.

Phoenix sits beside Leo at the window, both of their heads tilted together as they whisper behind the book they're looking at. I can't hear what Leo is saying, but it's funny enough that Phoenix squeezes her eyes closed and scrunches her nose as she tries not to laugh too loud. Leo looks at her like she hung the moon herself, beaming with pride that he could make her smile.

My heart swells, affection warming my chest. She's so beautiful. How can such beauty exist amid a world as depraved as this one?

Tonight went so wrong but seeing Phoenix waiting here by my side makes something shift into place. Something I've been missing.

I watch them for a while, not wanting to alert them of my presence, until Phoenix glances up from the book.

She gasps and rushes to my side. "You're awake. How do you feel?"

"Like I've been shot."

The corners of her mouth pull down. "Are the painkillers not working? Do you need more? Do you want some water? Tell me what you need."

I lift my hand to her cheek. "I just need you to stop frowning like that."

She closes her eyes and leans into my touch. "And I need you to not get shot."

Leo walks around to the other side of my bed and pats my leg. "Want me to get the nurse? She can have you flying high with the push of a button."

I shake my head. "Where's Dad?"

"He's down at the station. He said he'll handle everything while you recover."

"Handle what, exactly?"

Phoenix and Leo exchange glances.

Guilt sinks into my stomach like a lead ball, and the room falls silent.

"He didn't make it, did he?"

Phoenix shakes her head. "He lost too much blood. He was dead before he got to the hospital."

Fucking Christ.

Leo squeezes my knee. "It wasn't your fault, brother."

"I should've just arrested them when I had the chance last week. If I would've done something differently, then maybe…"

But all the *shoulda, coulda, wouldas* in the world can't undo what happened.

I fell short.

Again.

Leo's eyebrows press together. "Phil said you did everything you could've done. You tried to defuse the situation, but the kid pulled a gun on a cop."

The kid. He was just a kid.

I squeeze my eyes shut and swallow past the lump in my throat as my emotions threaten to spill over. "You know, I'm really tired. You guys can go home."

The curtain slides open and closed, and I wait for the sound of their shoes shuffling against the tile to disappear. But then the mattress dips on one side.

I open my eyes to find Phoenix climbing onto the hospital bed.

"What are you doing?"

"I'm staying here with you—and don't tell me not to because I won't listen, and you can't make me because you're injured and there's nothing you can do about it." She moves around the wires I'm hooked up to, and lies down beside me, nuzzling her head into the crook of my neck.

Every muscle in my body relaxes, and I wrap my arms as far around her as the wires will let me. Having her here, feeling her next to me, knowing she's with me settles my restless soul.

"I know you're not okay, James," she whispers against my skin. "And you don't have to be. I'm here. I've got you."

A tear escapes me as everything surges to the surface, and I don't move to swipe it away. I don't have the strength to hide it. Not now, not from her.

I bury my face in her hair. "I tried to stop him."

I fucking tried.

Phoenix tightens her hold on me. "Some of us can't be saved, no matter how hard you try."

Memories of my mother cooking, laughing, dancing, flicker by on a reel through my mind.

I tried.

"It's not your job to rescue everyone." Phoenix lifts her face to mine and kisses each tear as it falls. "You can't bear the weight of that responsibility. All you can do is try. You try, and you help, and you make a difference to so many people. But you can't save them all."

I drop my forehead to hers, breathing in a lungful of her sweet scent of lavender and mint.

"You're in control of you," she whispers. "Your thoughts, and your choices, and your actions. Only you. So, at the end of the day, when you lay your head down on that pillow, you should be proud of the man you are because you've done your best and given your all to everyone you meet, no matter the outcome."

"I only see pain and death whenever I lay my head down."

"That's why I'm here." She runs her fingers through my hair. "I'm going to help keep your demons at bay so you can get some rest."

I pull back and look into her dark eyes, concern and pain swirling around her irises like a storm. "You hate hospitals. You didn't have to be here."

"When Leo told me you'd been hurt, it wasn't even a thought in my mind. I had to be here with you."

I shake my head. "You might not feel like a phoenix, but I'm starting to think you're *my* phoenix."

She smiles—a real, true, genuine smile. "I told you: I've got your six."

I pull her head down to my chest, and she snuggles her warm body against me.

"And I've got yours."

"James Theodore Russo, get that perfectly round ass back in bed."

I freeze with one foot on the floor. "Who told you my middle name?"

"Your father."

"Of course he did." I shake my head. "It's been two days. I don't want to lie in bed anymore."

Phoenix lifts my leg and tucks it back under the comforter. "I don't care what you want."

I grunt. "Some bedside manner. Do you have another nurse on duty today?"

She smirks. "Yeah, his name is Leo. Want me to get him?"

"No, no. That's okay. I'll stick with the one I've got."

"Are you hungry?"

"No."

"Do you need to use the bathroom?"

"No."

"Do you want Tylenol?"

"No."

"Then what do you want, besides to get out of bed and tear open your stitches?"

She looks so adorable standing there with her hands on her hips. The bruising on her face has almost completely faded, and the gash on her forehead is scabbing off. She's been determined to take care of me once I was released from the hospital, and though I don't need it, I don't want to tell her to leave.

I like when she's here.

With me.

I tug her hand until her knees hit the mattress beside me. "I want to read together."

Her eyes widen. "Really?"

"Yes." I tap the book on my nightstand. "I've got my favorite right here. Go get yours."

She bolts out of the room, and I chuckle at how excited she is. It makes me wonder how much she's been missing out on in life if reading a book makes her this happy.

It also makes me realize how much *I've* been missing out on. When all my college friends were out partying and dating, I was mourning the loss of my mother. I exiled myself from everyone. I focused on getting a job and threw myself into work. I cut myself off from love and affection. Being around Phoenix has brought out a side of me I haven't thought about in years. The way my pulse spikes when she looks at me. The way my stomach clenches when she smiles. The way my skin ignites when we touch. The way I lose all sense when I watch her lips moving as she talks. I was a cold, hollow shell until she moved next door. I want to care for her, protect her. Make her happy.

And *fuck* do I want to kiss her.

Phoenix blows back into my bedroom. "Okay, it was a difficult decision but I think I have the perfect book for you to read. It's not cheesy. It's realistic and emotional, and it has adventure and some mystery. I hope you—" She pauses as her eyes flick to mine. "What's wrong? Are you okay?"

"Yes, why?"

"You look a little flushed."

Because I was just thinking about kissing you. "It's a little warm in here. I'm fine."

"Do you have a fever? I hope your wound isn't getting infected." She climbs onto the bed and presses her wrist against my forehead. Then she pulls up my T-shirt to inspect my hip. "You look okay."

"Just okay?"

"I was talking about your stitches." Her smile fades as she traces a slow circle around my wound. "The doctor said you were lucky. Another inch or two, and you might not have made it."

"But I did. I'm here." I reach up and tuck a wisp of hair behind her ear, toying with the ends of her silky chestnut strands. "So you don't need to think about that."

"I can't help it. I care about you."

I move her hand until it's resting over my racing heart, letting her feel what she does to me. "I care about you too."

A small smile tugs at the corners of her lips, and I'm tempted to lean forward and kiss her. To pull her onto my lap and feel her thighs on either side of me. To grip her hair and listen to her soft moans as she rocks her hips against mine.

But she clears her throat and pulls back. Handing me her book, she sits back against the headboard beside me. "Ready to read?"

I reach for my book on the nightstand and hand it to her. "Ignore the notes in the margins. I write down my thoughts as I read."

She flips through the pages, and her eyes widen. "You are full of surprises."

I take her book. "*On the Way to You.* You said there's some mystery in here too?"

She nods. "Kandi Steiner's writing is so beautiful. It's such an emotional story. I cry every time I read it."

"All right, Kandi Steiner. Let's see if you can make me cry." I prop my pillows against the headboard and lean back, grunting as a sharp pain shoots through my hip.

"Careful," she says. "Go easy." Then she flips to the first page in John Grisham's *The Partner* and settles in beside me.

"Come here." I wrap an arm around her, needing her close. "Get comfy."

She snuggles in, and my heart swells. I could get used to this, the feeling of her next to me, spending a lazy day reading in bed together.

After a few minutes pass, she glances at me. "You know, most guys think women who read romance have unrealistic expectations of men because of these books."

"That's because most guys don't have enough sense to find out what it is that women actually want." I lift a shoulder. "I think romance can be very real if you find the right person. If you can listen to what your partner wants and do what you can to make him or her happy, then you can have any romance scene in these books. It might not be a millionaire with a yacht, but I think anything is possible if you set those standards and make it clear what you're looking for."

A slow smile spreads across her face. "Officer Russo, are you a hopeless romantic?"

"Keep reading, and you'll find out."

13

Phoenix

Daily Affirmation: "I am proud of myself."

"I know you have a big day this afternoon, but will you take a ride with me?"

I stop what I'm doing and look up at James. "Of course. What's wrong?"

He rubs the back of his neck and blows out a breath through his lips. "Damon's funeral is today. I… I don't want anyone to see me there, but I feel like I need to go."

I cap the marker and set it down so I can reach for James's hand. "Absolutely."

James doesn't talk on the ride over to the cemetery. Light snow flurries around us, the sky a dark, gloomy gray.

When he pulls into the parking lot, he puts the car in park and turns up the heat. "Are you warm?"

I nod. "I'm fine."

He scans the field and points out the window at a handful of people gathered around a priest. "That's his mother."

I squeeze his hand. "You did everything you could to help those boys, James. He's not in that casket because of you. He made the wrong choice, and Phil only fired because you were in danger."

"I know." He shakes his head, and I wonder if he believes his own words. "She lost her son right before Christmas."

"If he was into drugs and guns, it sounds like she lost him long before he actually died."

"Maybe. But I'm sure she still held on to hope. I know I always did when Leo went off the rails."

"I'm so glad you have your brother back."

"Me too."

We remain in silence, watching the funeral until the casket gets lowered into the ground.

"The last funeral I went to was my mother's."

I nod. "Same with my dad."

"Aren't funerals awful?" His dark eyes glisten. "Everyone stands around a dead body, remembering the life that once was. It's fucking morbid."

"I want to be cremated. I don't want to be in the ground."

"I don't think I want to be in the ground either. Sprinkle me into the water."

I scrunch my nose. "Ever think about how many dead bodies we're swimming with in the ocean?"

He turns his head to look at me. "Not until just now."

I smile. "My dad used to tell me that we all swam in fish poop when I was a kid. It used to rile me up."

"I mean, he's not wrong," he grunts. "Leo's afraid of fish. Won't step foot in the ocean."

"Really? I can't picture him being afraid of anything."

"Oh, yeah. Screams like a little girl if he thinks something touches his leg in the water."

I laugh. "I can't wait to tease him about that."

His smile fades, and he casts his glance out the window. "Thanks for coming with me."

"I've got your six, remember?"

He puts the car in reverse and places his hand on the back of my headrest as he twists in his seat. But he pauses before he backs out of the spot, pinning me with his intense stare.

"I could never forget it."

"Wow. Look at this place."

I inhale a nervous breath. "Does it look okay?"

Sadie's eyebrows shoot up. "Are you kidding? It looks better than okay."

I wring my hands and glance around the room. "I tried to make it look festive. Do you think there are enough balloons?"

"Any more and we might float away."

"Oh, no. Are there too many balloons? Is it overkill?"

Sadie laughs. "No, no. You did a fantastic job decorating and setting up this entire event. These dogs are going to end up with loving families tonight. You should be very proud of yourself."

Leo strides over to us, chewing on a mouthful of something.

My eyes widen. "Are you eating already? Did you make a mess on the tables? Please don't make a mess."

He pats me on the back and talks around the ball of food in his cheek. "I'm just sampling the food. You know, in case the cheese is bad or something. Don't want anything to happen to the guests."

I shoot him a dubious look. "Gee, thanks. It's so nice of you to put your safety on the line."

Sadie chuckles. "You should eat something too, Nix. You won't have time to eat once the event starts."

I shake my head. "I want to go over everything one last time. Make sure I didn't leave anything out."

Leo jerks his thumb to the right. "I'm going to sample those pigs in a blanket. Make sure they're not serving rancid meat."

I roll my eyes and lead Sadie over to the main table by the entrance. Louie's Legacy Animal Rescue is the nonprofit agency helping me host this event. They find people to foster dogs to rescue them from shelters or life on the street, so that the animals get to live in a loving environment while they're waiting to be adopted.

A beautiful woman with brown hair and a warm smile stands up to greet me. "You must be Nix. It's so nice to finally meet you. I'm Tina."

I clasp her hand. "Hi, Tina. Thank you so much for working with me for this event."

"Thank you for calling us to help." She gestures to two women standing beside her. "This is Melissa and Olivia. They run Louie's Legacy."

Melissa shakes my hand. "We're going to find some great foster homes for these litters tonight."

"I hope so. I love what your agency does to help animals. I think it's a great alternative to a shelter."

"We think so too. The foster parents we work with are amazing. They potty train them and get them ready for their forever homes."

I reach into my back pocket and unfold the envelope I shoved in there. "I'd like to make a donation to the agency. Can I give you a check?"

Olivia's eyes widen. "Oh, yes. That is so kind of you. Thank you so much."

I pull out the second envelope and turn to Sadie. "And this is for you to help with the shelter."

Her lips part on a gasp. "Thank you so much, Nix. This is amazing."

I smile, and my heart swells with pride. "My father left me some money when he died, and I haven't been able to figure out what to do with it until now. I know it'll go to good use."

"It definitely will." Sadie nudges me with her elbow. "The boys in blue are here."

My head whips around as James and the cops from his precinct waltz through the front door. He's in a navy-blue T-shirt with the yellow state police logo over his chest and a pair of dark jeans. His large frame and handsome, chiseled face demand your attention—and judging by the way every woman in the room is staring, I'd say he has it.

But my favorite thing he's wearing is the rarely seen wide smile on his face when he sets his honey-colored eyes on me.

When he gets close, he dips his head and presses a soft kiss to my cheek. "It looks amazing in here."

"You think so? The balloons aren't too much?"

He shakes his head. "Just the right amount."

"How are you feeling?" I gesture to his hip. "What did the doctor say about the stitches?"

"He said they're healing nicely, and that I had a very capable nurse taking care of me all week."

Heat creeps into my cheeks, and I bite back a smile.

"Come on." He ushers me toward Leo at the hero table. "You need to eat something."

"No, I'm fine. I just need to—"

"Eat." He hands me a paper plate. "You can make yourself a plate, or I can make one for you and feed you in front of all these nice people. Take your pick."

I glare up at him. "You're extra bossy today."

"You should've seen him setting up the tables this morning." Leo mimics James's voice. "They're not centered. Where's your measuring tape? You have to make sure they're even."

James shoves his brother's shoulder. "They were crooked. You can't have crooked tables."

I grin and pinch James's cheek. "Your OCD is adorable."

He rolls his eyes, but he's smiling. "I just wanted to make sure everything was perfect. I know how much this event means to you."

My heart melts into a ball of mush in my chest. "Thank you, James. Seriously. I appreciate you."

"What about me?" Leo stuffs a wad of bread into his mouth. "I helped too."

I wrap my arm around his waist and hug him to my side. "Yes, you did. Thank you, little bro."

Once four o'clock hits, people start filling the space. Kids are dragging their parents by their arms from pen to pen, squealing in delight as the puppies crawl all over them. I make sure to talk with each family and tell them the dogs' backstory. I pull out all the stops and work my ass off to make sure every dog finds a home.

By the end of the night, only a few dogs are left, but even they are on hold for people who needed to go home and talk to their loved ones about bringing home a puppy.

My heart sinks when I realize I didn't get to say goodbye to my favorite pit bull. "Sadie, did you see which family the runt pup went to? I didn't see him go."

She shakes her head. "No, I'm sorry, Nix. It was so busy in here, I missed it."

"That's okay." I chew my cheek to stop from frowning. "I should be happy he went to a good home."

Leo and I fold up the tables and chairs, and the police officers carry them out to James's truck. I pack up the leftover food and send it back to the precinct with them to thank them for their help. Leo sucks helium from the balloons while we take down the decorations, and he hugs me goodbye when we're done.

"I'm gonna catch a ride home with my dad. James will take you back."

I give him an extra-tight squeeze. "Thanks for your help. Seriously, you're the best."

He grins. "I know."

I'm about to flip off the lights when James walks in with his coat zipped up. "You ready?"

I nod, giving the room a once-over. "Yeah, we're done here."

"What's wrong? You look upset."

I heave a sigh. "It's dumb. I shouldn't even be sad about it. But I didn't get to say goodbye to the puppy—the one with the heart-shaped nose. He got adopted, and I didn't even get to say goodbye to him."

A smirk tilts his lips. "You mean this puppy?" He unzips his jacket, and a tiny black-and-white head pops out of the opening.

My hands fly up to my mouth. "Oh my god. What are you doing with him?"

He scoops up the dog in one hand and places him in my arms. "I'm the one who adopted him—for you."

The dog licks my face, and his tail wags like crazy. "For me? You mean, he's mine?"

James nods. "I couldn't let someone else take him home. I know how much you love him. I told Sadie about my plan before the event started. She made sure to put a tag on his collar that said he was already adopted so nobody else would try to take him. And I had him checked out by the vet. She said he's perfectly healthy, and she gave him all his shots."

This man. "I can pay you back for that. And the adoption fee—I can Venmo you or get the cash."

"Just call it an early Christmas gift. I don't want your money."

Emotion strangles me as I blink up at James. "Why? Why would you do all this for me?"

"Because you deserve to be happy."

I glance down at the puppy in my arms and smile. Every cell in my body fills with love, and I know this dog is going to make me the happiest person alive. But what's more is that James knew it too.

James lifts his hand to my cheek, his thumb making idle strokes against my skin. "Anything that makes you smile like this is worth it."

I wrap one arm around his waist and sandwich the dog between the two of us. He crawls up James's chest and licks his chin.

"Thank you. This is the best Christmas present ever." I let out a sigh. "The gift I got you definitely isn't as cool as this."

"You didn't have to get me anything. Speaking of Christmas, I don't know if you have any plans, but I'd like you to spend the day with us. If you want to." He scratches behind the dog's ears. "You and this little guy, of course."

For the first time since my father passed, I feel like I belong somewhere. I feel wanted. I feel like I have a purpose, a sense of direction.

I feel *happy*.

I lift onto my toes and press a kiss to James's cheek. "There's nowhere else I'd rather be on Christmas."

14

Phoenix

Daily Affirmation: "I am letting go of people that no longer serve me peace."

I get my brother's voice mail for the second time today.

"Merry Christmas to you too." I end the call and let the sadness overcome me for a moment. Though I'm hurt over his choice to keep me out of the baptism, he's still my brother.

I bend down and clip the leash on my adorable puppy. "At least you love me, Wilbur." He licks my face, and I can't help but smile. "Who needs family when you have dogs, am I right?"

We head next door, and the Russo's door flies open before I can lift my hand to knock.

"Merry Christmas, Nixie!" Leo wraps me in a bear hug and spins me around on the porch.

"Be careful. I've got presents here."

He sets me down and takes the gift bags from me. "Which one's mine?"

I smack his wrist as we walk into his house. "Who says I got you anything?"

"You should've gotten him coal." Jim stands from his recliner and gives me a hug. "Merry Christmas, Miss Bridges."

I relish in the warmth of his embrace, missing my own father a little bit extra today. "Merry Christmas, Jim. Thank you for having me."

"Of course. And who might this little guy be?" He leans down to pet Wilbur.

"This is Wilbur."

Leo scoffs. "I can't believe you named him after a pig."

I shield Wilbur's ears. "You leave him alone. He loves his name."

Leo scoops the puppy up into his arms. "You're a cute piggy though, aren't you?"

"He'd be even cuter if he stopped stealing my shoes and destroying them in his crate."

Jim laughs, his round belly shaking with the movement. "Did you get him any chew toys? He'll stop messing with your things if he's occupied with something else."

"Oh, yes. I gave him many chew toys. The only toy he wants is my shoe."

"Ah, let him have your shoes." Leo holds up Wilbur like Simba. "Look at this face. How can you deny him anything?"

I ruffle Leo's hair. "Well, we know *you're* not going to be the disciplinarian when you have kids."

A dark-haired woman sitting on the couch chuckles. "You should see him with my daughter. She could ask him for the sun, and he'd figure out a way to give it to her."

I offer her a knowing smile. "Sounds about right. Leo is *go big or go home*."

She stands and offers me her hand. "I'm Denise. It's a pleasure to meet you."

Leo wraps his arm around her. "This is my mom's sister."

"It's so nice to meet you. I'm Nix. I live next door."

"Oh, I've heard an earful about you and I've only been in town for a few hours. I feel like I know you already."

My cheeks burn. "Not sure if that's a good thing or a bad thing."

She laughs. "Anyone who can make these boys smile is a very good thing in my book. Plus, you have a kick-ass name."

"Told you." James waltzes into the room with a young dark-haired girl sitting on his shoulders.

I stick out my tongue at him, and the little girl laughs. "She stuck her tongue out at you, JJ." Then her eyes go wide. "Is that puppy for me?" We all laugh as she squirms to get down, and James sets her on the floor.

I kneel down beside Wilbur. "This is my dog. I brought him over because I heard you loved puppies."

She gives me an emphatic nod. "I do. Mommy said I can get one when I'm old enough to pick up his shit."

Denise tries to hide her mortified expression behind her hand. "Madison, remember what I said about cursing?"

Madison nods. "Not in front of other people because they're going to think you're a bad mommy."

Denise grins. "Good girl."

Madison crawls into my lap as if I'm her own personal chair, and Wilbur climbs on top of her to lick her face. "What's the puppy's name?"

"Have you ever read the book *Charlotte's Web*?"

"That's the one where the spider dies at the end. It was really sad." She points up at James. "JJ cried."

His jaw drops open. "That was supposed to be our secret."

She giggles. "Oops."

I bite back a smile. "Well, I named him Wilbur, because he was the smallest puppy in his litter."

"Hi, Wilbur." Madison scratches behind his ears, and his tail goes wild. "Can you tell me when he has to poop? If I can show mommy that I can pick up his poop, then maybe she'll let me get a dog soon."

"Don't push your luck, kid," says Denise.

Leo lifts Madison and tosses her over his shoulder. "Let's go play with Wilbur and let JJ get to cooking so we can eat."

James grumbles as he heads for the kitchen. "Calm your tits, it's almost ready."

Madison giggles. "Yeah, Leo. Calm your tits."

Denise pinches the bridge of her nose as she flops down onto the couch. "Great. I'll be getting another phone call home from school about that one."

I brush off Wilbur's fur from my pants as I stand and follow James into the kitchen. "I'm helping, and you can't tell me no because it's Christmas."

He arches a brow. "Is that so?"

"It's a rule. You can't be bossy on Christmas."

He pulls me in for a hug and lowers his lips to my ear. "I think you like it when I'm bossy."

A shiver dances down my spine, and my breath hitches in my throat. "I'll never admit it."

He pulls back wearing a smug smirk. "Grab that head of romaine over there and start chopping."

I do as he says and start prepping the salad. "It's so nice that your aunt spends Christmas with you."

"It helps us all feel like a part of Mom is still here."

I nod. "The last good Christmas I had was the year before my dad passed. Then my brother moved away, and after that, my mom stopped decorating or even acknowledging that it was a holiday—even though I was still there. It was like I wasn't worth the effort."

James sets down the knife and comes to stand behind me at the counter. He wraps his arms around my waist and presses a kiss to my temple. "Hopefully we can make this a better Christmas for you."

I close my eyes and relish in his warmth. "I'm happy to spend it with you."

"Phoenix, I—"

"Oh, look at you two!" Denise saunters into the kitchen wearing a smile like the cat who ate the canary as James and I break apart. "Don't mind me. I'm just coming in to steal a piece of bread."

Madison bounces into the kitchen. "JJ, can we play Twister?"

James glances at the timer. "You've got seven minutes. Then it's time for dinner."

She squeals and yanks his arm until he's out of the kitchen.

Denise sidles alongside me at the counter. "Okay, I know we just met, but I need to know the scoop because James tells me nothing."

I laugh. "The scoop about what?"

"About you two."

I slide the lettuce off the cutting board and into a bowl. "I don't really know that there is a scoop. We've been... friends since I moved in last month."

She pops a cherry tomato into her mouth. "But you like each other as more than friends."

It's a statement, not a question, and I can't deny that my feelings for him have been growing.

"I'm not sure how he feels." I shrug. "He hasn't told me anything."

"James doesn't say it with words. He shows it." She jerks her chin in the direction of the living room. "Like that puppy in there. You think he hands out puppies to everyone like Oprah?"

I look down at my feet and smile. The whisper of doubt still lingers in the back of my mind—why would someone like him want to be with me? What do I have to offer *anyone*? But James has done nothing but show me how much he cares, and his flirting *has* been more obvious lately. Maybe it's time I believe the signs in front of me instead of going down the same self-sabotaging road I've been on all my life.

"That man has a heart of gold, but he locks it away behind a steel gate." Denise frowns and lowers her voice. "My sister would hate to see how devastated he's been since she left us. This isn't the life she'd want for him." She squeezes my hand. "Just be good to him, whether you're a friend or more."

"I will." I say it with absolute certainty, because I know that's what James deserves.

"Come on," she says, linking elbows with me. "Let's go see what kind of pretzel Madison has James twisted into."

I burst into laughter as soon as we step foot into the next room. Leo is holding himself up like a crab with James's ass in his face.

"Bro, I swear… if you fart right now, I'm kicking you in the balls."

James grunts. "If you would put your left hand on red already, we'd be out of this position."

Leo stretches his hand, and his fingertips are just shy of the red circle. "I can't reach it."

"Then fall and let me win!"

"Never!"

And all the while, Madison cackles with the spinner in her lap like it's the funniest show she's ever seen.

I slip my phone out of my back pocket and snap a quick picture.

Jim howls with laughter. "Send me that picture, Miss Bridges. I'm going to need it for blackmail one day."

"You got it, sir."

"Why don't you come and play with us, Nixie." Leo shoots me a wink. "I'd rather your ass in my face than my brother's."

James elbows him in his side, and Leo's wrist gives out. He crashes onto his back, and James jumps to his feet, pumping both fists in the air.

Madison cheers. "JJ is the winner!"

Leo frowns as he stands. "That's cheating. You should be disqualified for violence."

James nudges him with his shoulder. "Watch your mouth, and I wouldn't have to resort to violence."

"Maybe you're just worried I'm going to steal your girl." Leo drapes his arm around me. "What do you say, Nix? I'm the younger stallion with way more stamina than this old man."

Before James can move toward him, I twist Leo's nipple.

"Ow! Jesus, fuck, that hurts."

Madison giggles. "Jesus, fuck!"

"Okay, that's enough with the cursing." Denise lifts her daughter and hauls her out of the room like she's carrying a football.

Jim wipes the corner of his eye as he laughs. "This is the best Christmas we've had in a long time." He rests his hand on my shoulder. "I'm so glad you're here."

Emotion settles in the pit of my stomach. "I'm glad to be here too."

If my own family doesn't want me around, at least this one does.

Everyone clears out of the room, but James pins me with a devilish look.

I arch an eyebrow. "What?"

He walks me back against the wall. "That makes two compromising pictures you have of me now."

A shit-eating grin spreads across my face. "You can't blame a girl for looking when you have a rear end like yours."

His hands ball into fists at his sides, like he's restraining himself from reaching out for me. "I don't think that's very fair."

"I guess you don't always get your way, Mr. Bossy Pants." The timer beeps in the kitchen, and I pat his chest before squirming out of the way to head for the dining room.

"Presents! Presents! Presents!"

Leo lowers himself in front of the tree next to Madison and puts on a Santa hat. "Who said you're getting presents?"

Madison rolls her eyes. "It's Christmas. Everyone gets presents on Christmas."

"Only the good children get presents. Have *you* been a good child this year?"

She purses her little lips. "Yes. And I've been very response-a-vull."

Leo laughs. "Response-ible. With a *b*."

James sits on the couch beside me. I smile and he gives my knee a squeeze but lets his hand rest there. Goose bumps fly up my leg, and I'm glad he can't see them. I don't want him to know the way every little touch affects me.

Madison tears into all of her presents within minutes, and she jumps into my arms to thank me for the dog stickers I gave her with a matching dog notepad.

James leans over and whispers, "Thank you. You didn't have to get her anything."

"I wanted to."

Next, Leo sets a shallow square box in my lap. "Your turn, Nixie."

I peel the tape on the silver wrapping paper and slide out the box from inside. I gasp when I pop open the top. "Leo, this is beautiful." I inspect each of the charms on the silver bracelet: a dog, a book, a sneaker, and a police shield.

"I got each of your favorite things." He shrugs. "I couldn't find anything to remind you of me though. I'll have to keep looking."

I blink to keep the welling tears at bay. "This whole bracelet will remind me of you. This is so thoughtful. Thank you."

"You're always scratching that scar on your wrist. I wanted you to have something better to play with when you feel anxious."

I fling my arms around him and let a few tears fall while my face is buried in his shirt.

"Why are you sad?" Madison asks. "Do you not like the bracelet?"

I chuckle as I wipe my eyes when I pull back. "Sometimes people cry when they're really, really happy."

She scrunches her nose. "That's confusing."

We laugh, and I scoot forward to reach for Leo's gift. "Here you go, little bro."

He opens the membership to the gym I bought him. "Is this that new MMA place that opened up in town?"

I nod. "Now you can have somewhere safe to get out all that pent-up energy. I signed up for it too, so we can go together."

He plants a kiss on my cheek. "Thank you, Nixie."

137

I toss Jim the gift bag with the slippers I got him, and he wiggles his big toe that's sticking out of his current slippers. "Are you saying I need new slippers?"

I laugh. "These will keep your toes warm."

Madison scampers under the tree and comes back with the present I got James. "This is the last one. It's for you, JJ."

James stares down at the recipe book I half filled with his mother's recipes that I got from Jim. I also stuck in a few pictures of his mother.

"It's kind of like a scrapbook, so you can keep your mom's memories in one place." I flip to a blank page. "And then you can start adding in your own recipes. Create your own dishes to pass down one day."

"Thank you." He blinks and clears his throat. "I love this."

"Are we done now?" Madison asks. "I want dessert."

Denise shushes her. "You're going to make Phoenix think I haven't taught you any manners."

I smile. "It's fine. You should never stand in the way of a girl's dessert."

I help James dole out the desserts—a variety of pies and Christmas cookies—and when it's just the two of us in the kitchen, he reveals one last dessert.

"My mother used to make this. It's a homemade chocolate cake."

"You had me at chocolate." I don't even wait for him to hand me a fork when he cuts me a slice. I pick off a chunk of it with my fingers and pop it into my mouth. I hum, closing my eyes. "Damn. This is good."

"Is it? I haven't made it in a while."

"See for yourself." I slide the plate across the counter, but James takes my hand instead. He lifts my fingers and sucks my chocolate-covered thumb into his mouth, keeping his eyes locked on mine as his lips wrap around it. His warm tongue skates over my skin, and wetness pools between my legs.

I almost let out an audible moan.

"I thought you wanted to try the cake."

James releases my thumb from his lips with a pop, but he holds on to my hand. "I don't want the cake, Phoenix." He pulls me closer and flattens my hand against his chest to feel the thundering rhythm under my palm. "Does yours race this way when we're together too?"

I place his hand on my chest so he can feel it for himself. "Every time."

He slides his hand around to the back of my neck, drawing my mouth closer. I lift up onto my toes to close the distance between us and press my lips against his. A spark of electricity shoots through my entire body.

But Madison has other plans for us as she bursts into the kitchen. "Can we play hide-and-seek now?"

James and I jump back, flying to opposite sides of the island.

James clears his throat. "Sure, kid. Go hide, and I'll start counting."

She runs out of the room, and he gives me a tentative smile. "I didn't pick the best time to kiss you, with my entire family in the next room."

I let out a nervous laugh, still in shock from what just happened. "I didn't mind it."

"No?"

I shake my head and bite my bottom lip to keep the goofy smile from spreading across my face.

"So, you wouldn't mind if I kissed you again sometime?"

I squeeze his shoulder. "Just don't make me wait too long."

"I don't hear counting," Madison yells from somewhere in the house.

James shakes his head and walks out of the kitchen. "Aunt Denise, your kid is a cockblock."

Madison's head pokes out of the closet. "What's a cockblock?"

"Jesus Christ," Denise mutters.

We play several rounds of hide-and-seek, and then Madison declares it's time for teams. James and I hide so she and Leo can find us. James yanks me down the hall, pulls me into his bedroom, and we crouch down inside his closet.

I peek out from behind the door to get a look at his room. No surprise, it's neat and simple. Navy-blue comforter on his bed, plain white walls, and wood furniture.

On his dresser, I spot a picture of his mother. "Your mom was so beautiful. You have her eyes."

"That's about all I got from her. I look more like my dad, but Leo is the spitting image of her."

Maybe it's because we're crammed into a dark closet that I get the courage to ask, "Do you mind if I ask how she died? You've never mentioned it before."

He's quiet for a moment. "She committed suicide."

My throat goes dry at the sound of those three words, and my heart plummets to the floor.

His hand finds mine, and he grips it as he continues. "I was at my friend's house playing video games. She called my cell, but I sent it to voice mail because I was leaving soon. I figured she was just calling me home for dinner." He pauses. "I was the only person she called that day. My dad was at work, and Leo was at the skate park. By the time I got home, she was gone. I found her hanging by a rope in the bathroom."

My lungs constrict, and I can't get in any air. I can barely hear his voice over the sound of my pulse roaring in my ears.

She killed herself.

James's mother had depression.

She took her own life.

"I-I'm so sorry, James. That's… that's awful." I fight to keep my voice even as the tears stream down my face, but I can't make this moment about me. He just shared something tragic with me, and I need to be here for him.

"It's all I see sometimes when I close my eyes at night. The vision of her, just hanging there." He sucks in a deep breath. "I'll always wonder what she wanted to say to me when she called. Maybe she was calling for help. Maybe I could've stopped her if I'd answered. I've hated myself for ignoring her call."

This poor man. That's why he's always running around trying to save people. He couldn't save the one person who mattered most to him.

I take his face in both of my hands and press my forehead to his. "Don't hate yourself. Please, James. It's not your fault, and if your mother were here, she'd tell you the same thing. You are not responsible for what other people are going through."

"Why?" His voice sounds strained. "Why would a mother *choose* to leave her children?"

I swallow a sob. "It wasn't her choice. Depression isn't a choice. It's a sickness in your brain. I know because—"

Madison comes barreling into the room and flings open the closet door. "I found you! I found you!"

James wipes his eyes before we crawl out of the closet. "Good job, Mads."

"Let's play again!"

Denise leans against the doorframe. "That's enough fun for one night. We have to get back home before Santa comes."

"Santa! Santa! Santa?" Madison bounces out the door into the hall.

I feel like I'm going through the motions as I say goodbye to Denise and Madison, like I'm underwater and I can't really hear what anyone is saying.

"I'm going to head out too." I give the Russos a hug and thank them for allowing me to spend the day with them.

I clip Wilbur's leash to his collar and all but run back to my house. When I'm inside, I close the door and lean my back against it, letting out a long exhale. Thoughts swim in my head, worry churning like a brewing storm.

But a knock on the other side of my door pulls my attention. I swing it open and see an out-of-breath James standing on my porch.

My eyebrows press together. "Hey, what's wrong?"

His hand wraps around the small of my back, and he pulls my body against his. "I wanted to give you a proper good-night kiss."

Then his mouth is on mine.

This is more than the tender kiss we shared earlier. It's a deep, frantic, passionate kiss—like we'll die if we stop.

I just might.

He lifts me up and walks me backward into my house. My shoulders hit the wall in the entryway, and I wrap my arms and legs around him. My lips part as James slides his tongue against mine. He groans into my mouth, sending a delicious shiver down into my core.

I lose track of time, relishing in the feel of his hard body pressed against mine, his hand in my hair and the other gripping my waist, as our tongues wrap around one another's.

Finally, James pulls back, panting, and rests his forehead against mine. "I could kiss you for days."

"I wish you would." I lower my feet onto the floor, grounding myself as the reminder of our conversation about his mother creeps back into my mind.

How would he feel if he knew I tried to do the same thing his mother did?

What would he think of me?

Should I tell him? Does it even matter?

"Good night, Phoenix." He places a lingering kiss on my lips, and I wonder if it'll be the last.

15

James

I stare at Phoenix's mouth while she finishes her phone call.

I've been completely useless since our kiss last night—Phil made sure to tell me so during our shift today. But those soft, warm lips of hers have been calling to me like a siren. I was on her doorstep the second I got home, hoping she'd be as eager to see me as I've been to see her.

She answered the door with the phone sandwiched between her ear and her shoulder and waved me inside. Now, I'm watching her like a lion while she paces, waiting for the right time to pounce on my prey.

"I'll come by this week so we can hang for a bit." Phoenix's eyes dart to mine before she glances down at her feet. "Yes, I will. I'm sorry, okay? I'll make it up to you. Okay, bye." She shakes her head as she sets down her phone. "Sorry. That was my friend, Drew."

I wrap my hands around her waist. "Everything okay?"

"We haven't spoken much lately, and he's a little upset with me."

"You were busy with the adoption event. I'm sure he'll understand." I kiss her nose. "How was your day?"

"Better now."

I lower my lips to hers. "I've been thinking about you all day."

She melts against me, and I cradle the back of her head, tilting her mouth up to mine. We haven't talked about what we're doing, or what's happening between us, but for now, kissing her is all I can focus on.

But Phoenix pulls back too soon. "Let's go sit on the couch and talk."

"Sure." I take her hand in mine as we walk into the living room and lower ourselves onto the cushions. "What's wrong?"

"I've been thinking about what you told me about your mom yesterday. About how she died."

"Oh." My stomach knots itself. "And what are you thinking?"

"There's something you should know." She swallows and rubs her palms against her thighs. "About me."

I shift in my seat. "What is it?"

"Remember when I told you that I had a falling-out with my mother?"

I nod.

"Well, the reason is because…" She squeezes her eyes shut, and I give her time because I can see this is a difficult subject for her. Then she pulls up the sleeve on her left arm, revealing the thin scar etched into her skin. "Two years ago, I tried to take my own life."

A high-pitched whistle pierces my ears.

My body stills.

I forget how to breathe.

I blink down at the mark on her forearm in disbelief.

She tried to take her own life?

Phoenix tried to kill *herself?*

Tears well behind her lids as she continues. "I have depression. I've had it since I was a kid. I managed it as best as I knew how, but my mother never believed in mental health issues so she didn't guide me to get proper help. I just thought something was wrong with me, and that it was my fault that I couldn't figure out how to make myself feel happier. Then as I got older, my dad got sick, and that took a toll on me. When he died, everything got ten times worse. My mom shut me out, and we grew even further apart. And one day, I'd just had enough of trying to find the will to live when it seemed like I had nothing to live for. So, I tried to kill myself. I would've succeeded if my mother didn't walk in on me in the bathroom."

Her bottom lip trembles and a part of me wants to wrap her in my arms and hold her while she cries. But the other part of me—the wounded son who lost his mother because she didn't want to live anymore—overpowers all else. I feel blindsided. Deceived in some way. Anger flares deep in my gut and spreads throughout my body like a comforting blanket to soothe my pain.

"You... you slit your wrist?"

A tear slides down her cheek as she nods. "Yes."

"Why would you do that?"

"I just wanted the pain to stop. I didn't know what else to do."

A bitter laugh rips from my chest, and it doesn't sound like my own. "You couldn't figure out that you needed to go to therapy instead of *killing yourself*?"

Her head jerks back. "In that moment, no. I couldn't. But I went to a mental health facility to get the help I needed. What I did wasn't the answer to my problem. I know that now. It was a mistake, and—"

"It was a mistake that almost cost you your life. How could you do something so selfish?"

"It's not selfish, James. It's *depression*."

"What about your family? Did you think about how they would feel after you died? No wonder your family doesn't want anything to do with you."

Her mouth falls open, and I know I've hurt her but I can't seem to stop my words from tumbling out. Everything I want to say is getting jumbled by the emotion I've buried deep with my mother's death.

"I can't believe this." I push off the couch to stand, and Wilbur jumps off with me, wagging his tail like we're going on a walk.

Phoenix muffles a sob and follows me into the hallway. "Wait. James, please don't leave. Let's talk about this."

"Talk?" I spin around. "How can you expect me to stay after what you just told me?"

"I... I don't know. I understand this brings up a lot for you, and that's why I wanted to talk to you about it."

"No, you *don't* understand. You don't have a fucking clue. Do you know why? Because you aren't the one who was left by choice. You're the one who made a selfish decision that affected everyone else in your life except you. You hurt everyone who loved you, and you told them that they didn't matter enough."

"I didn't mean to! That's not how depression works. It's *not* a choice." She chokes out the next words. "Do you think it was a happy moment for me? That I relished in the thought of dying? Because suicide wasn't me telling them that *they* didn't matter—it was me telling them that *I* didn't matter. I was drowning, James. I was alone, and I was drowning. And obviously, your mother was too."

Is that how my mother felt? It kills me to think of her feeling so hopeless when she had all of us here, supporting and loving her. Her limp body hanging from the noose around her neck flashes through my mind, and I picture Phoenix in her place. Cold and dead. This beautiful soul gone forever.

I stab the air with my finger. "You could've done better. You could've tried harder. Anything! You could've done anything except for killing yourself. How could you even think of doing that?" My own cheeks are wet now as I toss the words at her like daggers. "Phoenix, I can't be with someone like you."

She wraps her arms around herself like a protective shield. "You mean someone like your mother. Someone with depression."

"I already lost one person, and I won't put myself in that position again."

"I am not your mother. I was lucky to be given a second chance, and I got help. I go to therapy, and I take my medication. I won't allow myself to get to that place ever again. I won't—"

"It doesn't matter." I shake my head and yank open her front door. "I can't do this."

She wipes her tears with the backs of her hands and squares her shoulders. "So you're punishing me because of one mistake I made."

I step onto her porch and dig my heels in as deep as I can. "There are some things you can't undo."

Leo opens the door to the garage and stares at me. "What's your deal? You've been in here beating the hell out of that bag for over an hour."

"Fuck off." My arms burn, but I keep throwing sloppy punches at the hanging bag.

"You fuck off. Dad's worried."

"Dad's always worried."

"Yeah, but he's never worried about *you*. Something happen at work?"

"I said fuck off. I don't want to talk about it."

He walks into the garage and stands behind the bag like he's going to hold it for me, but he pulls it back as I swing. I falter and brace myself against him so I don't fall to the ground.

I shove him hard. "Don't fuck with me, Leo. Not now."

He bounces back and forth, wearing a dumb fucking smile. "Come on. You want to fight? Let's fight."

"I'm not fighting you."

"You know you want to." He smacks me in the back of the head. "Come on. Give me one good punch."

"Leo." I shoot him a warning glare as I start to walk away.

He sticks out his foot and trips me, and that does it. I whirl around and swing my fist, connecting with his jaw.

The fucker laughs. "There you go. Feels good, doesn't it?"

"It'll feel better when I knock you out."

"Not gonna happen." He dodges my next punch. "I have an iron jaw."

"Let's test that theory." I swing again and clip him on the chin before he ducks out of the way.

147

But I don't *want* to hit him. This isn't helping me feel better. I've been hitting the punching bag, waiting for the pain to go away, and it's not working.

I drop my arms. "This is stupid."

"Come on, bro. What's wrong? If it's not work, then…" He smirks. "Shit, it's Nix. That should've been my first guess. You're all bent out of shape over a girl. What happened? Did she shoot you down?"

Just the sound of her name has my heart thrashing against my chest. I feel terrible for the way I reacted to what she told me. I can't get the look on her face out of my head. I hurt her, and that's the last thing I ever wanted to do.

But how the hell was I supposed to respond? The woman I care about told me she tried to end her life, the same way my mother ended hers.

I shove my fingers through my hair, pulling at the roots. "God, I'm so fucking stupid."

Leo's expression sobers. "What did you do?"

Then I freeze. "Wait, did you know about this?"

"Still don't know what you're talking about."

I scrub my hand over my jaw. "Of course you know. You're like two peas in a fucked-up pod. You should've told me."

He holds up his palms. "I don't know what the hell you're talking about. You're not making any sense."

"That scar on her wrist. You got her a bracelet to cover it. Do you know what that scar is from?"

His shoulders fall. "I have a pretty good idea what it's from."

"So, she didn't tell you?"

He shakes his head. "She didn't really have to. It's obvious."

Anger rears up again inside me. "Well, it wasn't obvious to me."

Leo's jaw drops. "Wait, she told you?"

I nod once.

"And you're… mad about it?" He looks from the bag to me. "She tells you she was so fucking low that she tried to kill herself, and you're in here punching a fucking bag instead of holding her?"

Acid burns my throat. "I can't go through that again, Leo!" My voice cracks. "You didn't find her hanging there—you didn't see Mom until *after* I cut her down."

The color of her skin, the lacerations around her neck, her bloodshot eyes, and her lifeless body hanging like a piece of laundry. The image is burned into my mind like a brand, a searing hot memory of horror and agony.

"Just because I didn't see her doesn't mean I didn't lose her just the same." Leo grips my shoulders. "I'm so sorry you had to see that. I'm sure it haunts you, and it probably always will. But Phoenix is not the same as Mom. Mom never wanted to get help. She was sick, and she stayed sick. Phoenix is different. She wants to live. She's a fighter."

"How do you know that? How can you guarantee someone with depression isn't going to take a turn one day?" Bile rises in my throat. "I can't go down that road with her."

"Yes, you can. That girl over there? She's worth *everything*. And she makes you happy—truly happy. She makes you smile, and she makes you feel. I've seen it. You're different when you're with her. And you can't pass that up just because you're too fucking scared."

My head spins, and my hands shake. "What if she tries to end it again, and she succeeds? She did it once before. What's to stop her from doing it again?"

Leo shoves me, hard. "You! You'll stop her. And me! And Dad. We'll be the family she never fucking got to have. We'll give her what she's been missing all this time. Her piece-of-shit mother disowned her after she tried to kill herself, and her brother couldn't give a shit less that she's still alive. She cared enough to pour her heart out to you, and you turned your back on her the same way they did." He shakes his head. "You fucking asshole. She's not the same person she once was. She won't do it again. I fucking know it."

Each of his words hurt worse than the gunshot I took to the hip. He's right. I know he is. Yet he can't erase the fear gripping my heart.

"You can't *make* someone not kill themselves, Leo. No matter how much we loved Mom, she left us anyway. It's the same for Phoenix, and it's the same for you. You'll do drugs if you want to do drugs, no matter how many times I try to stop you. I can't stop her if she wants to die."

"Maybe not, but you can sure as fuck give her a reason to want to live." His chest heaves. "*You* can be that reason for her. *You* can help make her life worth living."

The words tear from deep within my chest as I hurl them at him. "And what if I'm not enough? Then what? What if I'm not enough to make her want to stay? I wasn't enough for Mom. Who says I'll be enough for anyone else?"

My confession hovers in the silence between us.

Leo tilts his head and his mouth opens. "Oh god, James."

I turn away, needing to look anywhere but at his knowing stare.

"*That's* what you've been carrying around since Mom died?"

My chest deflates, and my shoulders drop. "Why couldn't she just stay? Why couldn't she try harder? Why did she have to leave us like we didn't matter?"

The door creaks open, and both of our heads snap to Dad standing in the doorway. His red, watery eyes bounce between us.

Fuck.

He points his index finger at me as he takes slow steps into the garage. "You listen to me, and you listen good. Your mother was sick. There was nothing any of us could've done to help her because she didn't know how to help herself. She was in too deep and couldn't see her way out." He jabs his finger into my chest when he gets close. "But what she did had nothing to do with you or your worth. Not a goddamn thing. Do you hear me?"

My eyes burn, and my throat tightens as I try to push out the words. "How do you bear it? Every single day, how can you stand it that she left? You loved her so much, and she's just gone."

"Some days, I can hardly stand the pain in my chest." A tear rolls down his cheek. "But I know her pain was greater than any of us could understand, and I can only hope that wherever she is, she is free of it."

Leo covers his face with both of his hands. Dad wraps his arm around his shoulders and reaches for me with his other arm. He pulls us in close, and we put our heads together.

"Don't live your lives in fear or in sorrow. She wouldn't want that for you. Live your life like every day is your fucking last, boys. Dream big, take chances, and love with all you've got." Dad sniffles before he finishes. "Live your life *for* Mom, not as a hollow result of what she did."

Leo pulls away first, wiping his tears with the hem of his T-shirt before he walks out the door.

And I know where he's going.

Phoenix

Daily Affirmation: "I am capable of so much more than I think."

Wilbur barks at the sound of the doorbell. My foolish heart hopes it'll be James on the other side of the door, but my mind knows better.

He left hours ago, and I'm not sure he'll ever come back. Not after the things he said to me. I've been curled in a ball on the couch, wishing there was something I could do or say to change his mind. But that's the battle I've been fighting with my mom my entire life. Some people will never understand what depression is like because they don't want to try to understand what it's like—and that's just the way it is.

As soon as I crack open the door, Leo pushes his way in and engulfs me in a hug. My knees buckle as the emotion overcomes me.

"It's okay. I've got you." He holds me tight and presses a kiss to the top of my head. "Everything is going to be okay."

I sniffle as I pull back and look up into his dark eyes. "Does this mean you don't hate me too?"

151

"He doesn't hate you. He's giving you all the anger he wants to give Mom." He leads me back into the living room and pulls me onto the couch beside him. "And I couldn't hate you for doing what you did. I'm relieved as fuck that you didn't succeed in killing yourself. It breaks my heart to know that you felt that much despair. It's killing James too."

I rest my head on Leo's shoulder. "I don't want to talk about him right now."

"Then tell me what you want to do."

"I want to sit here and talk with my little brother, who I appreciate more than anything in this whole world."

"I'm not going anywhere."

"That's why I love you so damn much."

"I knew." He turns over my hand and lifts up my sleeve to inspect my wrist. "I knew what you did to yourself. I was just waiting for you to feel comfortable enough to tell me about it."

"It's not something I wanted to share with anyone."

And James's reaction proves why.

Leo twirls a strand of my hair. "We all want to stop the pain. Some of us are just more proactive about it than others."

A laugh escapes me. "You're sick for making a joke about this."

"And you're just as sick for laughing at it. The humor is how we survive."

I look up at the ceiling. "God, we're a sorry pair."

"Hey, Nix?" He nudges me with his knee. "Will you tell me what it felt like?"

My eyebrows press together. "To die?"

He nods. "Did you regret it while it was happening? Or did you feel relieved?"

I choose my words carefully, knowing he's trying to make sense of what his mother did. "I felt relieved. Tired. Weightless. Like I was drifting off to sleep, and everything was calm."

He lets his head fall back against the couch. "So, no pain then?"

I grip his hand and lie again. "No pain."

His Adam's apple bobs as he swallows. "Good."

Sadness and guilt seep into my stomach. "Leo, I'm so sorry your mom went through that. I'm sorry she's gone. I'm sorry she couldn't find her way out of the darkness. But I hope you know that it's not your fault, and she'd tell you the same thing if she were here."

He nods, and he swats away a tear as it springs free. "I don't take that responsibility like my brother does. But I just wish she would've opened up to me and told me what she was going through. I wish I was older when it happened. Maybe I could've helped her in some way."

"You were her son. I'm sure she didn't want to put that on you, regardless of how old you were."

"I miss her."

A ball of emotion clogs my throat. "I wish I could've known her."

"Me too." He laces our fingers. "I'm glad I could know you though."

I smile through my tears. "You might not have been able to help your mom, but you're helping me. Knowing that I have your friendship makes all the difference. Please know that."

He wipes his eye again. "Shit, Nixie. You're making me emotional when I'm supposed to be tough and manly."

A laugh bursts out of me. "Is that why you got all these tattoos? To make you look tough and manly?"

He grins. "Had to disguise the teddy bear inside me somehow."

"Nah, you're not a teddy bear. You've got a lion heart."

"Guess that makes James the cowardly lion then."

I say nothing. James *is* scared, and rightfully so. We shouldn't fault him for that—no matter how much it hurts.

"You gotta help him find his heart, Nix. It's in there. I know it is."

I bury my face in a decorative pillow and groan. "It's not my job to find his heart. He needs to dig deep and find his own damn courage if he wants to have any kind of happiness in life."

"He'll get over this temper tantrum. Give him time."

Time. I gave my mother time, hoping she'd come around—but it's been two years, and she hasn't. James might not either. And why am I always waiting around, hoping for people to *come around*? Why can't I be enough for someone to love on the spot, regardless of my mental health? Why can't we accept people for who they are, instead of punishing them for all their shortcomings?

"Like I said, I don't want to talk about your brother."

"Fine." Leo lifts his hips, slips his hand into his pocket, and pulls out a joint. "Then let's get high instead."

16

James

"How have you been since the shooting?"

I shrug and glance away. "Fine."

My therapist slips off his glasses and sets them on his clipboard. "Watching a teenage boy die isn't something you can easily forget. Have you had any trouble sleeping?"

"I always have trouble sleeping."

"I can prescribe something to help with that."

"No." I stare out the window just over his shoulder. "The boy shouldn't have died that night. I should've diffused the situation."

"Didn't you try to?"

"Yes, but I should've tried something different. Said something different."

"Or, could it be that the boy's choice to bring a gun to the skate park, and his choice to pull the trigger are the reasons for what happened that night? Could it be that you had nothing to do with the outcome?"

"It was a series of unfortunate events, but I could've done something to stop it."

"Hmm." He scribbles something into his notepad. "How has life been outside of work? Your brother is back home, sober, you said. How has that been?"

My knee bounces. "It's been nice having him back. But I don't know how long this will last."

Dr. Parker tilts his head. "It's difficult when it comes to addiction. But that doesn't mean you can't enjoy the present while it's here. There's no way to tell what the future will bring."

I let out a humorless laugh. "You're not kidding."

His eyes narrow. "What's going on with you? You're more closed off than usual today."

I scrub my hands over my face. "Long story short, I met a girl, but it turns out that she has depression and tried to kill herself two years ago."

"She shared that with you?"

I nod. "I told her about what happened to my mother, and then she told me that she almost succeeded in doing the same thing."

"That was brave of her. And how did you react to that?"

"Like a jackass."

Dr. Parker smirks. "Meaning?"

"Meaning, I told her that I couldn't be with someone like her because I didn't want to lose her the same way I lost my mother."

"Ah. I imagine that was scary to hear." He writes in the notepad again. "What has her life been like since the incident?"

"Her family disowned her, and now she's living on her own right next door to me. She said she goes to therapy, and she's on medication."

"Family is tough when it comes to suicide."

I let out a sigh. "But she doesn't seem depressed. Not like my mom did. I wouldn't have known she was on medication if she didn't tell me."

"That's the point of medication. It helps people feel *normal*, for lack of a better word." He pauses. "If she's in therapy and taking medication, that shows she is in control of her sickness, and that she's taking all the necessary steps to maintain her mental health."

I wipe my palms on my jeans. "She does seem in control of it."

"So, why the poor reaction to this news? I mean, I can understand that you were shocked. No one wants to hear that the person you care about tried to harm herself, especially when the subject hits so close to home for you. But… why cut her off because of it?"

"How can I trust that she won't try to do it again?"

"How can you trust that she won't cheat on you? Or that she won't want to break up with you one day? Or that a bus won't hit her on the way to work? You can't know what's going to happen, and you can't stop it. You just have to have faith that you'll make the best decisions for yourself, and what will be, will be. Much like the night of the shooting, and your mother's death—you can't control everything, James."

"Why does everyone keep telling me that?"

Dr. Parker laughs. "Because it's true. Listen, you have every right to be cautious when entering a relationship with someone who has a history of mental health issues. Being open and honest with each other is important, which she has done by telling you about her past. She's taking all the necessary steps to lead a healthy life, and she hasn't given you any reasons to doubt that. James, I don't think your problem is with her, or with depression. I think your problem stems from the abandonment you felt when your mom died. You haven't dealt with that or let go of it. In fact, you've let it spider out into every facet of your life. Work, family, now love. When will you stop carrying around your mother's death like it's your cross to bear?"

I rub the back of my neck. "I don't know how."

"I can help you if you're ready."

I think about Phoenix and the way my heart blazes for her. I think about the kind of life I've had after my mother died, the dull, mundane life I've cocooned myself into. I think about my father, the lonely man who has no one to share his time with.

"I'm ready."

Phoenix

Daily Affirmation: "I forgive those who have done me wrong with ease."

It has been said that the best love songs are written about heartbreak.

The same can be said about books. People love those soul-crushing, gut-wrenching, oh-my-god-this-is-the-most-painful-thing-I've-ever-read-and-I-might-fling-my-Kindle-out-a-window-if-they-don't-end-up-happy books as we're sobbing into a package of Oreos at two o'clock in the morning on a twelve-hour reading bender.

Some of us are masochists like that.

But the reason people like it is because everyone goes through pain and suffering at one point or another. It's relatable. And we want to root for the heroine to make it out alive, because if she does, then so can we.

I'm going to write a book about my life. It's not that I think my story is anything special. But I want to write a book that can help people who are struggling through the same thing I've been through. Maybe someone will read this and choose to keep fighting. Maybe it'll be a suicide survivor like me. And just maybe, someone who doesn't have depression will read it and it will change the way they view the disease.

I want to write about the darkest, lowest time in my life, and then show what happens when you survive it.

I crack open my journal and start writing. I don't have a direction, or an outline, or a beginning and an end. My plan is to write about the experiences I've had and go from there.

I don't really know what I'm doing, but the words pour out of me all afternoon and it helps keep my mind off James—even if the hero I'm creating in this story seems to be turning out a lot like him. By the time the sun sets and I'm in bed, I'm still writing.

Until a text pops up from James.

James: Hi. Is it okay if I come by? I want to apologize in person.

My chest aches, but I set my phone back down and ignore his text. A minute later, my phone buzzes again.

James: You have every right to be mad at me, but please just let me apologize.

I switch my phone to silent.

James: You know I can see you reading my texts.
Me: Then you can also see that I'm ignoring you.
Me: And don't be a stalker.

I get up and shut my blinds without looking at him through the window.

James: Phoenix, I'm so sorry. You don't deserve the things I said to you. I was caught off guard, but that's no excuse. I shouldn't have left. I should've listened to what you were saying instead of pushing you away. I know it couldn't have been easy telling me about your past, and I wish I would've reacted differently.
James: Please let me say this to your face.

My heart urges me to respond. I know he didn't mean the things he said. James isn't a malicious person. I can understand that my suicide attempt was a trigger for him, and I know he needed time to process. Still, I can't pretend that his reaction didn't hurt.

Me: I really didn't appreciate the way you spoke to me.

159

James: If I could take it all back I would.

James: I'm heading over to your house now. I'll sleep on the porch if I have to.

Me: I'm tempted to let you.

But I'm already moving down the stairs with Wilbur at my side.

Forgiveness is what sets me apart from my mother. She's cold and closed off, and I refuse to treat others the way she has treated me. She cuts people out of her life as if they never existed. But my heart is open and full of love, even when it's bruised and broken.

If James wants to apologize, then I'm going to hear him out because everyone deserves a chance to be heard.

I open the door and try to remember how to breathe. James's honey-colored eyes are bloodshot, and the skin underneath is a deep purple. His hair is a disheveled mess, and he looks like he hasn't slept in days. He's been struggling, and if I didn't matter to him, he wouldn't have lost an ounce of sleep over me.

"Phoenix, I'm so sorry I hurt you."

"I know you are."

"Then let me explain."

I step back to let him in, and then I lead him into the living room.

James sits at the edge of the couch facing me and braces his elbows on his knees. "When you told me about what you did, all I could think of was my mother. It's like it brought me right back to the day I found her, and all the anger and pain and resentment came rushing out at once. I guess I've been holding on to a lot more than I realized." He reaches for my hand and holds it between both of his. "But you didn't deserve to hear any of the things I threw at you, and I need you to know that I didn't mean them. I was surprised, and I wasn't thinking straight. I never want to cause you any pain or sadness, and I hate that I did."

I nod as my bottom lip trembles. "It means a lot to me that you're able to reflect on what you said and take responsibility for it. My mother was furious with me for trying to take my own life. But honestly? I think it was more of an inconvenience for her than anything. She didn't care if I lived or died. She was worried about how it looked to her friends. She doesn't believe that depression is as real as cancer. Do you know what she said to me when I woke up in the hospital? She said, *If you want to die, then you'll be dead to me.* Those were the last words she spoke to me."

James's eyes widen. "But you're her daughter."

"Blood doesn't mean shit to some people." I shrug. "I've struggled my whole life with feeling less than. I wasn't happy like my brother. I wasn't as social as him. I didn't make my mother proud like he did. My brain just isn't hardwired the same way. So, when you walked out on me the other day, it felt like you were confirming all my worst fears. You confirmed what my mother taught me: That I'm not good enough for someone to love."

James shakes his head. "No. That's not true at all. My reaction was about me, and my issues."

"I'm not going to hurt myself again, James. I need you to understand that. I'm not the same person I was two years ago. The depression will never be gone, but I'm managing it. I'm in control. And I'm working on myself to be better every fucking day. I'm in therapy facing shit I don't want to face, and it's hard. But I'm still doing it. I get up and I keep fighting." I suck in a brave breath and prepare myself to say what I need to say. "I need someone who's willing to fight *with* me. I can't be with someone who's going to shut down or shut me out when things get real. I need you to talk to me. If something I say makes you mad? Good. Yell at me. Let's fight it out together. I don't want to hand my heart to someone and have him leave it on my doorstep as he turns his back on me."

"I shouldn't have left you like that. Like a fucking coward." He shakes his head. "You shared a piece of yourself with me, and I don't want you to think that I'm only interested in the good parts. I want to see all of you. I want the broken, jagged pieces, the ones you think are ugly and ruined, the ones you hide from everyone else—especially those. I want to be the one you can trust your heart with."

A tear slips down my cheek. That's all I've ever wanted. For someone to see the darkness in me and accept me—scars and all.

James tilts my chin and holds my gaze. "I told you I've got your six, and that means no matter what. I'm sorry that I made you feel otherwise. I am going to work on my issues with my therapist."

"You see a therapist?"

"I've been seeing one since my mom died. Nobody knows."

"You mean your dad and brother don't know?"

He shakes his head. "Not even my partner knows. There's a stigma attached to therapy when it comes to cops. We see the worst of the worst, yet we're expected to be strong enough to handle it all on our own."

"Well, I'm glad you're talking to someone. It really helps."

His eyes hold mine. "Do you forgive me?"

James might've hurt my feelings, but he's here trying to make things right. He opened up to me, and he cares enough to try.

"I do. I appreciate your apology and your honesty." I wring my hands in my lap. "But I need you to be sure that you want to be with me. If you can't because of everything you went through with your mom, then tell me. I get it. We can just be friends, if that's what you want. I'll understand."

"Honestly, I'm scared shitless. I'm scared of what'll happen to me if I let you all the way in. I'm scared to lose you. I'm scared that I won't be enough to make you want to live. I'm scared I'll find you the way I found my mother."

His Adam's apple bobs as he swallows. "But you're worth that fear, because I don't want to go back to living my life without you in it. These past few days without you have been hell. Not a moment goes by that I'm not consumed by thoughts of you. And no, Phoenix. I don't want to be friends with you. That's the last fucking thing I want. I can't imagine a worse torture than being *just friends* with the woman who haunts my dreams every night."

He pulls me onto his lap, and I straddle him with my legs on either side of his hips. "I *yearn* for you. My fingers itch to reach out and touch you. My tongue craves your taste. I want you on me, your hair surrounding me, your scent filling my lungs." He pulls me close, and his lips speak against mine as he says, "I ache for you *everywhere*. It takes all of my willpower not to devour you whenever we're together."

My heart thrashes against my chest like a wild, caged beast.

Yes.

I slip my fingers into his hair. "What if I told you I want to be devoured by you? What if I told you I felt the same?"

"Then I'd tell you that I'm all in." His fingers dig into my hips, and his eyes tighten. "Just promise me that if you ever feel your control slipping, if you ever reach a point where you feel like you're losing yourself again, I want you to tell me. Because I'll be here to bring you back from the darkness."

Another tear falls as I nod. "I can promise you that."

"There's a lot I don't understand about depression, but I'm open to learning. I want to know. I want to know *you*."

I press my forehead to his and close my eyes. "Your mother is missing out on you, James. You are a wonderful man. She'd be so proud of you if she were here."

"I think we've been focusing on all the things we've lost for too long. I think it's time we start enjoying what we do have."

I smile. "I think so too."

We remain on the couch for the rest of the night, talking, asking questions, and listening to one another's stories. And for the first time, someone shows me what it feels like to be heard—someone without depression, someone not in my therapy group, someone not being paid to listen to me. James doesn't make me feel judged, or weird, or ashamed. He sees me, and all my scars.

And it's because I stood up for myself and told my truth. It's more than mattering to someone else—it's the fact that I showed *myself* that I matter.

And why shouldn't I?

My family gave up on me, but that doesn't mean I have to give up on myself too.

I can find people who accept me as I am, like Leo.

I can find people who will change their perspective for me, like James.

I can find friends who know what it's like to be different, like Drew.

And I can find it within myself to love my brokenness.

163

Bring Me Back

It's now that I realize I'm the one person I needed to have my back all along.

I've got my own damn six.

17

Phoenix

Daily Affirmation: "I choose to be happy and to love myself today."

"Fuck."

I glance over at James. "What?"

He holds up Kandi Steiner's book. "Emory is at the bar with another woman."

I squeal. "Keep reading."

"I don't like the direction this is heading. Is he going to spend the night with this random chick?"

"I can't tell you. Just keep going." I clutch my chest. "Isn't her writing so beautiful? It's like poetry."

"It is." He heaves a heavy sigh. "Fine, I'll keep reading."

We continue reading in silence until I notice a change in his breathing. His shoulders rise and fall with his short, quick breaths. I steal a peek at which page he's on and stifle a laugh. It's Emory and Cooper's first sex scene. I let him keep going and watch out of the corner of my eye as he turns each page more quickly to get to the next.

Finally, I can't contain myself any longer. "You okay over there?"

"Yeah, why?" His voice sounds gruffer than usual.

"You seem a little flustered."

"First of all, I don't get *flustered*. Second, this is… steamy."

I laugh. "It is."

"You like this stuff?"

"Don't you?"

"Are you going to write these kinds of scenes into your book?"

I nod proudly. "I sure am."

"Hmm." He sticks the bookmark into the book and closes it. "Do you like that *Fifty Shades of Grey* type of stuff too?"

I arch a brow. "You know what *Fifty Shades* is?"

"Everyone knows what *Fifty Shades* is."

"Well, I'm not into BDSM or pain." I shrug. "But I'm sure I could be into more than just the missionary position with the right person."

"You've only had sex in the missionary position?"

I grimace. "I haven't had the greatest sex life. With the few guys I've dated, it was about *their* pleasure, or they didn't know what they were doing."

"And you didn't tell them that they were doing it wrong?"

I shake my head. "I didn't want to make them feel bad."

"So, you let yourself feel bad instead."

I blow out a sigh. "I guess so."

"Promise me something." He sets our books aside and pulls me onto his lap. His hands settle on either side of my face, his thumbs smoothing over my cheeks. "Promise me you'll tell me what feels good to you."

My stomach clenches. "I promise."

He drags his nose down the side of my neck, sending goose bumps flying along my body. "And I promise that you will always feel good with me."

A shiver dances down my spine as he continues speaking against my skin.

"Those other guys didn't know what they had. They didn't know how to appreciate a woman like you." He bites my shoulder. "A body like yours." He licks my neck. "But I'm going to taste every inch of you, learn every curve." He pulls back and gazes into my eyes. "I'm going to show you how you deserve to feel, every single time I touch you. You will always get what you need with me."

I swallow, my skin slick with sweat just from his words, from the promise of pleasure at the hands of this beautiful man.

My hips rock against him, yearning to ease the mounting ache between my legs.

His fingers dig into my hips. "I think about you every night, and all the ways I'm going to ravage you."

My mouth falls open. "You fantasize about me?"

His low laugh rasps in my ear. "Yes, babe. I've got plans for this body."

I suck his plump bottom lip into my mouth and bite down on it. "I'd like to know more about these plans."

"You name the time and place, and I'll be happy to show you."

Just as our tongues dive for one another's, Leo's loud voice booms in the hallway outside James's bedroom door. "Get your clothes on if you're fucking in there. I'm coming in." He bursts into the room wearing a smug grin. "What are you two doing?"

I slide off James's lap. "Reading."

Leo laughs. "Yeah, looks like it."

James glances at the alarm clock on his nightstand. "Fuck, I have to get ready for my shift."

"Guess it's just me and you tonight, Nixie." Leo winks. "Maybe I'll be your New Year's Eve kiss since the big guy has to work."

James pushes off the mattress and shoves his brother back into the hallway. "Bring your lips anywhere near her, and you won't make it into the new year."

I laugh and shake my head. "I'll see you later, Leo."

James closes the door in his face, but Leo keeps talking. "You're bringing chips and dip, right?"

"Yes. And root beer for your dad."

James wraps his arms around me and presses his lips to my forehead. "Thanks for spending the night with them. I hate leaving Dad on holidays. I feel like he gets lonely."

"Well, he won't be lonely anymore."

"You know, I'm going to have to talk to this Steiner lady if Cooper and Emory don't end up together by the end of the book."

I smile. "It's a romance. They have to end up happily ever after."

He arches an eyebrow. "Then how do you explain *The Notebook*, or *Titanic*?"

"They did end up together in *The Notebook*. It was just a really sad ending because they were old." I curl my lip. "But *Titanic* was... dumb."

"Dumb? Wasn't it supposed to be an epic love story?"

"She could've moved the fuck over and shared that door with Jack. *Titanic* doesn't count. Rose was an asshole."

He tilts his head back as he laughs, and I welcome the sound of his deep laughter. The corners of his eyes crinkle, and dimples frame his wide smile. The sight stills my heart and makes it hard to catch my breath.

"You look so beautiful when you smile."

His expression sobers, and he leans down to kiss me. "I smile because I'm with you."

My body warms, and I close my eyes, allowing this foreign feeling to sink into my chest. "I'm glad I didn't injure you too badly when I hit you with the bat the night we met."

He chuckles, and his warm breath tickles my lips. "I'd suffer through the head trauma all over again if it meant we'd end up here."

"Good. Now, go save lives. Be safe."

"Yes, ma'am."

After the ball drops, I head back home.

Jim was already passed out in his recliner with a snoring Wilbur, so Leo and I whispered Happy New Year to not disturb them.

I place Wilbur in his crate when I reach my bedroom, and he curls up in a ball and passes back out. James should be home in an hour, and he said he'd come by to give me my first kiss of the new year.

Just the thought of his lips has me fanning myself. My mind has been in the gutter all day thanks to our conversation earlier. It's been a long time since I've felt this turned on. The medication I'm on tends to lower my libido, but more than that, I haven't been interested in being with anyone. I was too busy focusing on my health to put work into being with anyone else.

But James has awakened my dormant sexuality.

"Might as well put it to good use." I flop onto my bed and open the journal I've been using to jot down ideas for the book I'm working on. Maybe if I write a steamy scene, I'll be able to get it out of my system.

Bad idea.

The more I write, the more turned on I get. My skin is hot and my heart is racing. I'm tempted to slip my hand into my shorts and relieve this ache, but I want to finish writing the scene before I find my release.

I left the door unlocked for James so he can let himself in when he gets here, but I'm so engrossed in my scene, I don't hear anything until he walks into my room.

Flustered, I flip the journal closed and jump up to greet him. "Hi, you're here. How was work?"

"Fine." He pauses. "You okay?"

I let out a nervous laugh. "Yeah, why?"

"I don't know. You look weird."

My nose scrunches. "Uh, thanks?"

"No, I mean something's off."

Oh, I was just fantasizing about you in my journal. No big deal.

"I'm good."

He arches a brow and scans the room. "Were you sleeping?"

I shake my head.

"What were you doing before I got here?"

My eyes dart to the notebook on my pillow. "Nothing."

Nothing besides picturing you touching me.

His eyes narrow. "You were sitting here doing nothing?"

I hike a shoulder. "Yeah. What's wrong with a little quiet time?"

His eyes flick to my bed. "Why do you keep looking over there?"

"No reason."

Then he spots the notebook. "What's that?"

"A notebook. It's filled with paper. People in modern societies use it to write in."

He smirks. "Yes, I know what a notebook is, smart-ass. I mean, what is that notebook in particular?"

I inch toward the bed, trying not to make any sudden movements. "It's the book I started writing." I take another step forward. "It's just a bunch of ideas and random scenes right now."

"So, if you were working on your book when I walked in, why wouldn't you just say that?"

I fiddle with the hem of my T-shirt. "I don't know."

He cocks his head to the side, his eyes bouncing from the notebook to me. "Are you sure everything's okay?"

I nod vigorously as I continue creeping toward the notebook. "Just tired I guess."

Almost there. One more step and I'll be able to—

James lunges forward and snatches the book off my bed before I can. "What's in here that has you acting like this?"

My eyes go wide. "Give that back."

He holds it above my head, wearing a playful smile. I jump and try to grab the book out of his grasp, but he's too damn tall. He holds it open above his head while he cranes his neck to read it.

I watch helplessly as his eyes move from left to right over the page, heat burning my cheeks. "It's just some ideas I've been working on. It's nothing." I jump again, but he swats me like a tiny gnat.

The smile drops from his face.

I swallow hard.

He continues reading, and his eyebrows jump. "This definitely isn't nothing."

I drop my head, too embarrassed to look him in the eyes.

His finger touches my chin, tipping my head up until I meet his gaze. "You're writing about me?"

I nod.

"Do you want this? What you wrote about? Is this what you like?"

I chew my bottom lip and give him another nod.

God, do I want this.

His eyes darken, no longer the light-honey color I've become accustomed to. "Will you read it to me?"

"What?" My voice is a whisper.

He hands me the notebook. "I'd like for you to read it to me, if you're comfortable."

My hands shake, and my breaths quicken.

"I want to know what you like." He walks me backward. "I want to know what turns you on." My calves hit the bed, and he stops, skimming his thumb over my lips. "I want to hear it from this sweet mouth of yours."

I shiver as a wave of heat rolls over my skin.

"Will you do that for me?"

"Yes."

James removes his belt, setting it on my nightstand along with his gun. He lowers himself onto the bed and props himself up against the headboard. Then he pats the space between his legs. "Come here."

I oblige and lean back against his chest. My heart pounds so loud in my ears, I can barely make out the sound of my own voice when I begin reading. "A movie plays on the screen in front of us, but I'm not paying attention to it at all. The only thing I can focus on is James's hand on my leg. He draws idle circles across my skin. I squirm because it tickles, but he grips me tighter so I can't move away."

James trails his hand along my skin, stroking my bare thigh and mimicking the words I just read.

"His fingers inch closer to the inside of my thigh each time he circles around."

Goose bumps fly down my leg as his fingers follow my words.

I pause and lick my lips, preparing for the next part. Electricity and anticipation crackle in the air around us. I let my head fall back against his chest as I continue reading. "He kisses my neck and licks my ear while his other hand disappears under my shirt."

James gives my neck a gentle bite as his hand slides underneath my shirt, smoothing over my stomach and traveling higher until he takes my breast into his large hand.

"The tips of his fingers skim my panty line, and my legs fall open, begging for him to keep touching me."

James's middle finger slips underneath my shorts and traces the outline of my cotton thong.

"Then he slips a finger into the side of my panties, and groans when he feels how wet I already am for him."

I hold my breath waiting for James to do the same, and when he does, he lets out a deep rumble in my ear. His thick finger slides over me in slow, languid circles.

I whimper and my voice shakes. "I tell him how good that feels, and beg him not to stop, spreading my legs wider."

I'm breathless as James works me exactly how I instruct him to. "He tells me how sexy he thinks I am, and whispers dirty things in my ear."

His hot breath is at my ear. "You're incredibly sexy. You feel so warm and wet. I can't wait to make you come." He brings his fingers to his lips and sucks them into his mouth, letting out another deep, satisfied groan. "Fuck, you taste so sweet. Will you take off these shorts so I can see you?"

I shimmy out of my shorts and thong in one swift movement and let my knees fall apart.

"That's my girl." James slides his fingers over me, coating them and humming in approval. "Keep reading."

My words come out in broken clips. "He plays with me, switching from long, firm strokes, to light teasing ones. I tell him how turned on I am, and how good he's making me feel."

"Tell me, Phoenix. I want to hear it."

I twist my neck to meet his hungry gaze, and trace his lips with my tongue, nipping at his full bottom lip. "You're making me so wet, James. I've been dying for you to play with me just like this. To feel your hands all over me. I've thought about it for so many nights."

"What else do you need?" he rasps, thrusting his hips under me to rub his hard bulge against my ass.

I yank off my T-shirt, and I guide his left hand back to my breast. "Swirl your thumb over them like this."

I moan, arching into his touch, and he grins against my cheek. "Look at you, spread and bare for me." I meet his gaze in the mirror across the room. "You are the hottest fucking thing I've ever seen."

I toss the notebook to the side and recite the rest from memory. "When I'm a writhing mess in his hand, James starts to rub me faster. I take his hand from my breast, and wrap my tongue around his finger, imagining it's his cock in my mouth."

I let out a loud moan as he pushes his index finger into my mouth. My hips move wild under his touch, and when I release his finger from my mouth, he returns it to my nipple, rolling the wetness over the hardened bud.

"What happens next?" he asks.

"I want to come so bad, but James brings me to the brink, and then slows his fingers, teasing me until I can't take it anymore."

James bites my neck and then chases the sting with his tongue. "Are you ready to come?"

"Yes, James. Make me come."

"I've got you. Let me hear you."

I let go and succumb to his touch. The mounting pleasure between my legs explodes and my orgasm racks my body, sending a flash of white-hot heat through me. I throw back my head and let my moans fill the room, calling his name so he knows this moment belongs to him. I grip his wrist, keeping him there and riding his hand until I finish, until my body is tingling and sated.

"You're beautiful, Phoenix." He showers me with kisses as he whispers in my ear. "That was the sexiest thing I've ever witnessed."

"So, I should put that scene in my book?"

He chuckles. "You should definitely put that scene in your book."

I turn around and meet his gaze. "I want to make you feel good too."

But he shakes his head. "This was *your* fantasy. We'll have plenty of time for mine."

I stifle a yawn. "Will you stay with me tonight?"

"Of course."

I watch as he strips out of his uniform, heat reigniting in my core all over again at the sight of his sculpted body.

He smirks as he slips into bed beside me in nothing but his black boxer briefs. "Keep looking at me like that, and you'll have another scene to add to your book."

I give him a sleepy grin. "I can't help it when you look like that."

"Are you really writing your book about… us? About me?"

I nod and snuggle against him. "You're the ultimate book boyfriend."

He wraps his arms around me. "And what about a real-life boyfriend?"

I crane my neck to look into his eyes, questioning him with my gaze.

"I'd like to be your boyfriend."

Affection warms my chest. "I'd like you to be my boyfriend too."

"Good." He presses a chaste kiss to my lips. "Sweet dreams, my phoenix."

"Happy New Year," I whisper as I drift off.

If the way we started this new year is any indication, I'd say this year is going to be the best one yet.

18

James

"He's not here, man."

My eyes scan the skate park, hoping to catch a glimpse of Cory's blond hair. "Maybe they found a new place to cause trouble."

Phil nods. "Or maybe he learned his lesson. His friend died because of the poor choices they made. I'm sure he feels guilty about it."

"*I* feel guilty about it."

"Don't. He sealed his fate once he lifted his gun to a cop."

"It could've gone differently."

"It's part of the job."

"Kids dying isn't part of the job."

"It is when they're carrying weapons."

I scrub my hand over my jaw, knowing I won't be able to change Phil's mind. "I just wish I knew if Cory was okay."

Phil smirks as he makes a U-turn. "I think being with your girlfriend is making you soft, Russo."

I chuckle, unable to hide my grin at the word *girlfriend*. "Maybe soft isn't a bad thing."

His chin jerks back. "Last time I checked, *soft* is a very bad thing. You saying you're having trouble in the bedroom?"

I roll my eyes. "No trouble in that department… at all." My mind wanders back to New Year's Eve. The way Phoenix looked, with her legs spread wide and my hand between them. The way she sounded, with my name on her tongue as she moaned from the pleasure I was giving her. The way she felt, so soft and wet as my fingers slid over her. The way she tasted, dripping from my fingers.

Fuck, I'm dying to have her again.

My head falls against the seat. "Do you believe in destiny?"

Phil nods. "I think God has a plan for us all."

"I feel like our paths were destined to cross after everything we've been through. How can it be a coincidence that she went through the same exact thing my mother did? And she moved in right next door."

"It is pretty freaky." He flicks on the blinker and turns out of the parking lot. "You fuck her yet?"

"No. Asked her to be my girlfriend though."

"Ah, being a gentleman. I'm really happy for you, man." He shakes his head. "I never thought I'd see the day when someone would be able to crack James Russo's cold, black heart."

"Fuck you. My heart is not cold or black. She's just… I don't know. I feel better when she's around. At peace. Like something was missing from my life, even though I didn't know what it was, and now that she's here, I can't picture my life without her."

"You're falling for her." Phil pins me with a pointed stare. "You know that, right?"

Am I? I care for her. I'd do anything for her. The thought of losing her terrifies me.

"It scares me," I admit. "Loving her. Losing her."

"That's because you lost the woman you loved the most." Phil gazes out the windshield as he pulls up to a red light. "But you don't always lose it. Love doesn't always end in tragedy."

My eyebrows hit my hairline. "Wow. Maybe you're the one who's going soft."

Phil laughs. "Not a chance in hell, bro."

While we continue patrolling the neighborhood, I get a text from Phoenix.

My Phoenix: So, tell me about this fantasy of yours.

Me: I'd rather show you after our date tonight.

My Phoenix: Give me an idea. Is there anything specific I need to know?

Me: Keep your kitchen counter clear.

My Phoenix: Why don't we skip dinner and go straight to dessert?

Me: Nope. I'm taking you on a proper date.

My Phoenix: Maybe I don't want you to be proper.

Me: But you always complain that I'm "bossy."

My Phoenix: Mr. Bossy Pants has grown on me.

Me: Then you'll see him tonight.

My Phoenix: Good.

My Phoenix: One last question: Black or nude?

Me: Depends on what we're talking about.

My Phoenix: That I can't tell you.

Me: Then surprise me.

And surprise me she does.

When I ring her doorbell to pick her up for our date, Phoenix answers the door in a tight, long-sleeve black minidress with black thigh-high boots. Her chestnut hair falls over her shoulders like a silky dark curtain.

The air leaves my lungs.

She makes a slow turn so I can see the way the slinky material hugs her plump ass.

"God, you look… amazing."

"Leo bet me twenty bucks that you'd make me go upstairs and change."

I shake my head and snake an arm around her waist. "I want everyone to witness your incredible sexiness."

"Really?" She lifts onto her toes to meet my lips with hers.

177

"Really." I suck her bottom lip into my mouth and release it with a pop. "And then I want them to see you with me and know that they can't have you."

Her modest smile warms my heart.

"I love the dress." I smooth my hand up her arm. "Guess you went with black."

She smirks and shakes her head as she walks past me and onto the porch. "No. I didn't."

My dick stirs in anticipation.

"This place is beautiful."

"My mom loved it here." I glance around at the flickering light from the candles dancing on each table. "I haven't been here since she passed."

I took Phoenix to my favorite Spanish restaurant, and we sat on the same side of a dark-red booth near the back. It's the perfect private, intimate corner.

When the waiter arrives to take our order for appetizers, Phoenix squeezes my hand. "Order whatever you want for us."

It means a lot to me that she trusts me to know what she'll like. Whether I'm teaching her how to cook, or leaving meals on her porch, feeding her has become something I deeply enjoy. I love knowing I can take care of her. And I love that she lets me.

I do as she requested, and when the waiter leaves our table, I tip her chin. "I know I should wait until the end of the date to kiss you, but I'm not sure I can resist."

"Please don't make me wait." She closes the distance between us and presses her soft lips to mine.

Phoenix sparks something inside of me, and I can't quite articulate what it is. It's not just a physical attraction—and *fuck* am I attracted to her. Every cell in my body reacts to the feel of her mouth moving against mine. But it's more than that. More than anything I've ever felt.

When I kiss Phoenix, it's like I can feel my soul catch fire.

This burning desire to care for her, to give her everything inside of me.

"I have a bone to pick with you." She pulls back to look into my eyes. "I finished your book."

I lean my elbows onto the table. "And what do you think?"

"*Surely, someday she would find him.*" She blinks. "Are you kidding me? *That's* how it ends? After all that, you don't even know if they're going to be together?"

I chuckle. "But he didn't have to hide anymore. He got everything he wanted."

"Except her. What if she took all his money and ran? What if she wasn't the person he thought she was?"

"I like the ending because it leaves it up to your interpretation. Everyone sees something different."

"Well, I hate that. I need happily ever afters." A slow smile spreads across her face. "But I did enjoy reading your notes in the margins."

"You were supposed to ignore those."

"I couldn't help myself. I love seeing the way your mind works. It made me love the book, to read it from your perspective."

I sip my water. "I love how the author makes us root for the bad guy, and how we realize that he's not really the bad guy we thought he was."

"I was rooting for Patrick too. I hope he finds his happy ending somewhere in fiction land."

I grin and hug her to my side. "I love that you believe in happy endings for everyone."

"We all deserve one." She rests her head on my shoulder. "It makes me think about my mother. My father died way too soon, and now what? What about her happy ending? Is she going to be alone forever?"

"I think that about my father too. I hate seeing him so lonely."

"Is that why you moved back in with him?"

I nod. "I know he's a grown man who can take care of himself, but it broke my heart to think of him in that house all by himself."

"He's lucky he has you and your brother." She squeezes my hand. "And now he has me too."

"You make him smile. He's liked you since the very first day he met you."

"You mean when I made him handcuff his own son?"

I laugh. "Yes."

"Did you finish *On the Way to You* yet?"

"I did." I blow out a long breath. "Kandi Steiner made me cry. That scene with Emory on top of the cliff got me bad."

She splays her hand on her chest. "Wasn't it so heartbreakingly beautiful?"

"That's a good way to describe it." I shake my head. "I wonder if my mother went through that before she died. I wonder if she was sitting there contemplating whether she should go through with it, or if she was just certain in her decision."

"It's not an easy decision. It's not an impulse. We're brought to that moment over time, and even when we're there, it's still the hardest thing to do."

My stomach twists, and my heart aches. "I hate that you were at that point."

"Me too."

I tip her chin and kiss her lips. "But I'm so damn happy you made it to me."

"So am I." Phoenix nudges me with her shoulder. "You look really good tonight, Bossy Pants."

"Thanks. So do you." I slide my hand across her bare leg. "You always do though."

She leans in and brings her lips to my ear. "What's for dessert later?"

I squeeze her thigh. "You."

She smiles. "Come on. For real."

"Oh, I am for real." My hand slides up her leg a fraction of an inch. "Mixed with a little key lime pie."

Her eyes widen. "You're going to teach me how to make key lime pie?"

I nod. "You mentioned that it was one of your favorite desserts."

She puts her hand over mine and pushes it higher up her leg, bringing my fingertips to the hem of her dress. My fingers continue their ascent, grazing against the material of her thong.

Only, I don't feel any material.

Soft, warm skin greets me instead.

My head whips to the right to look at her. "You're not wearing any underwear."

"I asked you if you wanted black or nude." She fights to conceal her grin. "I went with *nude*."

"Jesus Christ." I run my knuckles over her most sensitive spot, loving the way she hums in my ear and pushes herself against my hand. "You're killing me."

The waiter arrives at our table and drops down three plates. Phoenix stiffens in the seat beside me. But I don't let up.

"Is there anything else I can get you at the moment?" the waiter asks.

I glance over at Phoenix as I slip a finger inside her. "Is there anything you need?"

She shakes her head and swallows as a pink flush crawls from her chest to her cheeks. "N-no, thank you. This is p-perfect."

"Great." The waiter smiles. "Are you ready to order your main course, or do you want to wait to order?"

I curl my finger and run my thumb over her clit at the same time. "What do you think, babe? Are you ready for the main course?"

Phoenix stifles a moan and grips my wrist. "I think we're okay for now."

The waiter nods. "Of course. I'll come back in a bit to check on you."

"Thank you." I wait for him to leave our table before slipping my finger out of her and bringing it to my mouth for a taste. "Mmm. Fucking delicious."

Phoenix whimpers. "Tease."

I chuckle. "Says the one who didn't wear underwear."

"Let's skip the main course and ask for the check so we can get home."

"As much as I'd love to tear this dress off of you, we're not rushing through dinner." I lean in and bite the cusp of her ear. "Now be patient like a good girl."

I thoroughly enjoy teasing Phoenix for the remainder of dinner, despite the fact that it's torturing me as well.

When we get back to her house, I unload my bag of ingredients onto the island.

"We're going to mix these with sugar and melted butter to make the crust." I place the box of graham crackers in front of Phoenix. "Start crushing these up."

"Yes, sir."

My dick twitches. It's been straining against my pants all night after my stunt under the table at dinner. I try my best to focus as I whisk together the pie ingredients, but with Phoenix beside me in the privacy of her house, my restraint is slipping.

I dip my finger into the pie filling and bring it to her lips. "How does this taste?"

Her tongue snakes out, and she takes my finger into her mouth in an agonizingly slow motion.

"I don't know. I think I need another taste." She dips her finger into the bowl and swipes it against my mouth. Then she reaches up and rolls her tongue across my lips.

It's the shot at the starting line.

I dig my fingers into her hips and hoist her up onto the counter. She tugs at my shirt, pulling it over my head, and then we come back together, our tongues finding each other as we kiss and nip and suck. I slip my hands into her hair and grip it tight, jerking her head up to give me better access to her mouth.

"I want you, James. I've been craving you ever since the other night in my bedroom."

"Same, beautiful." I pull up the hem of her dress and peel it off of her in slow motion. "I haven't been able to think of anything else."

She reaches behind her back and unclips her bra, tossing it to the floor as I reach for the can of whipped cream. I spray a dollop over her nipple, and she gasps as I lean down and suck her hardened peak into my mouth.

Phoenix smiles. "This your fantasy?"

I spray a trail from her belly button downward and lick it off. "Every time we've cooked together, it's been all I've wanted to do: Spread you out on this countertop and taste every inch of you." I skim my tongue over her clit. "I want to devour you, Phoenix."

She shivers and gazes down at me from under hooded lids. "I'm all yours."

I growl with possession. "Yes, you fucking are." I slide her ass to the edge of the counter and throw her legs over my shoulders. Then I bury my face in her.

She arches her back and cries out as she grabs two fistfuls of my hair. I drag my tongue all over her, lapping up her sweetness. I alternate between light, teasing licks, and long, firm strokes. Every time I pull back, her grip on my hair tightens and she pushes my head against her. Her hips rock and I can barely breathe as she fucks my face. This woman knows what she wants, and she's using me to get it—and it's the absolute sexiest thing I have ever witnessed.

I watch her face as she squeezes her eyes shut and finds her release. She screams my name as the orgasm racks her body, and her thighs squeeze my head to keep me where she needs me. By the time she's done, my dick is throbbing from how turned on I am.

Phoenix slides off the counter and drops to her knees. She yanks open my pants and pulls them down with my boxers in one swift motion. My dick hangs between us, and her eyes widen.

I smirk. "This is what going down on you does to me."

She reaches for the can of whipped cream and sprays a cold peak onto my crown. My jaw drops as she licks it off and then wraps her tongue around me as she sucks me into her mouth. She takes me in far and twists her hands around the remaining length.

"Oh, fuck." My hands slide into her hair, brushing it off her face and gathering it all at the nape of her neck. "Do that again."

Phoenix swirls her tongue around my tip, and then takes as much of me as she can, working her hands at the base. Every now and again, she'll suck on the head, just bobbing in short pulses, not letting the rest of me inside her mouth until I can't take it anymore. All the while, she gazes up at me as she moans, showing me how much she's enjoying this.

My grip on her hair tightens as I get closer to my release. "Baby, I'm gonna come."

She takes two handfuls of my ass and pushes me all the way to the back of her throat. White-hot heat courses through my veins, and my hips thrust forward as I come.

And Phoenix swallows everything I give her.

I brace my hands on the countertop, catching my breath, while Phoenix stands in nothing but her black boots. I pull her against me, letting my hands trail down her smooth back. Then I toss her over my shoulder and carry her to the staircase, leaving our clothes strewn on the kitchen tile.

She squeals. "Where are we going?"

"To the shower. I'm not done with you yet."

19

Phoenix

Daily Affirmation: "I am worthy. I am brave, bold, and beautiful."

"Wow. You went from *he's just my neighbor* to getting eaten out on the countertop."

I shake my head on a laugh. "That's not exactly how it happened, but yes—feelings have developed."

Drew sighs. "And you're really able to forget about all those awful things he said to you?"

"He didn't say them to hurt me. He said them because *he* was hurting. Plus, he apologized."

"An apology makes it all better?"

"I think it shows that he can own up to his mistakes and try to fix them. If anyone knows how important that is, it's me."

"I don't know, Nix." He sighs. "I want you to be with someone who treats you right. Someone who gets you."

I frown. "I think it's important to give people the chance to get me. I don't expect someone without depression to automatically understand everything I've been through."

"Don't you think it'd be easier to be with someone who does know?"

"I'm not going to hold out in the hopes of meeting a man who just so happens to have mental health issues like me."

"Maybe you don't have to hold out." Drew pauses. "Maybe you already know someone like that."

My lips part on a silent gasp. "Drew…"

"I was trying to wait until I got out of this place to tell you in person. I wanted to give you some time to get settled in your new house. I didn't expect someone else to swoop in and beat me to it."

My mind races. "I had no idea you were even into me like that. I… I thought we were friends."

"We *are* friends. But somewhere along the line, I realized that I wanted more." His voice lowers. "You're beautiful, and smart, and kind. How could I not want more?"

"Did I lead you on? Did I give you the impression that I felt the same?"

"No, no. These feelings are my own. I guess I was just hoping that you'd realize how you felt about me during this time apart, and then we'd be together when I got out."

My heart sinks. "I'm so sorry, but I don't feel those kinds of feelings for you."

"But you could. Maybe I could take you on a date, and we can see what happens. I'm just asking for a chance."

"I can't do that, Drew. I'm really sorry."

He's quiet on the other end of the line. "Is it the cop?"

"He's part of it." My feelings for James wouldn't allow me to feel anything for anyone else, but I have to be honest with Drew so he doesn't get a false sense of hope. "You're my best friend. That's all I want us to be."

"It's okay. It was a long shot anyway. Nobody wants to be with the crazy schizophrenic dude."

"That's not true. Don't say that. And you're not crazy. We'll find you someone great when you get out. I'll spend the summer helping you."

"Don't worry about me, Nix. Seriously, I'll be fine."

"Drew—"

"Hey, I'm gonna go, okay? Let me go with my tail between my legs and lick my wounds."

"Please tell me we're still friends." My bottom lip trembles. "I don't want to lose your friendship."

"Of course, we're still friends. Just promise me one thing."

"Anything."

"Promise you'll put me in the book you're writing and make me totally awesome."

A smile spreads across my face. "Done."

"Bye, Nix."

"Bye."

I drop my phone into my lap and replay each conversation I've ever had with Drew, trying to figure out why I didn't pick up on any hints about his feelings for me.

I look down at Wilbur as I scratch behind his ears. "Oh, Wilbur. Life is so much simpler when you're a dog."

"Are you ready?"

I muster all the courage I have inside me and give James a quick nod. "Let's go."

I swing open the door and step inside the room.

The marks from my father's hospital bed are still indented on the carpet. It's a lot like his memory—he's gone, but the marks from where he used to be are everywhere.

My eyes bounce around the empty walls. "It's so bare."

James sets down his spackling tools and lays the tarp on the floor. "It won't be when you're finished in here."

I walk over to the sliding glass doors and gaze down at the choppy water below. "We used to sit out here on the balcony and watch the fireworks on the Fourth of July."

"It's a great view." James stands behind me and wraps his hands around my waist, resting his chin on the top of my head. "Maybe we can do that this summer."

I close my eyes and smile. "I'd like that."

"Do you have pictures of him?"

"They're in a box in the closet." I tug his hand to pull him toward the closet doors and pause in front of them. "His clothes are in here too. I want to donate them. But maybe I'll keep a few for myself." I let out a bitter laugh. "My mother wanted to get rid of everything. After his funeral, she brought literal garbage bags back to the house, as if she could just toss him away. We had such a big fight."

"What happened?"

"I told her that he left this house to me, so everything in it was my property. She stormed out, and I packed up his things by myself."

"What did your brother do?"

I slide open the closet door and shrug. "He always sides with her."

"Have you heard from him since Christmas?"

"All I got was a text saying *Merry Christmas* with a picture of the baby."

James covers my hand with his. "It sounds like he's so preoccupied with his new life that he doesn't realize how much you're hurting. Maybe you should try to have a serious talk with him. Lay all your cards on the table and be honest with him about the kind of relationship you want to have with him."

"And if he doesn't want the same thing?"

"Then at least you know where you stand."

I flick through the hangers and land on my father's winter coat. He always wore a brown leather bomber jacket with beige fleece around the collar. "I used to make fun of him, calling him Maverick from *Top Gun* whenever he wore this. He'd grumble about being taller and better looking than Tom Cruise."

"Try it on." James holds it out for me. "I bet it'll look great on you."

I slide my arms into the sleeves, and the scent of baby powder puffs up around me. My eyes glisten as I stare at my reflection in the hanging mirror across the room. It's a tad long on the sleeves, but it fits.

"Well," James says. "There's no denying it now: He definitely wasn't taller than Tom Cruise."

A laugh bubbles out of me. I slip my hands into the pockets, and my fingers hit the plastic wrappers of his favorite Wint-O-Green Lifesavers. I pull out a handful. "Oh my god. We'll probably find these mints in every pocket he had. He was obsessed with them."

James chuckles. "Want to bet on how many we'll find? I say one hundred."

"Deal. I say we find two hundred."

After we make two piles of clothes, one to keep and one to donate, I pull out a container with hundreds of pictures.

James picks one up and grins. "You were a chubby baby, huh?"

I snatch it out of his hand and feign a scowl. "I wasn't chubby. I was healthy."

He laughs and kisses my cheek. "You were adorable. Still are."

I gaze down at the picture—my father holding me in his arms wearing a proud smile—and I can't help but wonder if my mother felt proud of me then too. If she ever did. Was it my depression that ruined it, or was she incapable of loving me all along?

James holds up my parents' wedding album. "Maybe your mother would like to have this."

I shrug. "It's not like she wanted it back then."

"Maybe she feels differently now. Maybe she wishes she didn't give it all up."

I roll my eyes. "Then she shouldn't have been such a cold bitch."

James sets down the album and takes my hands in his. "I know she hurt you, and I hate the way she treated you when you needed her the most. But maybe it isn't the end of your relationship. She might regret the things she said."

I grunt. "Or she might still be stubborn as she always was."

"She might. But you never know until you try." He presses a kiss to the top of my hand. "Her and your brother are the only family you have. If they see the strong, capable, healthy woman you are now, you can change their minds about how they see you. About depression." He shrugs. "I think it's worth a shot."

I gaze into his sincere eyes and lift my hand to his cheek. "I appreciate you for pushing me to talk to my family."

"But?"

"But I'm not sure I can do it."

"And that's okay. It's your decision, and I will stand by you in whatever you decide. But I want you to be happy, and I know you'd be happy if you had a relationship with your mom and your brother. I'd hate to see you not have that opportunity because you're too scared to try."

I nod. "I just don't know that it's possible to have the kind of relationship I'd want."

"Maybe you need to let go of the expectations, and just let it be whatever kind of relationship it's going to be. Maybe something is better than nothing at all."

We let the conversation stop there, and we continue sorting through the pictures.

Going through my father's things helps heal a cracked piece of my heart. By the time his closet is empty, I'm fifty dollars richer.

The man was hoarding three hundred and sixty-eight Lifesavers.

Later that night, I'm lying in bed thinking about what James said earlier. After two years in therapy, I'm definitely stronger and wiser than I've ever been. I'm a different person within my sameness. And in therapy, Dr. Erica taught me to push myself through the uncomfortable and vulnerable parts of life. She'd say, "Getting to the other side of that hurdle is how we grow. It's not easy, but it's worth it to push yourself to be a better version of yourself and do the things you didn't think you could do."

Maybe reaching out to my mother is my next hurdle. Whether she answers or not, I can still feel peace knowing that I tried.

So, I pull out my notebook and start writing.

Dear Mom,

I don't know if you'll even read this. There's a chance you ripped it up and threw it in the trash without opening it. But knowing that there's a chance you might read it—that you might want *to read it—is what's driving me to write this letter to you.*

I want to start by saying I'm sorry. I'm sorry for everything I put you through. It must've been really difficult to raise a daughter with depression, and not know what to do to help her. You must've been really worried about my well-being and my future. And you must've been terrified when you found me on the floor in the bathroom the day I tried to take my own life. I wish I could've been better for you. I wish I could've been an easier child. I wish I could've made you proud like Tyler always did.

Do you ever wish you could've been better for me?

I wish you could've tried harder to understand what I was going through. I wish you could've loved me unconditionally. Maybe then I would've known it was okay to love myself. But we can only do what we're capable of, and what you gave me was all you could. For that, I forgive you.

I got out of therapy in November. I've been living at the shore house, and I'm doing really well. I've been going through Dad's things. I came across this photo album and thought you might like to have it.

Maybe you'd like to have me back in your life too.

I'd love to hear from you.

—Phoenix

I seal the letter with the album in a large envelope, and write a similar one to Tyler, enclosing a picture of us dressed up as Mario and Luigi on Halloween.

When I send the mail out the next morning, I let go of my expectations with it. Whatever will be, will be. I can't control the outcome—I can only control my own actions and emotions.

I'm happy.

I'm worthy.

I'm healthy.

I'm strong.

I'm proud of myself.

I'm going to be the Phoenix my father always knew I could be.

20

James

Going through Phoenix's family belongings the other day made me want to go through my mother's boxes.

Guilt rises in my gut as I gaze down at all of her old stuff. "It's sad, isn't it? That we've kept her hidden away in a box all this time?"

"We thought it was best for Dad. But now I'm not so sure." Leo glances up at me. "Do you think he'd want to see all of this?"

"I don't know, but we can ask him. He might like to remember these pieces of her."

"How do you remember the good without remembering the bad?"

I shrug because I still haven't figured out how. "Maybe we don't need to forget the bad. Maybe that's where I've gone wrong all this time. Maybe we should remember Mom for all that she was—the happy and the sad parts, because that's who she was."

Leo smirks. "Being with Phoenix has done you some good, big bro."

"She makes me want to be better. She makes me think about everything in a way I never did before." I brush my fingers over the satin strap on Mom's apron. "I wish I knew her when Mom was still alive, so I could've tried to understand her more."

Leo nods. "I wish we could've done a lot of things differently, but that doesn't mean it would've made a different outcome."

193

"You're right."

Leo tosses another picture onto the pile. "You tell her you love her yet?"

My heart wrenches in my chest. "No."

"Don't be a chickenshit. She needs to hear that."

I scoff. "I'm not being a chickenshit. I'm just waiting for the right moment."

"There is no right moment. Look at what we're doing right now." He gestures to Mom's things sprawled out on the floor around us. "This should serve as your reminder that life is short, and you shouldn't hold back from the things you want to say and do."

"I'm not like you."

He rolls his eyes. "I know. You don't have to tell me how superior you are."

"That's not what I mean."

"Then what?"

"I'm not fearless like you. I'm cautious and scared, and I worry about the outcome of every move I make." I swallow. "I wish I could be more like you."

Leo's eyebrows hit his hairline. "You think I'm fearless?"

I nod. "You would've told your girlfriend you loved her as soon as you felt it."

"What's the point in holding it in? It doesn't make you feel it any less."

I smile. "No, it doesn't."

If anything, it's been swelling bigger and bigger, ready to explode at the surface.

"Why don't you tell her when you're fucking her? Girls love that romantic shit."

I clear my throat. "Yeah, good idea."

But Leo sees right through me. "Wait a minute. You've been with her, haven't you?"

I shake my head. "Not that it's any of your business, but no."

His eyes widen. "How? How have you not?"

"She's in control of that decision. I'm waiting for her to make that move."

"Damn. That must be hard." He gestures to my pants. "So hard, it's probably about to fall off."

I laugh. "Shut up. There's more to life than sex. You should take a page out of my book for once before you catch a disease and *your* dick falls off."

"Not a chance." He side-eyes me. "I wonder who got the bigger dick. How long is yours?"

I push off the ground to stand. "Okay, that's enough."

"Fully erect, not flaccid. Come on."

I walk toward the door. "I'm taking a lunch break."

"It's big, isn't it?" Leo rubs his palms together. "Mine is huge, bro. I bet Dad's is massive."

"Never refer to Dad's dick again."

I walk out of the garage and tap out a playful text to Phoenix.

Me: I think you should send me a sexy picture of yourself.
My Phoenix: You think so, huh?
Me: It's only fair since you have two of me in your phone.
Me: And make it a good one. I don't want to have to use my imagination.
My Phoenix: You're fully dressed in the pictures I have of you. How is that fair?
Me: Maybe if you do what you're told, I'll send you a better one.
My Phoenix: Maybe if you go upstairs, you'll get more than just a picture.

I take the stairs by twos, and head to my bedroom. I lock the door behind me and send another text.

Me: I'm here.

My phone buzzes with an incoming call.

195

"Hi, beautiful."

Phoenix's voice is low and soft. "Come to the window."

Heat rushes over me as I stalk to the other side of my room.

Phoenix is standing in front of her window with the phone pressed to her ear, in nothing but a towel. "I could send you a picture, or I could give you a show."

My eyebrows lift. "What kind of show?"

She drops the towel. "One I think you're really going to like."

I step closer to the glass, my eyes roaming over her luscious curves. "Why don't I just come over?"

She shakes her head. "You're going to stay right there like a good boy."

My dick twitches. "I like it when you're bossy."

She grins and cups her breast with her free hand. "I'll let you touch yourself while you watch."

I sandwich the phone between my ear and my shoulder as I fumble with my sweatpants, pushing them down and following suit with my boxers.

I grip my dick in my hand and squeeze. "Your body is so sexy, Phoenix."

Her fingers circle her nipple, and then they skate across her chest to the other one. "I think about you whenever I touch myself. I pretend it's you."

My breath catches in my throat. "Show me."

She trails her fingers down her stomach, her gaze locked on my hand as I stroke myself. "You're so big." The tip of her finger slides over her clit. "I don't know that you'll fit."

I stifle a groan. "I'll make you so wet and ready, you'll be able to take all of me. Don't you worry."

Phoenix rubs herself in light, languid circles. She lets out a soft moan, and my dick swells.

"I'm ready to try, James. I want to feel you inside me. I want to be close to you."

I close my eyes for just a moment as I thrust into my hand, imagining how it'll feel to have her wrapped around me. "I'm going to make love to every inch of you."

"Tonight." She pushes a finger inside herself and rocks her hips. "I need you tonight."

I pump myself faster, anticipation burning low in my stomach. "I work tonight, sweetheart."

"After." She slips in another finger and brushes her clit with her thumb. "Come over in your uniform."

"Another fantasy?"

"Yes." She's breathless and moaning as she works her fingers inside, and I clench my jaw hard, wishing so bad that her fingers were my own, that I could feel her and taste her. "Say you'll come here. Tell me you'll give me what I need."

"I'll be there. I'm going to bury myself so deep inside you that you'll feel me for days after. Every time you walk, every time you move, you'll think of me and count the seconds until I can fill you up again."

She moans loud. "James."

My dick swells, ready for a release.

"I'm gonna need you to stop."

I freeze. "What?"

A devilish grin spreads across her face as she removes her hand from between her legs. "Don't finish. Let's wait until tonight."

My forehead falls against the windowpane as I close my eyes. "You planned this?"

Her laughter flutters through the phone. "I don't want you tame when you come over tonight. I want you banging down my door, ready to tear my clothes to shreds."

I stare down at my swollen crown. "That won't be a problem."

"And James?"

"Yes, beautiful?"

"Bring your bossy pants."

Phoenix

Daily Affirmation: "I am giving myself permission to grow into the person I know I'm meant to be."

"Slow down, boy. Easy. I have to get the mail."

I pull back on Wilbur's leash. I've been taking him on runs with me, and it seems like he's getting stronger by the day.

"Bill, bill, another bill." I sift through the mail until I spot a blank envelope. No name, no stamp, or return address.

I tear it open and pull out a white folded sheet of paper. My jaw drops when I unfold it. It's a sketch.

Of me.

Soft pencil strokes make up my hair and facial features, fading into the edge of the paper at the bottom of my neck. It looks exactly like me.

Whoever drew this is incredibly talented. But who would do this? Can James draw? And why would he give me a picture of myself? Why would he stick it in my mailbox?

Something low sounds in the back of my mind, like a faraway siren.

A warning.

Unease creeps into my gut.

I tug Wilbur's leash and hurry inside to call James.

"Hey, gorgeous."

"Hi." I unclip Wilbur's leash and hang it on the hook by the door. "How's work?"

"Just counting the hours until I can see you."

Someone makes kissing noises in the background, followed by a loud, "Ouch! That hurt, fucker."

I laugh. "Hi, Phil."

"Hi, Phoenix. Got a hot sister or cousin for me?"

"No, but I have a brother."

"Not into men, but thanks anyway."

James grunts. "All right, let me get back to work."

I pull at the string on my hoodie. "Hey, did you leave a picture in my mailbox?"

"A picture?"

"Like a drawing."

"No. I can't draw to save my life. I failed finger painting as a kid."

I chuckle. I don't want to alarm him, especially when I don't know who this is from. The man worries enough.

"Okay. It must have been sent to the wrong address or something."

"Yeah, I get a lot of junk mail too."

"Be safe, you two. See you later."

"Can't wait to see you, beautiful."

Phil pipes up again. "Bye, beautiful. I love—"

James ends the call, and I shake my head as I laugh.

I go upstairs, shove the picture in my drawer in my nightstand, and try to push it from my mind for now. I have the day to myself, and I want to spend it working on my book.

I'm writing the first sex scene.

It's been so hard not to get myself off, especially after teasing James earlier. But it'll be worth it when he comes in like a crazed animal.

I've had sex because it's what I thought I was supposed to do. Lose your virginity and find out what all the hype is about. I've had sex because it's what a guy wanted. I wasn't really into it, but I didn't want to disappoint him by saying no. I've had sex because I was trying to feel something other than pain and sorrow. And sometimes, I was trying to feel something because it was better than feeling nothing at all. I've had sex for all the wrong reasons.

But now, with James, I'm not just giving him my body. I'm giving him my mind. My heart. My soul. I'm giving him a piece of me I'll never get back because I've never let myself go there with anyone before. It's not about an orgasm. It's not about a fleeting moment of euphoria. It's about feeling so completely at one with someone—so absolutely certain that you belong to him, and he belongs to you.

He sees me for who I am. For what I've done. For who I want to become.

He accepts me.

He supports me.

He cares about me.

He has my back.

He has given me so much, and I'm going to show him the kind of love he deserves, because he deserves it all.

When James finally walks into my house, my heart thumps in anticipation as I hear each step he takes on the stairs. I'm waiting for him on my bed in nothing but my silk robe. I've instructed him to come in his uniform, but that's as much as I've let him know about my fantasy.

His lips curve up when he sees me waiting on the bed. "Hi, my beautiful girl."

"Hi, officer."

He takes slow steps as he walks toward my bed. "I like the robe."

"You'll like what's under it even better."

He takes his bottom lip between his teeth as his eyes trail down my bare legs. "You thought you were cute with your little stunt earlier, didn't you?"

"Maybe." I open my robe and bare myself to him. Then I lift my hands over my head and clasp them together.

As if he can read my mind, he unclips the handcuffs from his belt. He looks into my eyes as he clicks the cuffs around my wrists. The bite of the cold metal sends a shiver down my spine. I'm splayed out for him, completely bare, and I squirm under his heated gaze as it roams over every bare inch of my body.

"God, you're beautiful." He tilts my chin with his knuckles and lowers his mouth to mine. He kisses me, slow and deep, while he skates his fingertips along the dips and curves of my skin.

I reach out to pull him closer and hook my wrists around his neck, longing to feel his body against mine.

But he presses my wrists back down onto the pillow and bends over to swirl his tongue over my nipple. "Be a good girl, Phoenix. I said no touching."

I rub my thighs together to ease the building ache between my legs and let out a frustrated sigh. "You're no fun."

He smirks and sucks my nipple before releasing it with a pop. "Oh, I'm going to show you just how fun I am."

He leans a knee onto the mattress beside me and unclips his baton from his belt. Starting at my ankle, he slides it up my shin and over my knee, inching higher.

Then the baton stops, and he taps it against my thigh. "Open."

I widen my legs, but only a little, knowing he wants more.

He arches an eyebrow, and a devilish gleam flashes in his eyes. "I can't wait to fuck the stubborn right out of you."

I lift my chin. "Good luck with that."

He trails the baton along the inside of my thigh and coats the smooth tip of it in my wetness. "I won't need luck."

I open my legs wider on instinct and release a moan.

James palms himself over his pants, watching his baton tease me in slow circles. I lift my hips, grinding against it for more friction.

"James." His name is a breathy moan as pleasure mounts deep in my core.

"I know, baby." His voice is raspy, and he's got a wild look in his eyes, like his control is slipping.

I want him to lose it.

I open my legs as wide as I can and draw out his name on another moan, begging for more.

He tosses the baton onto the bed and works the buttons on his shirt and strips out of his uniform like it's on fire and he can't get out of it fast enough. He towers over me—the wide span of shoulders, his smooth round chest. I lick my lips as my gaze lands on the deep *V* shape just above his boxers, leading down toward the bulge straining in my direction.

Reaching into his boxers, he pumps himself. I stretch forward, breaking the rules once more, and jerk his boxers down just under his ass so his dick springs free. It's long and thick, with a perfect smooth crown.

He climbs onto the bed and kneels beside me, stroking his length just inches in front of my face.

"Open that sassy mouth for me."

I do, and he pushes himself between my lips. I wrap my tongue around him and crane my neck to take him farther inside.

He lets out a primal groan, watching me from under hooded eyes, and his hips jut forward.

I stare up at him, entranced, turned on by seeing how turned on *he* is in this moment, watching him unravel.

With my hands tied over my head, my body at his mercy, I've never felt sexier.

He forgets about the baton and slides his fingers over my clit. "So fucking sexy, baby. My cock in your mouth, your legs spread wide with that beautiful, wet pussy." He grunts as his eyes rake over me. "You were made for me."

I moan in agreement, sucking him deeper.

His fingers slip inside me before they glide back up over my clit, making languid circles and sending sparks to every nerve ending in my body. He's teasing me, making me beg for it.

"James, please."

He reaches for the condom on the nightstand, and after he rolls it on, he coats himself between my legs, rubbing himself over me, back and forth.

But before he continues, he unlocks the cuffs around my wrists. "I want your hands all over me."

I claw his back and grip his ass, lifting my hips to meet his. He looks down to watch as he pushes his tip inside me, slow and controlled. I hold my breath, taking him inch by inch, relishing in the way he stretches me until he's all the way in.

His eyes close, and he drops his forehead to mine like he's saying a silent prayer. Then his eyes open and bore into my soul, something so vulnerable reflecting in his honey-colored irises. "I want to savor this moment. I always want to remember how it feels to be this close." He pauses as he swallows. "I never want you to forget that you're mine."

As if I could ever forget. I take his face into my hands and give him a deep, passionate kiss. "Then fuck me and show me who I belong to."

His eyes darken, and he laces our fingers as he presses my hands into the mattress above my head, pinning me beneath him. He pulls himself almost completely out of me, and then he drives back in with such speed and force that I gasp. He pulls out and plunges into me, again and again. His grunts grow louder, sweat beading along his skin. I open my legs wider to accommodate him.

He releases one of my hands to hike up my knee, throwing my leg over his shoulder, pushing himself as deep as he can get. His punishing rhythm is exactly how I need it. I see stars. I've never been this close, this connected to anyone.

He releases a strangled groan. "You feel so fucking good."

I grab a handful of his hair, rolling my hips to meet each of his thrusts. "I'm yours, James."

"And I'm yours."

Thrust.

"You have me."

Thrust.

"Always."

Thrust.

"Always?" I ask, breathless.

"Always, Phoenix." He drives into me and locks his eyes on mine. "This is forever."

An overwhelming surge of emotion clogs my throat, and hot tears sting my eyes. There's so much I want to say, so much I need him to know. But in this moment, I can't get the words out.

So, I give him my body and hope he can feel all that's inside my heart.

He kisses me hard and rubs his thumb over my clit as he plunges into me over and over. Pleasure builds deep in my core as a wave of ecstasy rises until I can't fight it anymore. It crashes over me and pulls me under.

I cry out, letting James hear what he's doing to me. And when my orgasm fades, I watch as he succumbs to his own. A beautiful mixture of intensity and vulnerability is etched onto his face, and his eyes are ablaze as he gives me everything he's got.

We're both out of breath as he eases off of me and curls himself around my body, holding me tight. We're too wrapped up in the moment to speak, and there's a long moment of comfortable, sated silence as we lie together.

Then James's low voice floats into the air. "I know you said you didn't like the ending of my book, but I like the last line, 'Surely, someday she would find him.' I've been drifting through my life these past several years, like I was wandering a desolate island after a shipwreck. I didn't know if I'd ever find love, or if anyone was out there for me. Then you walked into my life—albeit with a baseball bat—and you found me. Everything clicked. It's like our paths were meant to cross, like everything we've endured has been for the sake of something bigger.

"You make me incredibly happy, and I will give you everything I have in me to make you happy too." He hugs me tight. "I love you. You have my heart, Phoenix. Do you understand?"

I blink through my blurry vision and turn in his arms to face him. "I do understand, because I love you too, James."

And all I can think about for the rest of the night is the fact that I almost missed this. My life was almost cut short, and I would've missed out on knowing James.

On falling in love.

On this second chance at life.

And for the first time, I'm so damn grateful that my mother found me and got me to the hospital in time.

21

Phoenix

Daily Affirmation: "I am letting go of people that no longer serve me peace."

"I'm so proud of you, Leo."

He drops his chin and hides his smile. "Thanks."

"You're taking this EMT thing seriously and you're going for it. This is going to be a whole new chapter in your life."

"I just can't wait for this to bring in more women. A hot EMT with tattoos? They won't be able to resist."

I laugh. "Fine, you can downplay this, but I won't. I'm really proud, little bro."

He shields his eyes from the sun, scanning the dog park. "Wilbur's getting big."

"He is. I love his little puppy stage, but I'm excited to see how big he's going to get. The vet thinks he'll be between eighty to a hundred pounds."

"Damn. He'll be the biggest dog in this place."

I lean my elbows back against the bench. "So, you're just looking to mess around with random women? You're not interested in finding someone to be in a relationship with?"

He shrugs. "I don't know if a relationship is for me."

"Why not?"

"I'm not relationship material."

"Says who?"

"I don't know. I'm not the one who women want to settle down with. I'm the fun one. The one with the tattoos who you don't bring home to mom."

"But where are you getting that from? Is that what women have said about you, or is that your own insecurity?"

He rubs the back of his neck. "Come on, Nixie. You don't look at me the same way you look at James."

"You're definitely different, but that doesn't mean you're not the same in your heart." I squeeze his arm. "You have a lot to offer. You've been the best friend I've ever had. That's exactly what you need to be a good boyfriend."

He side-eyes me. "You mean that? The best friend part?"

I nod. "I wouldn't say it if I didn't mean it."

He glances out across the park. "Hey, where's Wilbur?"

My back goes ramrod straight. "He was right there, playing with the chocolate lab."

My eyes dart around as I spring to my feet. "Wilbur! Here, boy."

Leo gestures to the left. "You go that way, and I'll look over here. He probably saw a squirrel and ran into the woods."

"Wilbur!" I call his name over and over again, furious with myself for not watching him more closely. "Come on, boy. Where are you?"

I search the area, and then Leo's voice calls from the other side of the park. "He's here! Nixie, I found him."

My heart drops to my feet as I take off running in their direction. Leo holds Wilbur in his arms as he licks his face like nothing's wrong.

"Is he okay? Is he hurt?" I scoop him into my arms and check his body. "What the heck happened?"

"I'm telling you, he must've seen something and tried chasing it."

I clip his leash on his collar and put him on the ground. "Okay, that's enough dog park for one day."

I can't let him out of my sight again.

"Let's go by Miss Mindy's on the way home." Leo slings his arm around my shoulder. "I heard they have puppy treats there."

"You're gonna spoil your nephew."

He grins. "We gotta beef him up if he's going to be your guard dog."

"I don't need a guard dog. I live next door to a family of cops."

But I might've spoken too soon, because later in the afternoon, I find another anonymous envelope sitting in my mailbox.

My hands shake as I unfold the paper. I suck in a breath when I see the detailed sketch of Wilbur playing at the dog park. My stomach churns, and I feel sick.

I groan and rub my forehead. Wilbur paws at my leg, looking up at me as if he's asking what's wrong.

"Your dad isn't gonna be happy, Wilbur."

"Why didn't you tell me about this sooner?"

I grimace. "I'm sorry, okay? I thought it was just a fluke. But then I got this one from the dog park today."

"Someone sketched a picture of you, Phoenix. This isn't a fluke. This is purposeful and planned." James jabs the paper with his finger. "This person is stalking you."

I place my hand over my chest. "A stalker? Are you serious? But it's just a couple of pictures."

"That's how it starts. Whoever it is knows where you live. They followed you to the park today. Think about it, babe. Who knows where you live?"

"I literally have no idea. My mom and my brother." I shrug. "I haven't spoken to anyone else since I got out of Clearview."

"What about your friend? Does Drew have your address?"

"No." I pause, chewing my bottom lip. "Plus, he's still in Clearview."

James's eyebrows shoot up. "He's your friend from the mental health facility? What is he in there for?"

I toy with the hem of my shirt. "Schizophrenia."

He pinches the bridge of his nose and inhales deeply.

"That doesn't mean he's behind this, James. I was in there too, you know. Just because he's schizophrenic doesn't mean he's a stalker." I hold up the blank envelope. "And this isn't addressed. There's no stamp on it. Someone had to have put it in my mailbox. So, it can't be Drew."

James nods. "You're right, I'm sorry. This just really worries me. I don't like this."

"Can you take this to the station? Maybe get it checked for fingerprints."

"We've both touched it, so the chances of finding a viable fingerprint are slim. I can try though." He grabs his keys off the counter. "But I'm going to install some Ring cameras around your house."

I nod. "Cameras are good. Then we'll be able to catch who it is."

"You're coming with me. I'm not letting you out of my sight until we handle this."

Adrenaline courses through me. "Do you really think I'm in danger?"

"I don't know. Anything is possible, and I'm not taking any chances."

I glance up at him as we walk to the front door. "Is it weird that you're kind of turning me on right now?"

He smirks. "Now is not the time to get turned on."

I grip his large bicep. "I can't help it. I like it when you're in cop mode."

He stops on the porch and tips my chin. "I'm not going to let anything happen to you, Phoenix. I'm going to protect you."

Then he lowers his lips to mine, and I feel the verity of his words throughout every cell in my body.

James spends the rest of the afternoon installing my new cameras—and I spend my afternoon *watching* him.

I stretch out on the couch. "I missed an opportunity. I feel you should've been doing this shirtless."

He glances over his shoulder as he screws the last camera into place in my living room. "You keep looking at me like that, and you're the one who's going to be shirtless."

I grin. "Maybe we can test out these new cameras after you're done. See how clear the video is."

He raises his eyebrows. "You're not kidding, are you?"

I shake my head. "Not one bit. Just call it research for my book."

"You're insatiable, and I love it."

Just as I'm about to peel off my clothes, my phone buzzes on the coffee table.

My mouth opens. "Oh, shit. It's Tyler."

James climbs down from the step stool. "He probably got your letter."

My heart leaps into my throat. "I wonder what he's going to say."

"Only one way to find out."

I grip his wrist. "Stay with me?"

"I'm right here, baby." James lowers himself onto the couch and holds one of my hands while I answer the call with the other.

"Hey, Tyler."

"Hey, Nix. How are you?"

"I'm doing well. How are you guys doing over there?"

"We're good. I, uh, got your letter. Is this a good time to talk?"

I nod as if he can see me. "Sure."

Tyler lets out a long sigh, and I hold my breath waiting to hear what he has to say. James squeezes my hand, grounding me to the moment.

Whatever Tyler says isn't a reflection of my worth.

His feelings are his own, and I tried my best.

"You said in your letter that the reason I moved away was because I wanted to get away from you. That's not true. I moved away because I had to get away from Mom. I know she treated you much worse than me, but she was still hard on me too. I felt like I had to be perfect, like if I did something she didn't approve of, then she'd look at me differently and never forgive me. She held me to this impossible standard, and it wasn't healthy. I was anxious and wound too tight. I hated leaving you with her, but I had to get out."

I let out the breath I was holding. "I didn't know you felt that way."

"I regret not sharing that with you. I think I felt like you had so much on your shoulders that I didn't want you to feel like you had to worry about me. I was supposed to be the big, strong older brother. In hindsight, I realize it could've been something that brought us closer together." He pauses. "After you tried to kill yourself, Gabby insisted I go to therapy. I'd been through my own trauma growing up with Mom, but it was scary almost losing you like that. I couldn't stop thinking about it—about you. It made me sick to think about you not being here anymore, and I beat myself up for it for a long time. I felt like there was something more I could've done to help you. I should've been there for you, been a better brother. I shouldn't have left you with Mom."

My eyes widen. "Tyler, what I did had nothing to do with you, or Mom for that matter."

"Then why did you do it?" His voice lowers. "Why did you do that to yourself?"

"I was in a bad place, and my depression was filling my head with hopelessness. I was detached from reality, and I felt like I had nothing to live for. Like you and Mom would be better off without me."

"That's not true, Nix."

"I know that now. Took me a while to figure it out and get my mental health in check. Clearview really helped." I smile through my blurry vision. "Thank you for convincing me to go there."

"I couldn't leave the hospital until I knew you were going to be in good hands." He sniffles. "I hated the part in your letter where you said I made you feel like I didn't give a shit about you. When you were in the hospital,

Gabby and I were trying to have a baby, and she had a few miscarriages. Things were really stressful, and I didn't know how to juggle everything. You deserved more of my time and attention. Then when you got out of Clearview, we were getting used to having a newborn in the house, and our lives were turned upside down. But things are more stable now. I'd like to rebuild what we had when we were kids. We used to be best friends."

A tear rolls down my cheek. "I'd love that, Tyler. And I don't expect you to drop everything in your life for me. You went through some really important grown-up shit, and you had every right to be happy and enjoy it. I just want to be a part of that life too."

"So do I. Gabby and I were talking after I received your letter, and she said we should take a trip to the shore house this summer. Jenna will be a little older, and traveling shouldn't be too bad. If you're okay with that idea, of course. I know it's your house."

I clamp my hand over my mouth to muffle my sob. "This house will always be yours too, Ty. I'd love for you guys to come visit. I'm dying to meet my niece."

"I'm sorry about the baptism. It didn't feel right without you. You should've been there."

"How was Mom?"

Tyler chuckles. "Over the top, as usual. She asked about you."

"Oh?"

"She asked if I invited you, and I told her exactly what I told you. She acted surprised, as if I was crazy for thinking she'd cause a scene. Sometimes, I wonder if she acts the way she does on purpose, or if she truly can't help being like this because she's delusional."

"I'll never be able to understand the inner workings of that woman's mind."

"Have you spoken to her since you got out of Clearview?"

"No, but I sent her a letter like I did you. I don't expect a response, but it felt good sending it."

"I'm proud of you, Nix. I don't know that I would've been able to do that after the way she treated you. I give you a lot of credit."

I glance over at James and smile. "I have someone in my life who helped me to realize that I should live my life doing the things I want to do, and if people don't react the way I want them to, then that's on them. At least I tried."

"Wow. That's some grown-ass woman shit right there. You're not a little kid anymore."

I laugh. "I haven't been one for a long time."

"You'll always be my little sister though." Sincerity saturates his voice. "I'm really glad you sent me that letter, Nix. I've been wanting to talk to you, but I didn't know what to say, or how to start. You've always been better at words and feelings than I have. I've always looked up to you."

I choke in disbelief. "I'm sorry, what? You—the great Tyler Bridges—looked up to *me*?"

"It's true. You have always embraced who you are. You didn't try to be anyone else. You had depression, and you were open about it. You didn't let Mom or anyone else sway you."

I slump back against the couch and blink up at the ceiling. "I... I don't even know what to say to that."

"I admire you, Nix. Dad did too. Mom only paid attention to me because she knew she could control me. I had to unpack all of that in therapy too."

"I'm proud of you for going."

"So." I hear amusement in his voice. "Who is this person in your life? Does my little sister have a boyfriend?"

My cheeks heat as I rest my head on James's shoulder. "Yes. His name is James."

"And he's treating you well?"

I close my eyes. "So well."

"Good. You deserve all the happiness. I'm so glad you're doing better than when I last saw you."

"Me too."

After Tyler and I say goodbye, I can't fight the surge of emotion that overcomes me. It feels like a huge weight has been lifted off my shoulders.

"This is because of you, you know." I press a tender kiss to James's lips.

"No, it's because of you."

"You pushed me to do it."

"Doesn't mean shit if you didn't choose to make that step on your own. You did this. You're rebuilding your life, and you're taking control."

"I like taking control." I push him backward on the couch and straddle his hips. "Now, let's test out these cameras."

22

Phoenix

Daily Affirmation: "I deserve to be free from the past, and today I am allowing myself to move on."

"Do you smell that?"

James smiles. "Books?"

"It's my favorite smell in the world." I stop and turn to face him in the aisle. "Aside from your cooking, of course."

"I used to go to the library as a kid, and the first thing I would do is smell the book before I checked it out."

I wrap my hands around his arm. "I love that you love reading as much as I do."

"I can't wait until I'm reading *your* book one day." He gestures to the romance section in front of us. "On one of these shelves."

"I don't know if I'll get that far. Maybe a couple of people will download it on Amazon."

"Don't sell yourself short. You were born to do great things, Phoenix Bridges."

I laugh it off, but deep down, James's words nestle deep into my bones. Maybe I was born to do great things. Maybe that's why I survived my suicide. Maybe I'm going to help someone somewhere someday.

"I can see why you loved this place growing up." James glances around the old bookstore in my hometown in New York. "It has history."

"And it's super cozy. My dad brought me here every Sunday, and we'd sit by the fireplace and read side by side." The memory brings a smile to my lips. "It was my favorite thing we did together. Then when his cancer got bad toward the end, he wanted to be at the shore house. So, I'd bring books to him, and read at his bedside."

James pulls me to his chest and holds me for a moment. "I'm sure he loved you very much. I wish I could've known him."

"Me too. He would've loved you."

"You think so?"

"I know so." I stretch up onto my toes and kiss his lips. "It's impossible not to love you."

"Did you think you'd be saying that when you launched a baseball bat at my head?"

I grin. "No, but I did take note of how strikingly handsome you are."

His eyebrows lift. "You did?"

I nod. "I thought you were a hot criminal. Those gray sweatpants get me every time."

He tilts his head back and laughs. "Good to know."

We spend the afternoon reading in the same nook my father and I used to read in. I was reluctant at first to come back to New York, but James said it would be fun to see where I grew up. I have a lot of good memories here, so there's no reason not to visit.

When we finish at the bookstore, we head down the block to my favorite diner.

We're halfway through an early dinner when my gaze lands on a familiar pair of blue eyes staring back at me, and my fork falls to the plate with a loud clank.

James leans in. "What's wrong?"

I wipe my lips with the edge of my napkin, unable to look away from the woman across from me. Her mouth doesn't give way to a smile. Love doesn't emanate from her gaze. Her hand doesn't motion for me to come over, nor do her legs stand to come over to me. Nothing about her body language would even hint at the fact that she's my mother. She breaks our stare first and continues eating as if she never saw me.

"My mom's here."

James twists around and follows my line of sight before turning back to me. "Why don't you go over there and ask if she received your letter?"

A lead ball sinks into my stomach. "I'm sure she got it."

"This is your chance to confront her." James covers my hand with his. "Give yourself closure, once and for all. I'll go with you."

I shake my head. "I think I need to do this by myself."

"Then I'll be right here if you need me."

I slide out of the booth and push one foot in front of the other until I'm standing at my mother's table.

"Hi, Mom."

"Hello." She doesn't look up.

"Did you get the package I sent you?"

She nods once and takes a sip of her tea. "Thank you for the album."

"I was hoping to hear from you after you read my letter." I wring my hands. "You did read it, didn't you?"

She sits back against her chair and lifts her eyes to mine. "I didn't really have anything to say."

My mouth drops open, yet I don't know why I'm surprised. "So, I guess nothing has changed then."

She shakes her head. "Why would anything have changed? I told you how I felt the day you woke up in the hospital."

And there it is. The honest and painful truth.

"I've done a lot of changing and growing in the last two years, Mom. I realize now that what I did wasn't the answer to my problems. I've built a really great life for myself. I'm healthy. I'm renovating Dad's house. I fell in love. I'm even working on a book I plan on publishing one day. I'm truly happy."

She scoffs. "Your depression is cured, just like that?"

"No, depression can't be cured. It still creeps in sometimes, but it doesn't mean that I can't also laugh, and have fun, and love my life." I pause. "I guess I just hoped that my mother would want to be a part of it."

"What's the point?" She rummages through her purse and sets her wallet on the table. "Your life is great, and so is mine. We don't need each other."

And just like that, our conversation is over.

"You know what? You're right. I don't need you." I shake my head with a bitter laugh. "I can't believe I let myself think you would've been capable of change."

Mom's eyes dart around the restaurant as the volume of my voice goes up. "Phoenix, don't make a scene."

Of course that's what she's worried about.

I try to bite my tongue, but one last comment slips out, and it's the sharpest dagger I can find. "Dad was too good for you. I'm glad he's not here to see what you've done to your children."

I spin around and walk back to James. "Let's go." I toss several twenties onto the table and grab my coat. "I can't stand to be here with her for one second longer."

James

"Just give me a minute."

I stand as I swing my jacket around and slip my arms into the sleeves.

Phoenix shakes her head. "Don't, James. It's not worth it."

I tip her chin, forcing her to look into my eyes and hear my words. "You are *always* worth it."

217

I stalk over to Phoenix's mother, my insides twisted into a knot after how she just spoke to her own daughter.

To *my* girlfriend.

Phoenix's mother lifts her cold eyes to mine when I pull out the chair at her table and plop down into it.

"I just wanted to have the privilege of looking into your eyes when I tell you this: Your daughter is the most wonderful human I've ever met. She's smart, caring, and loving. She's so strong and courageous. I'm sorry that I couldn't meet her father. I know he's the one who had a hand in how Phoenix turned out, because it sure-as-shit isn't you."

Phoenix's mother places her hand on her chest, acting like I offended her. "Excuse me, I will not—"

"Don't interrupt me." I hold up my index finger. "I wasn't done speaking yet."

She clamps her mouth shut.

"I convinced your daughter to reach out to you. I told her that a relationship with her mother was worth fighting for, but that was my mistake. I missed out on a relationship with my mother because she passed away too soon, and I was trying to prevent Phoenix from going through the same thing. But I didn't realize that she wasn't dealing with the same kind of mother I had.

"A mother is supposed to love her children unconditionally. She's supposed to support them in the best of times and help them through the worst of times. You abandoned her when she needed you most, and I'll never be able to fathom what kind of a mother does that. The only good thing you did was call for an ambulance when you found her on the bathroom floor. You are the reason she's alive today, and for that, I thank you from the bottom of my heart.

"But you are missing out on her, on all that she is, because you're too stubborn and set in your ignorance to see that. And it's such a goddamn shame to watch you wreck the relationship with the only person who would stand beside your deathbed and hold your hand." I push back my chair as I stand, scraping the legs along the floor. "You're going to have a very lonely life, and you're the only one to blame for that. My girl deserves so much better than you, and I'm going to spend the rest of my life giving her all the love you never did."

I turn around and return to Phoenix, taking her hand in mine. "Now we can go."

Phoenix is quiet the whole ride home. She hasn't cried, and she hasn't looked at me since we left the diner. I give her time to sit with everything that transpired today, but when we get home, I start to worry that I upset her.

I stop on her porch and turn to face her. "Are you mad at me?"

Her eyebrows press together. "At *you*? Why would I be mad at you?"

"I don't know. Maybe I crossed a line speaking to your mother that way."

She shakes her head and wraps her arms around the back of my neck. "No, James. I'm not mad at you. No one has ever stuck up for me like that before. I actually loved what you said to her."

I lower my lips to hers. "You did?"

"I did. Especially the part where you said you were going to spend the rest of your life giving me all the love she never did." She swallows. "That part was my favorite."

"I meant every word." I lift her into my arms, and she wraps her legs around my waist. "You'll never question your worth with me."

She kisses me, urgent and passionate, gripping the back of my head, and sweeping her tongue against mine. "I need you right now, James."

"I've got you, baby."

And I know what she needs, because I need it too.

I take the stairs by twos with Phoenix in my arms, and when we get to her bedroom, I strip off her clothes and toss them onto the floor behind me.

"Get on the bed and let me look at you."

She crawls onto the bed and props herself up on her hands and knees, her hips swaying and taunting me as she glances at me over her shoulder. "Like this?"

"Exactly like that." I smooth my palm over her ass and give it a loud smack before kissing away the sting. Then I lie down underneath her, with her knees on either side of my head. "Now lower yourself and put this pretty pussy in my mouth."

Phoenix does as I command, and I lap up her arousal, humming in approval. "Lower."

Her legs widen, and she sits on my face. I grip her ass cheeks in each hand and spread them, trailing my tongue along her seam and circling around her tight hole before trailing back around to her clit.

Her hips rock in rhythm with my tongue as her loud, unrestrained moans fill the room. She reaches back and grips a fistful of my hair to hold me still as she fucks my face.

"That's my girl," I murmur against her skin. "Take what you need from me."

Phoenix rides me until I think she's ready to come, and then she surprises me by leaning forward and sucking my dick into her mouth. The feeling of her warm tongue wrapped around me while tasting her at the same time is absolute ecstasy.

But just as the pleasure mounts, she releases my dick with a pop. "I need you inside me, James." She locks her eyes on mine. "And don't be gentle."

I roll on a condom as quick as I can and slam into her from behind. I grip her hair in my fist and shove her into the mattress as I drive into her over and over again. She cries out, calling for *more*, and *harder*, and *deeper*. I give her everything I've got—everything she needs.

The more I think about the fact that no one has fucked her like this, that no other man has been able to give her the pleasure she deserves, the more of a Neanderthal I become with every thrust.

Mine.

Mine.

Mine.

I will do everything in my power to protect her, to never let her feel an ounce of pain ever again.

She's mine, and I am hers.

Nothing will change that, and nothing will take her from me—whatever may come.

.

23

Phoenix

Daily Affirmation: "I belong here on this earth."

"I owe you an apology."

I sandwich the phone between my ear and my shoulder and switch Wilbur's leash to my other hand. "No, Drew. You don't owe me anything."

"Just let me say this, okay?"

"Okay."

He exhales a long breath. "I shouldn't have told you that I wanted to be with you. I think I panicked when you started seeing James because for the past two years, it's been me and you. We were both fucked up when we got to Clearview, and we were going to get out and take on the world together. Partners in crime. But then your life started to take shape while I'm stuck in here, and it felt like I was losing you. It made me think about what my life will be like when I get out of here, and I got scared. But I know there's nothing romantic between us, and I'm sorry for making you think that I was hiding these feelings all this time. I just don't want to lose you. As my friend, and nothing more."

"Drew, you will never lose me. Ever. Whether I'm single or have a boyfriend, or even if I get married someday. We will always be friends. I will never abandon you."

"I have one more confession to make."

I arch a brow. "Oh?"

"I think I'm gay. Or bisexual. I don't know. I've never let myself entertain that possibility because my parents would disown me." He laughs. "But now that they already have disowned me, I guess I can be whoever I want to be."

"You absolutely can be whoever you want to be, whether or not your parents approve." I smile. "Thanks for sharing that with me."

"Speaking of parents: Have you heard anything since James told off your mother?"

"Nope. And I don't think I will." I jog up the porch steps and twist my key in the door. "She's just not capable of being what I need her to be."

"Well, it's her loss. I'm glad James was there to give her a piece of his mind, because I have a thing or two I'd like to say to her."

I laugh. "It's not worth it, honestly. I don't want someone like her to be a part of my life. I'm letting it all go. I have my relationship with Tyler, and that's all I care about."

"I'm proud of you, Nix. You've really done the work and grown and healed from all your shit. You give me hope."

"You will grow and heal too, Drew. You can do this. There's a light at the end of the tunnel."

Wilbur starts barking as soon as I set down my keys on the entryway table.

"Damn, that dog is loud."

He runs into the hallway, barks, and runs back to me.

I laugh. "He sees the birds out the window. They're the only things he barks at."

"Okay, well, you have fun with that. I'm gonna go. It's time for dinner."

"Talk to you tomorrow."

Wilbur continues barking.

"All right, all right. Calm down, dude." I bend over to rub his favorite spot behind his ears. "You can't be friends with them. Birds and dogs don't mix well."

My phone buzzes with an alert from one of the Ring cameras.

Indoor motion detected.

I glance down at Wilbur again. The hair on his back stands on end, and his tail sticks out behind him in a rigid line.

Shit, did a bird fly in here?

"What do you see, Wilbur? What's wrong?"

He barks again, directing his attention toward the hallway.

I shoot out a text to James and let him know I'll be needing his assistance when he gets out of work if there's a bird in the house.

"Come on, boy. Let's go see what you're barking about."

I walk down the hall and glance around the kitchen. Then I spin around to head into the living room.

My feet falter.

My mouth goes dry.

Adrenaline spikes in my veins.

A pair of blue eyes are staring back at me in the middle of my living room.

It's not a bird.

Wilbur stands in front of me, barking at the stranger.

"Shh." I lean forward slowly, showing the intruder that I'm only moving to soothe my dog. "It's okay, Wilbur." I push him until he's behind me. Protected.

"W-who are you?" I hold up my hands on either side of my head, staring down the barrel of the gun being pointed at me.

"I'm the guy who's going to kill your boyfriend."

My stomach roils.

Why would someone want to kill James?

He moves around the coffee table and steps closer to me. He can't be more than fifteen or sixteen years old.

He's just a boy.

My hands shake, and my lips tremble. "Are you Cory? The one who lost his friend?"

"I didn't *lose* my friend. My friend was taken from me." He stabs the air with his gun. "Your boyfriend killed him."

"He didn't mean to." My voice comes out as a broken whisper. "He was just trying to help."

Cory chokes out a bitter laugh. "Cops always mean to kill people. They love getting to show off their power and shoot their guns." He waves his gun in front of my face. "Well, I've got a gun now too."

A tear slips down my cheek. "That's not going to bring your friend back. You know that."

"I'm not trying to get my friend back. I'm not stupid. I know he's dead." He sucks in a breath through his nose and puffs out his chest. "I'm getting justice."

"This is revenge, not justice."

"Shut the fuck up, bitch!"

I flinch, and Wilbur barks.

"Shut your dog up too, or I will."

"No, please. He's only barking because he's scared." I bend down and scoop Wilbur into my arms. "It's okay, boy. It's okay."

"You're going to call your boyfriend and tell him to come over here." Cory takes another step closer, and Wilbur lets out a low growl. "But you're not going to tell him that I'm here. You're going to act like everything is perfectly fine."

I can't lure James here. Not without telling him about Cory, and not without protection and backup.

Think, think, think.

"He's at work right now. He never answers when I call him at work."

Cory clenches his jaw. "I said *call him.*"

"He'll know something is wrong if I do. Cory, please don't do this. You're going to ruin your life if you kill someone."

"Don't act like you give a shit about my life."

"I do." Another tear falls. "I used to be like you, Cory. My father died, and my mother was pretty rotten to me. I was depressed all the time, and I couldn't take it anymore. I was angry and in pain all the time. But instead of wanting to hurt someone else, like you, I wanted to hurt myself. So, I tried to kill myself."

Cory snorts. "Obviously you didn't succeed."

"I almost did. But I got a second chance. I was able to start fresh, and I got help. You can get help too. You don't have to feel like this all the time. You don't have to hurt other people just because you're hurting."

Cory presses the gun against my forehead. "Your psychobabble isn't going to work on me. You're acting like you want to help me because I'm pointing a gun at you."

I hold Wilbur tight to my chest as he whimpers and squirms to get out of my grip. "I do care, Cory. I care because I know what it's like to feel hopeless. I know what it's like to get a do-over. This can be *your* do-over. Put the gun down and walk away. I won't tell James anything. I'll even help you. You can turn your life around. You don't have to do this. This isn't the only path for you. I know it feels that way, but it's not."

His bloodshot eyes bounce between mine.

Come on, Cory. Put down the gun and walk away.

But then the front door opens, and all hell breaks loose.

"Honey, I'm home."

"James, run!" I try to warn him before Cory grabs me by my neck and pulls me in front of him. The cold metal of the gun digs into my temple.

James comes into view, and his shoes squeak on the floor as he comes to a stop. The color drains from his face, and the bouquet of roses he's holding drops to his feet. "Cory?"

Cory's grip on me tightens. "Make a move, and she's dead."

I blink through my watery vision as the tears stream down my face. "It's okay, James. It's gonna be okay. Just listen to what he says."

James's eyes narrow. "Let her go. Take me instead."

"Aww, what a good guy. So selfless." Cory chuckles. "I think I'll kill her first, and make you watch. Just like you made me watch my best friend die."

"I didn't want your friend to die." James holds up his palm in front of him. "That wasn't supposed to happen. I was trying to convince him to put his gun down. I even put mine down if you remember. Just like I'm going to do right now: Put your gun down. We can fix this. Damon didn't let me try to fix it last time. But you can."

I can feel Cory's body shaking against mine as his voice cracks. "He didn't need to die. You should've done something."

"I tried, Cory. I tried. You saw me try. All I wanted was to get the gun out of his hands so we could work out a plan together." James's eyes well. "Let her go and we can figure this out together. Please, Cory. I can help you. Just let her go. She's innocent in this."

Cory steps back and shoves me in front of him. "Go." Then he points his gun at James. "But you're staying."

James yanks my arm and pulls me behind him. "Go, Phoenix. Go now."

"I can't leave you," I whisper.

"You have to. I mean it. Get out of here."

I let out a helpless growl and run to the front door. I swing it open, set Wilbur down on the porch, and tie his leash to the railing.

I pull my phone out of my back pocket and send a frantic text to Leo:

Me: Call 911. Cory is here with a gun. No lights or sirens.
Me: James is with us.

Then I step back inside my house and slam the door shut.

Like hell I'm leaving.

James

Thank God she's out of here.

I don't care what happens from this moment forward as long as she's safe.

"Unclip your gun," Cory says. "Do it slowly."

I move my hand to my holster and do as he says, placing my gun on the end table next to me. At least it's close by.

"If you really want to help me, then give me money." Cory sniffles. "Ten thousand."

"What do you need the money for? So you can snort yourself into an overdose by the end of the weekend? What good is that going to do for you?"

"It's none of your business what I do with the money. I'm the one holding the gun, so you're gonna do whatever I say."

He's becoming more agitated by the minute, and if I push him too far then he'll snap and do something impulsive. I need to keep him talking until Phoenix calls for backup, which I know is the first thing she'll do.

"I don't have ten thousand dollars in my back pocket, Cory. I'll have to get it from the bank, and right now the bank is closed."

Cory paces, keeping his gun pointed at me.

"What's your plan? Let's work this out together."

"I don't know, I don't know, I don't know!"

I catch movement out of the corner of my eye, and when I shoot a quick glance to the right, I almost let out an audible groan as dread rolls over me.

Is she fucking kidding me?

Phoenix is crouched behind the wall in the hallway when she's supposed to be far away from here.

I return my attention to Cory. "Come on. Remember our talk at the skate park? You said you wanted to pursue art. I saw those sketches you left my girlfriend. That was you, wasn't it?"

Cory nods.

"This isn't you, Cory. You're strung out right now but once you get clean, you can start a whole new life. You can turn your art into something great."

"Enough!" He squeezes his eyes shut and shakes the gun at me. "You're lying. It's just like Damon said the night he died: You just want me to put down my gun so you can arrest me. I won't have a future after this. It's too late now."

"It's not too late. As long as you don't pull that trigger, it's not too late."

"You have to die."

"No!" Phoenix jumps out from behind the wall and dives in front of me, shoving my gun into my hand.

The sound of a gunshot blasts through the air, but it misses me. I fall onto my back as I aim for Cory's arm, and shoot.

He drops his gun, and I scramble to snatch it away from him.

"James."

My head jerks up at the sound of Phoenix's voice.

I rush over to her, lying on the floor in a growing puddle of blood. "Fuck, baby. You're shot."

"I couldn't leave you." She glances down at her arm, and her eyes go wide.

I search for the bullet wound and spot it on her left arm below her shoulder. "It's gonna be all right. I've gotta get you to the hospital."

Leo, Dad, and Phil burst through the front door, their eyes roaming over the bloody scene in front of them. Phil rushes over to Cory while Dad calls for an ambulance.

Leo drops to his knees beside me. "What the fuck happened?"

"We have to get her out of here now." I lock eyes with my brother. "I need you."

I rip off my shirt, the buttons flying and scattering around us. I tie it in a knot around Phoenix's arm, and she cries out.

"It has to be tight, sweetheart. I'm so sorry." I scoop her up into my arms and jerk my chin toward the door. "Leo, you're going to stay with her in the back seat. Keep her awake and keep pressure on her arm."

Leo jogs out ahead of me and swings open my car door. "You sure you don't want me to drive? This way you can stay with her."

"No."

I'll get us to the hospital in time.

I have to.

"Come on, Nixie. Keep those eyes open." Leo cradles Phoenix's lifeless body in the back seat. "Fuck, she's losing a lot of blood."

I glance in the rearview mirror. "Leo, keep her awake."

"I'm trying."

The light up ahead turns red, but I floor it and speed through the intersection. I'm being reckless but all I can focus on is getting to the hospital as fast as I can.

I didn't make it in time for Mom. I'm sure as fuck not going to let that happen again.

"James." The desperation in Leo's voice terrifies me.

"Keep pressure on her arm. We'll be there in another minute. Phoenix, baby, I need you to hold on just a little bit longer."

I blow through another light and speed around the cars clogging up the lane.

When we finally get to the hospital, my tires barely screech to a stop before I'm out of the car.

I take Phoenix from Leo, both of them covered in blood. "We're here, baby. We made it. Everything's gonna be okay."

It has to be.

24

Phoenix

Daily Affirmation: "I have gratitude for every experience I have encountered."

Two years ago, I woke up in the hospital...

The lights above seared my eyes. My body felt heavy and I didn't have the strength to lift my arms or my legs. Muffled voices surrounded me. I couldn't make out what they were saying, or who they even were. It felt as if I was underwater, weighed down by a sandbag.

Then a shadow fell over me, blocking the blinding lights. I blinked to clear my vision, but it was too blurry to see anything. I forced my body to move, attempting to sit up, but everything spun and my stomach roiled. Then a deep, throbbing pain surged through my left forearm, and that's when I remembered.

I remembered it all.

My mother's unmistakable shrill voice cut through the fog. "Phoenix, are you awake? Can you hear me?"

"Stop shouting, Mom. You're going to scare her."

My heart ached at the soothing sound of my brother's voice.

I lifted my hand, reaching out for him. Hot tears stung my eyes as I croaked out his name.

"I'm here," he said. Warmth engulfed my hand. "She's cold. Get her another blanket."

I swallowed past the dry lump in my throat. "I'm sorry."

"Shh. Everything's going to be okay."

As my vision came into focus, I noted the firm line of Mom's mouth. The clench of her jaw, the crease between her brows. It's an expression I'd seen countless times—an expression I'd induced.

She was mad.

Deep down, I knew she would be. Mad at what I did, or mad that she couldn't fix me. Or maybe she was just mad that I'd survived. Like she was disappointed that I couldn't even successfully kill myself.

It was too much—the harshness of waking up, the pain, the guilt, and the tidal wave of grief. So, I closed my eyes and pretended to fall back asleep despite the questions swirling through my head.

I hadn't planned for it. I don't think anyone does. You're not supposed to witness the aftermath of your suicide.

I snuck a peek at my brother as he guided my mom to a nearby chair. He showed her his phone. "Look. This place looks nice."

"Do you really think a place like that is going to help? She's lived in a wonderful house with a wonderful family all her life, and none of that mattered."

She wasn't wrong. With a normal life like mine, why would anyone want to die? I've never been able to understand it. Depression is a crazy, traitorous disease. It tricks you into thinking things that aren't true.

Tyler pinched the bridge of his nose. "We're not psychiatric professionals. We couldn't give her the kind of help she needed, despite how wonderful her life was. These people can help her."

Mom's voice got louder as she stabbed the air with her index finger. "I'm not sending her to some mental institution. She's not crazy. She's just ungrateful. She doesn't know how good she has it. Do they have a pill to fix that?"

Tyler's eyes widened. "Do you hear yourself right now? Your daughter tried to take her own life, and you're not going to try to help her get better?"

"If your sister is hell-bent on dying, then nothing and no one is going to stop her."

That was Mom. If she couldn't control something, then she discarded it like trash. It had no place in her world.

Tyler's head jerked back. "Well, we have to try."

"There's no we, Ty. Your father's gone, and you live a hundred miles away."

"Oh, so this is my fault? I'm not allowed to have a life of my own?"

"That's not what I'm saying." She waved a dismissive hand. "But when you leave, I'm the one who's left here to deal with her. And I won't let her ruin my life the way she's choosing to ruin hers."

"She didn't choose this, Mom. Didn't you hear what the doctor said?"

I wanted to tell Tyler it was hopeless. Talking to Mom about depression is like telling her there are aliens on Mars. If she doesn't believe in it, then there's no possibility for it to exist.

"I've been through enough with that girl. Your sister can't be saved, and you need to accept that."

"Look, I know you're upset right now, but—"

"No." Mom shook her head. "If Phoenix wants to be dead, then she will be. She'll be dead to me."

But today, waking up in the hospital again after two years? It's much different.

Same sterile smell. Same sound of beeping machines. Same pain in the same arm.

Though instead of feeling scared and alone, I feel safe and loved.

James, Leo, and Jim sit around my bed in their respective chairs.

Leo's reading a romance novel.

Jim is asleep with Wilbur on his lap—perks of being in the hospital with a police officer.

And James is watching me from under heavy, tired lids, gripping my hand like he'll float away if he isn't tethered to me. Those beautiful eyes pierce my heart and see into my soul.

A smile creeps onto my face. "Hi, handsome."

"Hi, beautiful. How do you feel?"

"I've been through worse."

He stands and nudges my leg. "Scoot over."

"You're too big. You can't fit in here."

He smirks. "Yeah, I've heard that before, but we made it work."

Leo makes a gagging sound, and Jim plugs his ears with his index fingers.

I laugh and Wilbur's ears perk up. He dives from Jim's lap onto the bed, but James intercepts him.

"Easy, boy. Easy. Mommy is hurt." He puts him gently in my lap, shielding my wounded arm as Wilbur stands on his hind legs to lick my face.

"You were such a good guard dog," I tell him. "Wilbur knew someone was in the house before the Ring alert went off on my phone." I glance at the Russo men sitting around me. "What happened to Cory?"

Jim jerks his thumb toward the door. "They just got done patching him up in the ER."

"Now what?"

"Now, he'll serve time for possession of an unlicensed weapon and attempted murder."

I cover my mouth with my good hand. "He needs help. He's just a lost soul."

James's jaw tics. "He almost killed you."

"But he didn't, so now he's getting a chance to make things right."

Jim's eyebrows rise. "Are you saying you don't want to press charges?"

"I just want him to get the help he needs. If he gets clean and goes to a mental health facility, maybe he can still have a bright future."

James strokes my cheek with the back of his hand. "We'll talk about it another time. Right now, he needs to pay for what he did—on drugs or not."

I glance over at Leo, who's unusually quiet. "Hey, little bro. Whatcha reading over there?"

"This reverse harem you gave me has me all kinds of messed up. How can they share her and not get jealous of one another?"

I see through his joke and reach my hand out for him. "You okay?"

He gestures to his shirt as he comes to stand by my bed. "I never want to wear this much of your blood ever again, Nixie."

"Thank you for being there with me. I know I was in and out of consciousness, and I know you were scared, but I knew you had me, and I knew I was safe."

His dark eyes glisten. "I thought I was going to lose you."

I shake my head. "Never."

He lifts my hand to his lips and presses a kiss to my knuckles. "Love you, sis."

"Love you more."

Jim rises and his sons back away from the bed as he leans down and drops a kiss to the top of my head. "Thank you for what you did. I'll never forget it."

My bottom lip trembles and emotion clogs my throat, making it impossible to say anything in return.

Jim and Leo take Wilbur home, and James wedges his big body onto the hospital bed with me. I rest my head on his chest, inhaling a lungful of his familiar scent as we lie together in the quiet room.

His voice is low and deep when he speaks. "You jumped in front of me and literally took a bullet for me. I never want you to do that again."

"I'd do it a hundred times over if it meant you were okay."

He lets out a slow exhale. "I'm supposed to protect *you*."

"You protect everyone else. I've got your six, remember?"

He grunts. "Still, you can't go doing that. I can't lose you."

"You saved me right back. You got me to the hospital in time." I press my lips to his neck. "Ripping off your shirt and making a tourniquet out of it, all sexy and shit."

He barks out a laugh. "You were half-conscious. What do you know about me ripping off my shirt?"

"When you're this sexy, a woman would rise from the grave to witness something like that." I lift my head. "Oh, maybe we got it on camera. Check the Ring for the video."

James's eyes squeeze shut as he laughs. "What am I going to do with you?"

I snuggle into him, careful not to put pressure on my arm. "Just love me. Because I love you with my whole heart, and I will always take a bullet for you."

"Okay, well, let's hope that never happens again." He tips my chin and presses his lips to mine. "I love you, beautiful. More than anything in this world, with all of my heart and soul, I love you."

"You realize this was the third break-in in the past year. I think I should be in the Guinness Book of World Records."

"Save your twisted humor for Leo."

"Too soon?"

"Definitely too soon."

"Fine."

I stare up at the beige siding along the front of my house.

Home, sweet home.

After needing surgery on my arm to repair the damage from the bullet and spending the last few days in the hospital, I'm ready to get back to my normal life. I blow out a contented sigh and lean my head back against the headrest in James's car.

"Dad, Leo, and I cleaned up the mess in the living room." James squeezes my hand. "Are you nervous about going inside after what happened?"

I shake my head. "I just want to take a minute to appreciate everything. This house. My father for leaving it to me. You and your wonderful family."

"There's a lot to be grateful for when you stop and think about it."

"I want to keep doing that—stopping to be in the moment and appreciate everything I have. I never used to do that before."

James hums as we stare up at our houses.

Just a few months ago, I was scared to walk into this house. Now, it's the only place I want to be.

"All right. I'm ready."

James helps me out of the car, and I adjust my sling as I walk toward the house. Wilbur barks from inside the second my feet hit the porch, and he bounds out the door when James unlocks it.

I pat his head as I step inside. "I know, I know. I missed you too, bud."

James takes my hand and leads me down the hallway.

"Hey, what's the rush? What are you—"

"Welcome home!" Jim, Leo, Phil, and Sadie clap as my eyes bounce to each familiar face. A *Welcome Home, Phoenix* banner hangs over the mantel.

But my tears don't well until I spot one more person standing in the corner.

"Tyler. What are you doing here?"

My brother smiles and comes to stand in front of me. "I got a phone call from James, and he said you were hurt and needed surgery. I'm sorry I couldn't make it sooner."

I squeeze him with my good arm as tight as I can. "Ow. This hurts, but I don't care because I'm so happy to see you."

Tyler chuckles as he wraps his arms around me. "Gabby sends her love. We'll bring Jenna over the summer when she's a little older."

I pull back and look up at him. "How long are you in for?"

"The weekend. Just enough time to get to know your new boyfriend."

I flick my eyes over to James, who's watching us with those intense eyes of his. "He's pretty fantastic." I wave Leo over. "And so is this one."

Leo presses a kiss to the top of my head. "Welcome home, sis."

Tyler tilts his head in question, and I bite back a smile.

We all spend the afternoon together. Sadie tells us about the updates she's made at the shelter since my donation. Tyler shows us adorable videos of Jenna. And Phil cracks us up with his funniest police stories.

While we're all together, happy and healthy, my mind wanders to Cory. I can't help but wonder how he's doing right now and if he'll be okay.

Later on, after everyone says good night and Tyler is settled in his old room down the hall, I lie on James's chest. In the dim light of the moon streaking through the window, I listen to the rhythm of his heartbeat, strong and steady.

"You know how people say their lives flash before their eyes when they're about to die?"

He hums and turns to face me.

"I didn't see my dad, or my mom, or Tyler. No familiar memories from my childhood. No bright light." I touch my fingers to James's cheek, sliding along his cheekbone, tracing the edge of his jaw, and outlining his lips. "I saw you."

"You did?"

I smile at the surprise in his voice. "I saw you and our future. I saw all the things I want for us. And I thought what a shame it would be if we didn't get to have it. For the first time in my life, I didn't *want* to die. I didn't want to give up. I felt regret, like there were all these things I haven't had a chance to experience yet, and I wasn't ready to leave." I inhale a shaky breath. "I held on to you through the darkness, and you brought me back, just like you said you would."

"That was all you. Your strength and the fight inside you. It's been in there all along." He wraps his strong arms around me. "You were a phoenix long before you were *my* phoenix."

"Maybe that's true. Or maybe we can't become all we're meant to be until we meet the person who brings it out in us."

"And we can't meet those people if we're not here." James cradles my face as his words pierce my heart. "Look at the people you were surrounded by today. Look at who you've affected just by knowing them. My brother might not be here if it weren't for your friendship, helping him and pushing him—pushing me to support him in ways I didn't know how. Look at the things Sadie was able to do with the shelter because of your generosity, not to mention all the people's lives you brightened by hosting that adoption event. You took a bullet for me and spared my father from burying his son. You're the reason your brother is dealing with his childhood trauma from your mother, which will make him become a better father for Jenna. Look at how happy you've made me. Look at it all, Phoenix." A tear slides down his cheek and drops onto the pillow. "You couldn't have done any of those things if you weren't here, on this earth."

I see it now, but I know I couldn't have seen it then. I was too sick. My perception was too skewed. And that's all it comes down to—perception.

My mind won't settle, thoughts racing long after James falls asleep. Around midnight, I slip out of bed and tiptoe into the spare bedroom where my journal sits atop a folding table. I'll be turning this room into my writing space come spring.

My pen moves across the paper as I write as fast as I can:

You look at things the way your brain presents them to you, and it's not the way life actually is. That's the reason so many of us don't make it. It's impossible to overcome when you don't have the proper help.

Life isn't always sunshine and rainbows and cuddly puppies. Those things do exist, but in a dark tunnel when all you can see are dark clouds, pain, and despair, it makes life seem hopeless. We need to hold on to hope, hold on to the possibility that things can get better. We need to take hold of the power we possess and take control of the demons wreaking havoc in our brains.

Talk to someone.

Get help.

Stop making ourselves the victims in our own lives, and start being the warriors we are.

Depression will always be there, lurking and waiting for the right moment to rear its ugly head. Instead of hating myself for it and trying to hide it, I've made the darkness a part of me. It's not a flaw or something I need to be ashamed of. It just is, the way my hair is brown and my laugh is loud. It's who I am and what makes me the person I am today.

But it no longer consumes me.

I lose track of time as I write until James creeps into the room and watches me from the doorway.

"I love watching you when you're inspired."

I smile and close the book with the pen inside. "I had to get that out before I fell asleep."

"You ready to come back to bed?"

"I'm ready." I walk over to him and drape my arms around his neck as he swoops me into his arms. "Bring me back, James."

"I always will."

Epilogue

One Year Later

James

"All right. Dig in, everyone."

The corners of my mouth curve up as I watch Phoenix proudly set down the tray of sausage and peppers that she cooked for today's BBQ.

Wilbur sits at her feet, tail thumping hard against the deck as drool drips from his mouth.

"You did this to him, you know." Phoenix points the serving spoon at Leo. "I know you're the one who's been sneaking him table food."

Leo snatches the spoon out of her hand, feigning offense. "I have done no such thing." He scoops a heaping spoonful of sausage and peppers onto his plate. "But you're welcome, because he's a big, bad pit bull now."

I lean forward and smack the back of his head. "Guests get served first, idiot."

He gapes at me. "This isn't my house. I *am* a guest."

Tyler peers into the tray of sausage before glancing up at his sister. "You cooked this, and you didn't set the house on fire?"

My eyebrows shoot up as I turn my attention to Phoenix. "You told me you didn't set fires in the kitchen."

Phoenix's eyes widen. "It was one time, and I was twelve years old."

"Dad had to call the fire department."

"He shouldn't have let me cook on my own."

Tyler's shoulders shake as he laughs.

Phoenix snatches Jenna from his arms. "You're the only one who has my back here, kid."

Jenna babbles like she agrees with her aunt.

"You know I have your back." I lean over and tickle Jenna's tummy. "I just didn't realize I needed to keep a fire extinguisher handy."

"I was twelve!"

Jenna lets out a loud giggle, and everyone sitting around the table laughs.

"At least your man cooks." Gabby pats Tyler's hand. "Where can I get me one of those?"

Leo spreads out his arms wide on either side of his body, talking around a boulder of food in his cheek. "Right here, baby. I'm the younger version with more stamina and a bigger—"

"Mouth," Dad finishes, cutting him off. "A much bigger mouth."

Leo winks at Gabby. "You know what I'm talking about."

Phoenix smiles wide, looking around at our friends and family, and my heart swells. I'll never grow tired of seeing her happy.

Drew clears his throat from across the table and slides back his chair as he stands. "I'd like to raise a toast to Nix."

We all lift our drinks.

"Not only are you the best friend, sister, and girlfriend we know, but as of last week, you're officially the best author we know."

Dad blows a whistle through his teeth, and Phoenix's cheeks tinge with a pretty pink color.

"We're so proud of all you've accomplished, and we can't wait to see what's in store in your future." He lifts his Solo cup higher. "To you, you badass."

We cheer in accord and tip back our drinks.

Phoenix hugs Jenna close and rests her head on my shoulder. "Thank you for all your support. I don't know where I'd be without each of you helping me along the way."

I press a kiss to the top of her head. "You'd be exactly where you are right now because you are strong, and you can do anything you put your mind to."

She tilts her head up and brings her lips to mine. "I love you."

"I love you, beautiful."

Phil wipes the corner of his mouth with his napkin. "Nix, have you seen Cory at all lately?"

She nods, her smile diminishing like it always does when she thinks about Cory. "I visited him last week."

"How's he doing?" Dad asks.

"He's making progress since they got his meds regulated." She looks at Drew. "He's lonely there though. You know how it was in the beginning."

"He has you, Nixie." Leo rubs her back in small circles. "He'll be okay."

Tyler shakes his head. "I still don't understand why you didn't press charges. The kid almost killed you. He would've killed James if you didn't—"

"Drop it, Ty." Gabby holds up her hand. "We've been over this so many times. Phoenix doesn't have to explain herself again. She wants to help him instead of putting him through the system, and I agree with her. It'll give him a better chance at rehabilitation. Putting him in juvie wouldn't help his mental health."

Phoenix flashes her sister-in-law a grateful smile. "Everyone deserves a second chance, and I'm going to do everything I can to try to help him."

Tyler and Phil exchange a glance, but I shake my head at them. *Not here.*

My first instinct as a cop is to put someone like Cory behind bars. But after listening to how Phoenix feels and realizing that Leo could've ended up in the same situation had he not given up drugs, I had to try something different. Clearview helped Phoenix, as well as Drew and many others struggling. Cory deserved a chance too.

Phoenix perks up again. "What about you, little bro? How has your EMT course been going? I feel like I barely see you without your nose in a book anymore."

"It's going great. There's a hot chick in my class." He waggles his eyebrows. "She's totally into me, of course."

Dad grimaces. "It's a miracle you haven't gotten anyone pregnant."

"I'm safe, Dad. I use protection. You taught me how, remember?"

"I try to forget that time in my life. You were so inquisitive."

Sadie presses her palm to her cheek. "I'm dreading that part of parenting."

"Now, being a grandparent, on the other hand…" Dad swings his gaze in my direction, eyes bouncing between me and Phoenix. "That I'm looking forward to."

Phoenix chokes on her water, and Leo slaps her back.

I pinch the bridge of my nose. "Dad, we told you, we're not having kids. You can cut the guilt trip."

"Don't worry." Leo puffs out his chest. "I want at least five kids, so I'll make up for all the kids James doesn't have and carry on the Russo name."

Dad looks up to the sky. "God help us all."

As if she understood the entire conversation, Jenna lurches off Phoenix's lap and dive-bombs into my arms.

I chuckle and scoop her up. "You want to come to your uncle James, don't you, baby girl?" I stand with her and walk over to the edge of the deck, letting everyone enjoy their meals.

I press my lips against her soft, wispy hair and breathe in deep as I gaze out at the calm lagoon. It's incredible how much different life is now than it was last year.

"You know, Jenna, there's something you should know about life: Things always change, even when you don't realize it's happening. There's no way to predict the future, what will come, good or bad. But everything ends up right where you're supposed to be. So, when things seem bad, just have faith that they will turn around, because they will."

My restless soul is content now that it has found its counterpart. Everything's better with Phoenix.

Jenna opens her mouth and slobbers all over my cheek—her favorite game where she tries to bite me with her two tiny shark teeth, and I pretend it hurts as I howl in pain. Kid thinks it's hilarious.

Phoenix hums, sidling alongside us. "Why is it such a turn-on seeing men hold babies?"

"Men?" I arch a brow.

"*My* man." She slides her hand up my arm, squeezing my bicep. "Want to sneak inside and make some babies—minus the babies?"

I glance at the table.

"Everyone's busy eating," she whispers. "They won't even notice we're gone."

I grunt. "Leo will."

"Let him hold Jenna. He loves it."

True. Leo thinks he's the favorite uncle.

He's not.

I hold out Jenna in front of me. "Sorry, kid. I've gotta leave you with your second-favorite uncle."

Phoenix disappears inside the house, and I drop Jenna off with Leo.

He chuckles to himself, knowing damn well where we're going.

I get to the bedroom—*our* bedroom, since I moved in—and pull Phoenix close.

Her hands disappear underneath the hem of my shirt, sliding up my stomach to settle on my chest. "What were you saying to Jenna out there on the deck?"

I skate my lips over her neck. "I was telling her about life."

She lets out a soft giggle. "The meaning of life to a one-year-old?"

I bite her shoulder and drop the strap of her dress. "Not the meaning of life, smart-ass." I continue kissing across her collarbone to the other shoulder and drop that strap too. "I was just letting her know that when things seem bad, there's always a light at the end of the tunnel."

Phoenix peels off my shirt and peppers kisses all over my skin. "You're my light, you know that?"

"You're mine." I tug her dress until it's pooling at her feet and pop the clasp on her strapless bra. "I want to spend the rest of my life with you."

She moans as my fingers glide between her legs.

"I'm going to love you forever." I lick her nipple, swirling around her hardened bud. "I'm going to care for you." I graze my teeth over it before switching to the other. "I'm going to cook for you."

Phoenix hums. "That's my favorite part."

I give her ass a firm smack, and she grins. "You're only with me for the food, huh?"

"And this." She yanks down my shorts and palms my dick through my boxers.

"Food and sex. It's easy to keep you happy." I drop to my knees and drag my tongue over her clit, continuing to speak against her skin. "I'd give everything I have to keep you happy."

She hums, threading her fingers through my hair.

"Through all your ups and downs, and mine. Through the good times and bad."

She moans again, arching her back to give me more of her.

"I'm going to be there for you, loving you, through it all." I toss one of her legs over my shoulder. "We are forever."

She's breathless when she whispers my name. "James?"

"Yes, sweetheart?"

"I've always got your six."

"And I've got yours."

THE END

The National Suicide Prevention Lifeline is now 988
Or text HOME to 741741

Click here for <u>Louie's Legacy Animal Rescue</u> to volunteer or donate

* * *

Thank you for reading!
Keep reading for a sneak peek of my emotional bestseller
What's Left of Me

New to me?
I always recommend starting with *Collision*
Book 1 in *The Collision Series*

Need something funny and light instead?
Check out my bestselling rom-com
Hating the Boss

Want to gain access to FREE books, exclusive news, & giveaways?
Sign up for my monthly newsletter!

Come stalk me:
Facebook
Instagram
TikTok

Want to be part of my warrior crew?
Join Kristen's Warriors
A group where we can discuss my books, books you're reading, & where
friends will remind you what a badass warrior you are.

All of my books are FREE on KU:

Collision (Book 1)
Avoidance (Book 2)
The Other Brother (Book3 – standalone)
Fighting the Odds (Book 4 – standalone)

Bring Me Back

Hating the Boss – RomCom standalone
Back to You – RomCom standalone

Inevitable – Contemporary standalone
What's Left of Me – Contemporary standalone
Someone You Love – Contemporary standalone

Dear Santa – Holiday novella

1

Callie

I'm not getting out of bed today.

This is an amazing mattress. Just the right amount of firm-to-soft ratio. This comforter rocks too. It's puffy but not suffocating. These sheets are a high thread count. Breathable. I did good when I picked these out. I could stay here all day. Don't need to go grocery shopping. Who needs to eat when you have a mattress like this? Laundry? Pffft. I won't need clothes if I stay in bed. This is the perfect solution to all of life's problems.

But what is that awful smell?

A long, wet tongue slides across my cheek, and I groan. "Go back to sleep, Maverick."

With my eyelids still closed, I reach out and smooth my fingers through my retriever's fluffy fur. His tongue makes another pass over my cheek, and again, I'm hit with a blast of that stench.

My nose scrunches as my head jerks up off the pillow. "Maverick, did you eat your poop again?"

His head dips down, and he rests it on top of his front paws.

"Don't give me those eyes! They're not going to work on me this time."

He leaps off the bed and bounds into the hallway, tail swatting from left to right as he waits for me at the top of the stairs.

Guess I'm getting out of bed.

I flip the comforter off my body, swing my legs to the side of the mattress, and jam my feet into my plush white slippers.

Once I'm vertical, my head throbs like someone dropped an anvil on it. I grip the cool iron banister and take my time down the spiral staircase. Maverick waits at the bottom, his body thrashing like a shark from the momentum of his tail.

"You are way too awake for me right now, bud."

He *woofs* in response and prances into the kitchen ahead of me.

When I stagger into the kitchen, sunlight streams through the windows, reflecting off the marble countertop and searing my retinas. I yank the cord on the blinds and bury my face in the crook of my elbow, hissing like Dracula.

Maverick plops down at my feet, nuzzling my ankle with his wet nose. We both jump when we hear the creak of the front door, and then he takes off into the foyer.

Paul strides into the kitchen, saturated in sweat from his morning run, and I hold my breath until his lips curve up into a smile.

"Good morning, gorgeous."

Relief washes over me. "Morning. How was your run?"

Paul snatches a water bottle from the refrigerator and twists off the cap. "Four miles today."

His royal-blue Under Armour T-shirt clings to his broad chest, the muscles in his biceps flexing with his movements. His blond strands are damp and disheveled, and his skin glows with a golden sheen.

I lift an eyebrow. "How is it that you look this sexy after a four-mile run?"

He grins. "How is it that you look this sexy when you just woke up?"

I huff out a sardonic laugh, knowing damn well I resemble the Crypt Keeper at the moment.

Paul leans in with puckered lips, but I make an *X* with my forearms in front of my face. "The poop-eating bandit got me. You might want to stay back."

He looks down at Maverick, and as if he knows we're talking about him, Maverick ducks around the corner of the island.

"You're nasty, dog."

"I'll call the vet today. Maybe they'll know how to deter him from eating his own feces."

Paul leans his hip against the counter. "I think all dogs eat their own crap."

"We have to watch him better when he's out back. Stop it before he can get to it." I walk around the island so I can start on breakfast. "I read something once that said dogs eat their poop when they're lacking vitamins in their diet. Was it an article? Maybe Josie told me. I don't know; I can't remember. Either way—"

I stop moving and snap my fingers in front of Paul's face. "Are you even listening to me?"

Paul shakes his head, his eyes roving over my body. "I haven't heard one word since you stood up in those silky shorts."

I smile and set a frying pan on top of the stove. "Please. This isn't anything you haven't seen before."

"Yet it never gets old." He closes the distance between us and stands behind me, trailing his hands up my arms.

I hum at his light touch, welcoming it. "Let's hope you always think that."

"I know I will." He tilts my head to the side and presses his lips to my neck. One of his hands slips under my camisole, cupping my breast, while he tugs my shorts down with the other.

My head falls back against his shoulder, and a long exhale leaves my parted lips. "Don't you have a meeting?"

"Just means we'll have to be quick." His fingers slide between my thighs and press inside me while his thumb rubs circles on my clit at the same time.

My legs quiver, and I reach forward to grip the edge of the counter. Paul gives my back a gentle push until my chest is pressed against the cool marble, and then he slides his length inside me.

"I love you," he whispers at my ear, gripping my hips, pumping in and out of me in long, controlled strokes.

I arch my back to meet each of his thrusts, and his fingers return to my clit as he drives into me faster, harder, deeper. I moan, writhing against his hand, and his pace quickens.

I can feel the pleasure mounting in my core, the steady build like a rising wave. Soon, it crashes over me. I cry out as the spasms race through my body. Paul goes under too, grunting as his hot liquid fills me.

He holds me there, pressing soft kisses to my shoulder, my neck, my temple. "This is what I've missed. I'm so glad we can finally get back to how things used to be."

"Me too."

And that's my halfhearted truth.

I should relish in this feeling, the closeness, his gentle love, but my mind crawls toward the analytical place it always goes to, calculating the date, the time, the exact location in my cycle. My fingers itch to reach for my phone and click on the fertility app out of habit, but for the first time in three years, I don't.

And after last night, I never will again.

With a pat on my backside, Paul pulls away and tucks himself back into his running shorts. "I'm hitting the shower."

My eyes linger on his wide back and confident swagger as he leaves the room with his head held high, free from the anxious thoughts that plague me.

Guilt squeezes my chest when I think about everything that I've put him through over the past few years. The stress, the doctor's appointments, all my tears.

No more.

Paul's right. We need to get back to the way we used to be. Back before I became obsessed with starting a family. Before I plunged into depression and dragged him down with me. Before the people we were when we got married turned into strangers.

It's time to put it to rest.

And it's up to me to do it.

I can be better.

I can find happiness again.

I straighten my camisole, pull up my shorts, and start gathering the ingredients I need for breakfast.

The kitchen is my favorite room in this entire house. Beautiful marble countertops; tall, white cabinets; stainless steel appliances. Paul had the contractor create it based off of my exact vision. He says it's because he loves me so much. I say it's because he needs me to cook for him because Paul could burn water.

Sometimes it feels like I'm living someone else's life, like this is all a dream. Living in a mansion in Orange County, California, married to the Adonis that is my husband, not having to get up and work nine-to-five every day. I'm very fortunate to have everything I could ever need at my fingertips.

I didn't grow up with all this. I came from an average, middle-class family. But when I met Paul in college, everything changed. We've been together for nine years now, and I'm still not used to this lifestyle. I don't think I ever will be.

As I scoop the egg-white-and-spinach omelet with hash browns into the glass container, Paul struts back into the kitchen, dressed to perfection in his navy suit. I hand him his lunch bag, his breakfast, and his coffee mug.

He presses his lips to the top of my head. "Thanks, gorgeous. I'll see you tonight."

"Have a good day."

"Be good, poop breath," he calls over his shoulder.

Maverick barely lifts his head from where he's sprawled out by the back door, bathing in the sunspot.

The dog life of Riley.

When I hear the click of the front door, a long exhale whooshes out of me. I want to walk upstairs and climb right back into bed, but if I'm going to make things better, I have to start by looking the part. So instead, I drag myself up the stairs and into the bathroom.

It's been a while since I've cared about my appearance. Been a while since I've cared about anything other than becoming a mother.

Fake it 'til you make it, they say.

Flipping on the lights, I shimmy out of my pajama shorts and tear the camisole over my head. I suck in a sharp breath when my eyes land on my reflection in the mirror for the first time this morning. My stomach clenches at the sight of the dark-purple splotches along my left bicep, memories of last night flooding my vision.

Damn you, Maverick. I wanted to stay in bed today.

I blink away the hot tears before they get the chance to brim over, quick to replace the weak emotion with logic.

Paul drank too much last night, and everything we've been holding in for the last three years came to a head.

It was my fault.

I shouldn't have let things get to that point.

I shouldn't have spoken up.

I'll do better.

It won't happen again.

Needing a plan rather than wallowing in self-pity, I examine the span of the bruising and mentally scour through my wardrobe for the right sweater. Hopefully, today will be brisk enough to wear one without drawing attention to myself. Even if the weather's hot, I could get away with wearing one of my cardigans with three-quarter-length sleeves. Shouldn't be too conspicuous.

Deep breath in through the nose, and out through the mouth.

Maverick.

California king bed.

Walk-in closet.

Dream kitchen.

Yard with a pool.

Mercedes.

"I'm fine," I tell my reflection. "Everything's fine."

I twist the lever in the shower and step under the waterfall, letting the warm water cascade over my skin. By the time I lather and rinse, the urge to cry is gone and I can breathe easy again.

Wrapping the towel around myself, I swing open the bathroom door and head to my closet. My pale-yellow sweater covers the mess on my arm, and I leave it unbuttoned over my white-and-yellow floral maxi dress. I spend thirty minutes lining my eyelids, curling my lashes, and passing the flatiron over my blond waves, taming it the way I know Paul prefers it.

With my armor in place, I square my shoulders in the mirror and heave a sigh. "Good as new."

At the sound of my sandals clunking down the stairs, my overeager dog gallops toward the front door.

"Ready for your walk, Mav?"

He *woofs* and spins in a circle.

I'm clipping his leash onto his collar when a loud *boom* echoes outside. My shoulders jolt, and Maverick jumps to scratch at the door, barking like a madman.

"Are we starting with the fireworks already?"

The Fourth of July isn't for another week. Plus, it's nine o'clock in the morning.

I push the sheer cream curtain aside and peer out the window. A white pickup truck rolls to a stop in front of Josie's house across the street. Well, there are visible areas of white paint—the truck was white at *one* time—surrounded by burnt-orange rust spots eating away at the metal. The bed of the truck is covered by a blue tarp, securing the contents underneath with a yellow bungee cord. Thick, black smoke billows from the exhaust pipe, trailing all the way down the block.

The truck pops again as it idles, sending Maverick into another barking fit.

"All right, bud. Enough." I reach down to pat his head, keeping my nose glued to the windowpane.

The driver's door swings open, and a man steps out. A navy-blue baseball cap sits on his head, pulled down low over his eyes. His plain white T-shirt, which looks more like an undershirt, is wrinkled and smudged with brown stains. His jeans are ripped—not the kind of rips people pay for—and equally as filthy as his shirt. He strides around the front bumper and up the walkway that leads to Josie's backyard.

"He must be the new landscaper."

Maverick cocks his head to the side as if he's listening to me.

Josie's Lexus isn't in her driveway, so I find it strange that she'd give a stranger the passcode to get in through her back gate. Maybe she left it unlocked for him before she left. Seems odd, but we've been desperate to find a new landscaping company after one of the workers from our old company got caught having an affair with Mrs. Nelson down the street. If

Josie found someone dependable, I'm going to need his card. Paul will be thrilled. Our shrubs need trimming, and weeds are beginning to poke up through the pavers in our driveway.

"Come on, bud." I snatch my sunglasses off the entryway table and lead Maverick out the front door.

Once we cross the wide street, Maverick pulls ahead of me, his nose to the ground, sniffing his way up the path of pavers. The iron gate is ajar, and Maverick continues pulling me through the opening into the backyard.

The layout is like mine. Same-sized rectangular in-ground pool, similar patio furniture. But Josie's yard is full of life, whereas mine has barely been touched. Squirt guns, skateboard ramps, and balls from every sport litter her grass. It's obvious that a family lives here.

Josie often complains of the mess, but I'd give anything to step on a Lego block belonging to *my* child.

The landscaper is standing in front of the pool house with his back to me, one hand on his hip while the other tips the neck of a brown glass bottle into his mouth.

So much for finding a reliable landscaper.

I stop a few feet behind him, wrapping Maverick's leash around my hand a few times to keep him from pulling me any further.

"Don't think you should be drinking on the job, sir."

The man spins around and blasts me with a scowl that sends a shiver down my spine. Under the brim of his hat, I spot a deep, disgruntled crease that lies between his dark brows. His prominent, unshaven jaw pops, clenching as if he's gritting through physical pain while he glares at me with piercing steel-blue eyes.

The hairs on my arms lift in a whoosh of awareness, and fear slices into me.

I shouldn't have come back here alone.

Maverick's tail thumps against my leg as he leans forward to get to the stranger, clearly unfazed by the potential danger I've put us in.

"I… I'm sorry." I pull Maverick back. "I didn't mean to startle you. I live across the street."

Great idea. Tell the nice murderer where you live.

He doesn't respond. Doesn't introduce himself. He just keeps hitting me with that unwavering glacial stare. It's too much, too powerful to withstand, so I lower my gaze and take in the rest of him.

Strong shoulders span wide, adding to his towering height. His shirt is taut around his upper body. The muscles in his arms are well-defined striations, more than just swollen biceps and triceps. He's carved from stone, detailed and unforgiving. A work of art that people would travel from all over to stand in front of in admiration.

This man is beautiful.

Then again, that's probably what every woman said about Ted Bundy right before he killed them.

I should leave. Flee back to the safety of my home.

But I'm frozen, sucked in by the enigmatic energy surging around him like a tornado of rage and agony.

And I'm standing right in his path.

I swallow, my throat thick with apprehension. "I, uh, we're in need of a new landscaper. I saw you come back here and figured I'd come ask for your card." I swallow again, my gaze flicking to the beer bottle glinting in the sunlight. "It's a little early to be drinking, don't you think? I mean, you shouldn't be impaired while operating heavy machinery. Don't want to lose a foot in the lawn mower."

I choke out a laugh, desperate to make light of the situation, but it comes out strangled and strained.

The man doesn't laugh with me. He doesn't crack a smile. Not sure his facial muscles would know how if he tried to. One massive hand is curled at his side, as if he's gripping the leash on his composure, his self-control ready to snap.

"You've got some nerve coming back here like this." The man's voice is gruff with a sharp edge, like he gargles with a throat full of razors every morning.

My eyebrows lift in a flash of irritation. "Me? I'm a potential customer. One who wants to pay you for your landscaping services. Or I did, before I caught you getting drunk on the job."

Why am I arguing with the scary man?

He folds his arms over his chest, accentuating the corded muscles in his forearms. "And you assume I'm a landscaper because why?"

"Your truck, for one." I wave my arm in front of him. "You're too dirty to be pool maintenance. If you were a roofer, you'd have a ladder." I shrug like it's simple addition. "And this isn't your backyard, so unless you're here to rob the place…" My fingers touch my lips. "Oh god. You're not here to rob them, are you?"

He edges closer, the look of disgust twisting his features—the look he's directing at *me*.

I lift my chin and try not to flinch.

I've learned that flinching only makes it worse.

Maverick strains against his leash, his eager nose in the air, wide eyes begging the stranger to pet him. I have to use both hands to tug him back.

Some guard dog you are, Mav! This man is about to kill me, and you're trying to sniff his crotch and make friends.

The man points his index finger at me, revulsion rolling off his tongue with each syllable. "You self-righteous, pretentious little princess."

My mouth falls open, and my stomach bottoms out.

"You stand there in your designer clothes, your shoes that cost more than a month's rent, scrutinizing everyone behind your ridiculous fucking sunglasses, and you're gonna judge *me*?" He shakes his head. "My clothes are dirty because I work my ass off. My truck's a piece of shit because I have more important things to pay for. And I'm a grown-ass man, so I'll drink whenever the fuck I feel like drinking. All you rich motherfuckers act like you're better than people like me, but I know the sickening truth. I can lay my head down at night with a clear conscience because I'm not living a lie. I'd rather look ugly on the outside than be ugly on the inside like you."

His words pack a physical punch, hitting way too close to home. A tremor rips through me, and before I can stop it, a tear escapes from under my sunglasses.

It's time to go.

"I'm sorry." I whip around and bolt out of the backyard, dragging Maverick behind me.

My legs carry me across the grass as fast as my wedges will allow. I bunch my dress in my fist, hiking it up over my knees so my strides are longer.

When I reach my house, I slam the door closed behind me and press my back against it. My chest heaves as I gasp for air, my heart racing. A sob gurgles in my throat, but I swallow it down.

Maverick.

California king bed.

Walk-in closet.

Dream kitchen.

Yard with a pool.

Mercedes.

Maverick whimpers, nudging me with his cold nose. I sink down to the floor and fling my arms around him, burying my face in the comfort of his soft fur.

"It's okay, Mav. I'm okay."

Everything's okay.

I shouldn't have confronted him like that.

It's my fault for making him so angry.

My speeding pulse returns to normal after a few minutes of deep breathing, and I push off the floor. Maverick follows me into the kitchen as I swipe my purse and my car keys off the counter.

"Sorry, bud. You gotta stay here. I'm running to the store. Making a special dinner for your dad tonight."

I kiss the top of his head, and then I'm back out the door, head down, without so much as a glance at the pickup truck out front.

"Mmm. So good, babe."

My lips spread into a smile. "Figured I'd surprise you with your favorite dish tonight."

Paul's hand slides across the cherrywood table, and he entwines our fingers. "I love it. Thank you."

"How was your day?"

He tugs on his tie, loosening it, before popping his collar and slipping the loop over his head. "Good. Meeting went well. I think Haarburger's going to sign with us."

"That's great."

He dabs the corner of his mouth with his napkin. "How was therapy?"

"It went well."

His Adam's apple bobs up and down. "Did you, uh, tell her what we talked about last night?"

"I told her about our decision to stop trying to have kids. She thinks it's good that we're on the same page, that we're able to move on together."

"Not what I was referring to, Cal."

"Oh."

He's asking if I told her about the bruises he left on my arm.

I look down at my spaghetti. "No, I didn't mention it."

"Good." He sets his fork down beside his plate. "Because I meant what I said last night. It won't happen again."

I nod, unsure of what he wants me to say to that. It wasn't the first time he put his hands on me, nor was it the first time he promised that it won't happen again. I want to call him out on that. I want to ask him why he feels the need to hurt me in order to get his point across. I want to ask him why he can't control his temper. I want to ask him what happened to the sweet man I met in college. I want to ask him to get some help.

But sometimes, silence is easier than navigating around all the eggshells lying at my feet.

He picks his fork back up. "Did you call the vet?"

"I did. They said to watch him when he's in the backyard, so he doesn't get the opportunity to eat his poop." I lift my goblet to my lips and take a long sip.

"Did you ask why he's doing this?"

My stomach coils. "The, uh, the doctor said it could be due to anxiety."

"Anxiety. Like you."

"Yeah. He asked if we've been stressed, because dogs can pick up on our feelings."

Recognition flashes across Paul's face, his light-brown eyes hardening. "So what did you tell him?"

"I told him everything's fine, of course. He said we could put Maverick on a low dose of anxiety medication, but I said that won't be necessary. We'll just watch him better when he's outside. Won't happen again if we keep an eye on him." I force a smile and clasp my hands together. "Ready for dessert?"

He shakes his head and pushes his chair back as he stands. "I'm going to change. Got some emails to send out."

"Of course. I'll get this all cleaned up."

He's gone before the sentence leaves my lips.

Could've gone worse, I suppose.

I release a sigh and begin stacking our plates.

While I rinse off the dishes in the sink, I gaze out the window into the darkened yard. The pool house at the far end elicits the memory of the bizarre encounter in Josie's backyard this morning.

I've tried not to think about the rude stranger all day, but my mind keeps drifting back to him. Back to what he'd said.

He was right. I'd judged him by his appearance and made an assumption based on it. Shouldn't have been that big of a deal, though. He could've laughed it off like a silly misunderstanding. He didn't need to go off on me like he did. People judge books by their covers all the time.

Hell, he did the same thing with me, didn't he? He lumped me in with the wealthy people in this neighborhood, pointing out my expensive clothes and accessories, calling me a fake without knowing anything about me. I could call him a jerk and chalk it up to him being mean.

But his words carry weight.

I *am* a fake.

I *am* living a lie.

Who was that man, and how did he read me so easily?

More importantly, does Josie know that someone was in her yard today?

I dry my hands on a dish towel and dig through my purse to find my phone. Before I can tap out a text, I spot one already waiting in my inbox. When I click on it and read the words that pop up on the screen, my hand clamps over my mouth.

Josie: So, I heard you met my brother this morning.

Keep reading HERE for more of *What's Left of Me*

Acknowledgments

First and foremost, I'd like to thank my therapist, Erica. Without you, I wouldn't have been able to write this story. You helped me find the courage within myself to stand up and fight when I was at a really low point in my life, and I'll never forget the lessons you taught me.

To my wife, thank you for your constant support of me and my dream. You keep me going, even when I don't want to. You believe in me even when I don't believe in myself. I'm so thankful to have you. I love you more than life.

To Dorthy, Becca, and Mary—my forever Beta readers and sounding boards. Thank you for taking the time to tell me what you think of each part of my books and helping me work through the storyline when I'm stuck. And thank you for being my confidence when I have none.

To Taylor, thank you for making my covers, but thank you even more for having my back when I felt alone. I'm so thankful for your friendship.

To Kandi, thank you for allowing me to include *On the Way to You* in this book—and for writing it—and thank you for being such a fierce friend when I really needed one.

Shout out to ThirdEyeThoughts on Instagram for letting me use their daily inspirations for the chapter headers. Reading these affirmations each morning really helps start my day with a positive, self-loving mindset.

To BookTok and Bookstagram, thank you for supporting me and for spreading the word about my books. I appreciate every review, comment, video, and post. Let's keep showing the world how amazing romance books are!

To every bully and troll I've ever met: Thank you. You showed me that I can overcome your ugliness and hate. You showed me how strong I can be. You showed me that I have so many people who love me and have my back. I'm so sorry your life isn't filled with the same things I've been lucky enough to have, and I hope you're able to find happiness and peace one day.

And last, to me. I almost gave up on writing last year, and I'm so thankful I pushed through and kept going. This book will always serve as a reflection of my resilience and my strength. Self, I'm so damn proud of you.

Printed in Great Britain
by Amazon

19823623R00153